Only. That one word
held a lifetime of wistfulness.

Spoken in that soft deep rumble she'd grown to like so well. With his lips so close to her ear, the sound of his voice had all the intimacy of a touch. Or a kiss.

"Only?" Husky with emotion, her voice emerged in almost as deep a timbre as his. She could no longer resist the temptation.

His whiskeyed breath caressed her face. "You had more than enough reasons to turn me down." In the softest whisper, as if a thought had escaped directly from his mind, he added, "And I sure did want to marry you."

He wanted her? As a woman? The thought made Caddie's knees tremble.

Without a single pair of reliable legs beneath them, they collapsed onto the stairs. Neither of them seemed to notice.

Her lips found Manning as his ca━━━━━━━━━r hers....

Deborah Hale

Carpetbagger's Wife

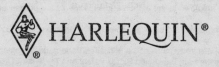

HARLEQUIN®

TORONTO • NEW YORK • LONDON
AMSTERDAM • PARIS • SYDNEY • HAMBURG
STOCKHOLM • ATHENS • TOKYO • MILAN • MADRID
PRAGUE • WARSAW • BUDAPEST • AUCKLAND

ISBN 0-373-29195-7

CARPETBAGGER'S WIFE

Copyright © 2002 by Deborah M. Hale

Please address questions and book requests to:
Harlequin Reader Service
U.S.: 3010 Walden Ave., P.O. Box 1325, Buffalo, NY 14269
Canadian: P.O. Box 609, Fort Erie, Ont. L2A 5X3

For Catherine Mann and K. Sue Morgan, wonderful Southern belles to whom I owe more than I can say.

And for my sister Patricia Galbraith, vibrant redhead and world's most devoted mom.

Chapter One

Northern Virginia, Spring 1866

"The house is still standing. That's something, at least."

Relief pushed the words out of Caddie Marsh's mouth. Tales she'd heard from Georgia and her native South Carolina had made her fear she'd find a gutted shell when she returned to Sabbath Hollow. Perhaps only the chimneys, listing above charred rubble.

Caddie paused at the crest of a gently sloping ridge overlooking the Marsh plantation. From where she stood, the place appeared as if war had hardly touched it. Four bold white pillars still held up a jutting triangular portico that shaded most of the spacious front porch. Arrayed in front of the house like attendants before a stately bride, flowering dogwood shimmered in the April breeze.

For the first time since Confederate troops had abandoned Richmond, Caddie allowed tears to rise in her tired eyes. After a long and bitter exile, she and her children were home at last.

The shambling old mare stopped in its traces beside Caddie, shook a graying mane and blew out its breath in what sounded like a sigh. On the driver's seat of the precariously loaded buckboard, eight-year-old Templeton Marsh roused from his doze. He pushed a stray lock of pale brown hair off his forehead, then rubbed his eyes.

"Are we there yet, Mama?"

Beside him, little Varina continued to sleep as serenely as she'd slept while Union batteries thundered at Cold Harbor.

Caddie's gaze rested on the children for a moment. A brooding warmth swelled within her bosom, both tender and fierce. Tender in her love for them. Fierce in her desire to protect them from the harshness of the world. They'd experienced too much of that already in their young lives.

"Yes, dearest, we're home." Caddie pointed toward the graciously proportioned mansion. "It must seem such a long time to you since we left for Richmond." To her, it felt like several lifetimes. "Do you remember Sabbath Hollow at all?"

Tem's brow wrinkled with an effort of concentration. "I...reckon I might." Clearly, he believed it was important to his mother, and he wanted to please her.

"Once we've been here a little while, I expect the memories will come back to you." Caddie did her best to reassure him with her smile and gentle tone.

Tem was such a grave, sensitive boy for his years. More than anything, Caddie wanted to give him and Varina back part of their stolen childhood. And the heritage of this fine old plantation that had been in the Marsh family since colonial days.

For an instant Caddie felt herself pulled into the warm embrace of the past, seeing Sabbath Hollow as it had looked when she first laid eyes on it. Ten years ago, as Delbert Marsh's newly wed bride. She could almost hear the laughter of guests and the mellow croon of a seasoned fiddle. Almost see the bewitching swish of silks and taffetas in a palette of colors as bright as a spring garden. Almost smell the mouthwatering pungency of oak and hickory smoke from the barbecue.

"Mama?" Templeton called Caddie back to the present.

She stirred from the sweet seduction of her memories with melancholy reluctance.

"What is it, dearest?" Caddie patted the mare's hindquarters to urge it forward.

"Why is one of the chimneys smoking?"

At that moment, a thick cloud with a dark underbelly enveloped the bright April sun, leaching every particle of warmth from the air.

Caddie froze in her tracks until the slow-moving front wheel of the buckboard prodded her forward. "I—I don't know."

For an instant her heart lifted as she wondered if some of the Marshes former slaves might have come back to the only home they'd ever known. If they'd be willing to work for their bed and board, she'd be able to manage so much easier.

It was an appealing notion, but common sense told Caddie not to get her hopes up. Slaves on this northernmost fringe of the Confederacy had fled in droves when the first Union army marched south.

Forcing her feet down the muddy lane, she swallowed a lump in her throat the size of a smoked ham. "I suppose we'd better find out, hadn't we?"

The closer they drew to the house, the clearer it became that the place was occupied by someone. Not someone very prosperous or industrious, Caddie decided as her gaze took in the peeling paint, shattered windows and broken railings that hadn't been apparent from a distance.

Would she be able to do any better? An insidious whisper of self-doubt taunted Caddie. With no money, no husband and two young children to care for, how could she expect to fix up the house and put the plantation back on the road to prosperity?

Stiffening her spine and tilting her chin defiantly, Caddie thrust those negative thoughts from her mind.

Somehow—that's how she'd manage.

It was the way she had survived and cared for her little family against the odds after Del had been reported dead in battle, and later when the Confederacy had fallen to the Yankees. By working hard, making do, swallowing her pride again and again without ever losing it. She had never failed at anything in her life, and she wasn't about to fail at this, either.

In the first place, she refused to give her enemies the satisfaction of having defeated her on a personal level. And in the second place, her children's future depended on it.

Just then, a woman sauntered around the corner of the house. Her dark hair hung loose and her brightly colored dress clung tight to her ample bosom. The gaudy garment looked far newer than Caddie's oft-mended calico, dulled by much wear and many washings.

The woman started at the sight of the horse and wagon, but quickly recovered herself and planted her hands on a pair of broad hips. "Git, now! We don't give handouts."

"Lydene?" The name retched out of Caddie, sour as vomit. Beads of sweat broke out on her forehead. With trembling hands, she pulled the bonnet off her tightly pinned hair before its ties choked her.

What the devil was Lydene Swade doing at Sabbath Hollow?

"Miz Caddie?" Lydene's mouth gaped open and her belligerently cocked elbows fell slack.

The two women stared at each other for a minute that seemed to stretch into hours. Caddie, bewildered, disgusted and furious. Lydene, embarrassed, triumphant and contemptuous. Just as they had looked at each other on that

long-ago evening when Caddie had discovered Lydene, naked, underneath an equally naked Delbert Marsh. That was
one memory from her past at Sabbath Hollow that Caddie
had no desire to rekindle.

Breaking from their stare, Lydene hollered over her
shoulder, "Lon! Git on out here. You'll never guess who's
come from Richmond for a visit."

With a sickening jolt, Caddie realized that she had failed
at one thing in life, after all. One of the most important
vocations of a Southern woman's life, and she'd made a
worse mess of it than General Sherman had made of Georgia.

Her marriage.

That must be his wife.

The man known as Manning Forbes pulled his impro-
vised fishing line out of the water. His heart beat a thun-
dering tattoo against his chest and his stomach contracted
into a lump as hard and heavy as a cannonball.

From his bivouac camp beside the creek, he watched the
slender woman lead her horse and wagon onto the lane that
wound its way down to the derelict plantation. The boy and
redheaded little girl resting on the seat of the buckboard
looked to be the right ages—the boy somewhat small for
his eight years.

Manning Forbes had been waiting for them. Waiting with
a mixture of anticipation and dread most good Christians
reserved for the Second Coming.

In the last day or two, he'd begun to wonder if they
would show up at all. Some instinct had warned him to
avoid the man and woman who'd made themselves at home
in the pillaged mansion. So he'd posed a few discreet in-
quiries around the neighborhood, instead.

Where had Caddie Marsh and her children gone? Were
they expected back at Sabbath Hollow anytime soon? He

hadn't received very satisfactory answers. Only puzzled, wary looks. Not surprising, perhaps.

With little choice but to wait and hope the Marsh family would come to him, Manning had occupied himself with an informal survey of the plantation. Assessing the damage done to it by the shifting tides of war. Weighing its assets and liabilities. Sizing up its potential.

He was confident he could make the place profitable again, if only he could win the cooperation of Mrs. Marsh.

Unbidden, his hand rose to pat the breast pocket of his coat. In it rested the last letter Caddie Marsh had written to her husband before the Battle of the Wilderness. Ever since the day of that terrible conflict, Manning Forbes had kept that scrap of paper on his person every waking hour.

Like the hair shirt worn by penitents of long ago, it reminded him of his transgression, and of the vow he'd sworn, to atone for it. A vow to protect and provide for Caddie Marsh and her children, no matter what it cost him.

He could think of only one honorable means to fulfil that vow, though he shrank from even the thought of it. Somehow, he would have to convince Widow Marsh to marry again.

But first he'd have to convince himself.

Caddie's shaken composure rallied as she watched her brother-in-law stroll onto the verandah.

She hadn't seen a Southern man so well dressed since the early days of the war. Lon's flaxen hair was smoothed in place with pomade. The wisps of facial hair on his chin and above his lip looked expertly barbered. He moved with the casual grace Caddie remembered so well.

"Why, Caddie, is it really you come all the way from Richmond?" Lon glided toward her and made an elaborate bow over her hand. "You should have sent us word you were coming. I could have ridden out to meet you."

From the first day she'd arrived at the Marsh plantation as a bride, Caddie had never felt comfortable around her husband's overindulged younger brother. Still, he was her children's only blood kin on the Marsh side. For Tem and Varina's sake, Lon would soon send that bold Swade minx packing from Sabbath Hollow.

"I didn't know you'd be here, Lon." Even if she had, Caddie could not have spared precious cash to mail a letter. Pride wouldn't let her admit it, though. "I wasn't certain you were still alive."

Pulling a slender cigar from his breast pocket, Lon trimmed and lit it. His lips stretched into a wide grin. "Take more than a few Yankees to get rid of Alonzo Marsh, my dear. I've got more lives than a cat and I generally land on my feet, too."

There *was* something sleek and feline about Lon—an air of smug self-satisfaction, an elegant disdain for the rest of the world. A single-minded concentration on his own interests. And charm that usually won him his own way.

Lon's gaze strayed to the buckboard wagon, heavily laden with supplies. "You fixing to stay a spell with us?"

"Us?"

"Me and my missus." Lon turned and held out his hand to Lydene, who sashayed over and plastered herself up against him. "You recollect Lydene, don't you?"

Caddie slammed down a lid of propriety on the feelings that boiled inside her. Did Lon have any notion what his bride had done with his brother? Or had that represented part of Lydene's attraction for him?

Not trusting herself to answer Lon's second question, Caddie seized on his first, instead. Indignation sharpened her words.

"I *am* planning to stay. Richmond's no fit place to raise children these days if a body has any choice, and I do. As

Del's widow, Sabbath Hollow belongs to me. It'll be Templeton's when he comes of age.''

As if to strengthen her claim, Caddie helped Tem down from his seat on the buckboard and put her arm around his thin shoulders. She needed to feed both her children a good hot meal and tuck them into bed, not stand around like uninvited guests to their own home.

"Hold on a minute." Lon's expression hardened. "If the war hadn't come, you and Del would have inherited Sabbath Hollow and I'd have got money from Pa to buy or build a place of my own."

His voice grew louder and angrier with every word. "But the war did come. The money's gone and so are Pa and Del. There's just the house in Richmond and Sabbath Hollow. You have one and I've got the other. Seems fair to me."

The spring breeze tickled Caddie's neck into gooseflesh. She could barely coax her reply above a whisper. "I sold the house in Richmond."

In bad shape, it had barely fetched enough for her to buy the old mare, the buckboard and a few supplies for them to start over up country.

Lon shook his head, as if in sympathy, but his lips clenched tight on his cigar. "That wasn't wise, Caddie. A woman on her own with two young'uns is safer in town or with her folks. You're welcome to stay here a spell, while I send word to your brother, Gideon. Then we'll see about putting you all on a train back to Jessamine."

So intent was Caddie on her brother-in-law's outrageous suggestion that she did not hear Varina stirring. At least not until Lydene scrambled to the buckboard and lifted the child down.

"Ain't you just as sweet as sugar pie?" Lydene crooned while Varina yawned and rubbed her eyes with dimpled fists. "Maybe you can just stay here with me and your uncle Lon when your mama goes back to South Carolina."

Caddie ripped her four-year-old daughter from Lydene's arms, pitching her voice low as not to upset the children. "Don't you ever touch my baby again, do you hear?"

Inside her, the heat of rage and the chill of fear collided, brewing up a thunderstorm of emotion she was powerless to control. When she turned her gaze on Lon, Caddie half expected bolts of lightning to shoot from her eyes and fry him where he stood.

"I am *not* going back to Jessamine, or Richmond or anyplace else. Sabbath Hollow is my home and my children's. Which means you are trespassing on our property, Alonzo Marsh."

"Now see here, Caddie—"

"Don't you *see here* me. I know you have land and a house from your ma where you can live just as well. Now, I want you and your...*her* to pack up and clear out. My children are tired from the trip. I want to tend to them and get settled."

Caddie felt Tem step back behind the protection of her skirts. Varina struggled against her tight grip.

Flicking the ashes from his cigar, Lon met Caddie's glare with a sneer. "If I say I like it here fine and I don't plan on leaving, just how are you fixing to make me go?"

How, indeed? Caddie's knees began to tremble.

She had soldiered through the hardscrabble months since Appomattox, lured on by a single goal. Like a flickering candle in the window of the future, guiding her through a stormy night when she longed to surrender to weariness and despair. Now, within sight of her haven, that last hope was being snatched away by her children's blood kin.

At least with the Yankees there'd been no illusion they were anything but enemies.

The soft click of a rifle cocking shattered the tense,

breathless silence. From behind her, Caddie heard a man's voice, quiet and calm, yet somehow just as menacing as the muted sound of the gun.

"If the lady wants you off her property, friend, *I'm* prepared to make you go."

A Yankee. Caddie could tell by the way he spoke. Even to run Lon off the plantation, she wasn't sure she could bring herself to accept help from one of *them*.

Lon's smirking mouth fell open. His cheroot dropped to the ground and lay there smoldering. Lydene looked as though she'd been kicked in the belly by a mule. What had gotten into them? It must be more than just the surprise of the Yankee's arrival or the sight of his weapon.

Slowly, Caddie turned.

What she saw made her head spin like a whirligig. Where had all the air gone? She could not seem to suck enough into her chest.

The man's gun wasn't pointed at Lon, as Caddie had half expected, but was aimed toward the ground. His stance proclaimed a desire to avoid violence, but a resolve to use it if pressed. That wasn't what made Caddie fear she might swoon for the first time in her life.

The man did not carry a spare ounce on his tall frame, least of all on his face, with its sharply chiseled features and fierce jutting chin. His thick, dark brows overhung deep-set eyes, shadowing whatever emotion they might have otherwise betrayed. Apart from a close-trimmed mustache, the lean contours of his face were clean shaven, which made him look slightly less familiar.

Slightly.

Caddie coaxed a question out of her mouth, which had suddenly gone dry as sawdust. "W-who are you?"

Part of her felt a fool for asking. Who could the man be

but Delbert Marsh? The husband whose reported death she'd never truly mourned.

Difficult as her life was now, it would become a hundred times more complicated if Del had suddenly risen from the grave.

Chapter Two

"The name's Manning Forbes, ma'am."

He had a hard job forcing those words out. Seeing Caddie Marsh up close robbed him of air and made his vocal organs balk. He hadn't been prepared for her to look so beautiful.

Another man might not have seen past the threadbare dress or the shadows of toil and worry beneath her eyes. Manning scarcely noticed those things. Instead, his gaze fell on the glory of her red-brown hair and the striking eyes that mingled misty gray softness with emerald fire. Something about the way she held herself stirred his admiration, too. Like the exiled aristocrats of old France, who had lost everything but their nobility.

Her children clung to her in the mute certainty that she would protect them at any cost to herself. Just watching the little family brought a wistful ache to Manning's belly—as though he'd been hungry for so long he'd begun to doubt the existence of food.

Clearing his throat, he continued. "I came to speak to you on a matter of business, Mrs. Marsh. When I overheard your discussion with this *gentleman,* I thought you might need my help."

Her gaze held equal parts fear and hostility, each vying for control. Manning shrank from the look in her eyes, even as he owned that he probably deserved it. Had he done a stupid thing, rushing to her aid, uninvited? It seemed likely. But when he'd heard the bullying contempt in the squatter's voice and the impotent desperation in Caddie Marsh's, Manning hadn't been able to stop himself from striding to her rescue. When she parted her lips, he braced himself to be sent packing.

Before she could get any words out, though, the squatter challenged him. "This little *misunderstanding* is between me and my sister-in-law, sir. You've got no call to meddle in our affairs. Certainly not at gunpoint. Whatever *business* you want to discuss, I think it's safe to say we aren't interested."

Sister-in-law? The word rocked Manning. He'd believed Mrs. Marsh and her children alone in the world, without menfolk to look out for them. If the children had an uncle, perhaps they wouldn't need him as urgently as he'd assumed. Particularly when that uncle looked to have come through the war unscathed.

A queer mixture of relief and disappointment washed over Manning. What if Caddie Marsh didn't need his help, after all? How would he ever make good the vow that had expanded to fill his empty life? Without a word, he stepped back and let his rifle barrel droop lower.

The dapper Virginian abruptly shifted his attention back to his sister-in-law, clearly satisfied that he'd dismissed Manning, and expecting him to slink away.

"Don't let's quarrel, Caddie. Not on the first day of your visit." The man had a voice like molasses taffy—warm and sticky. "You're welcome to stay a good long spell with us."

He took a step toward Caddie Marsh and her children. "We'd like to get to know young Templeton, here. He was just a wee scrap when you left for Richmond. The boy needs a man's influence what with his pa gone and all.''

Mrs. Marsh drew back from the man's approach, clutching her daughter in one arm, while groping for her son with the other. Reacting instinctively to a perceived threat, Manning swung his gun up and fired into the dirt at the other man's feet.

The Virginian jumped back and the women both screamed. The old mare shied as if startled by the sudden loud noise, but too tired to rear or bolt. The little girl in her mother's arms stared at Manning as she popped a small thumb between her lips and began to suck. Her brother covered his ears and blinked his eyes rapidly, making a manful effort to fight back tears.

Much as the child's quivering fear reproached him, Manning tried not to let the boy's uncle see him wince.

"Hold your horses, mister." His voice sounded harsh and threatening, even in his own ears, as he reloaded the rifle. "Move back from the lady and let her speak for herself. If she tells me to clear off her property, I will. Until then, I'm staying put. I suggest you do the same."

Snapping the breech of his weapon closed again, Manning made himself meet Caddie Marsh's wary, searching gaze. "What do you say, ma'am? Should I go?"

Caddie struggled to rein in her galloping pulse and to keep her words from leaping out in a breathless rush. The Yankee's warning shot was only partly responsible for her agitation. Now that she'd had a better look at the stranger, Caddie realized she'd been mistaken about his resemblance to her late husband.

Or had she?

Manning Forbes was a shade taller than Del had been...perhaps. His voice was certainly different than she remembered Del's. A difference that lay in more than just the stranger's Yankee accent...maybe.

What kind of woman, she silently chided herself, could let the memory of her children's father dim to such a bewildering degree in such a short time?

Prompted partly by uncertainty and curiosity, Caddie made her decision. "I'd like you to stay, please, Mr. Forbes."

"Have you lost your mind, woman?" barked Lon.

A twitch of the Yankee's rifle barrel chased the sharpness from his voice. "Come to your senses, now," Lon coaxed. "You don't want to wash all our family linen in front of one of *them,* do you? Send him away. Then you and I can discuss Sabbath Hollow peaceably."

Varina grew heavier in her arms with each passing minute, and Caddie's last square meal was a distant memory, but she couldn't bring herself to stay at Sabbath Hollow even one night as Lon's *guest.* Or Lydene's. It would set too dangerous a precedent.

Besides, she'd heard the unspoken threat in Lon's voice when he said Templeton needed a man's influence. If she gave this pair any leverage, they'd be scheming to get their hands on her children in order to secure their hold on the plantation.

"There's nothing to discuss," she replied. Lon was right about one thing. She didn't like airing their family squabble in front of a Yankee, but he'd left her no choice. "I am not moving back to South Carolina, now or ever. I'm also not a visitor at Sabbath Hollow and neither are my children. The plantation belongs to us and *you* need to leave."

"Now, Caddie…" With a sidelong glance at the Yankee's rifle, Lon kept his voice hushed. His tone sounded wheedling yet vaguely hostile. "How can I leave one of my womenfolk alone with an armed Yankee? Think what he might do to you."

Lord in heaven, she hadn't thought of that. She also hadn't thought it was possible for her heart to race any faster. This must be what Jessamine's foreman had called "betwixt a rock and a hard place."

As she studied on the problem, which seemed to admit no good solution, Manning Forbes spoke up. "I don't mean you or your children any harm, Mrs. Marsh. If it'll make you feel safer, you can take my gun."

That decided her. "Go, Lon. And take that woman with you."

Caddie strove to sound more resolute than she felt. Turning out kinfolk went so hard against the Southern grain. No matter how great a threat they represented to her children's future. No matter what other resources she knew they had at their disposal.

"Mr. Forbes has demonstrated he isn't spleeny about using that gun, and I don't reckon a Yankee would land in much trouble if he did shoot you. I'll let you hang on to the rifle for now, sir. You'll be a better shot than I am."

As if taking his cue from her warning to Lon, Manning Forbes cocked his rifle and took aim. Lon looked from Caddie to the Yankee and back, like a gambler trying to predict the strength of his opponent's hand. Would he see through her bluff?

Likely. From that long-ago honeymoon barbecue when she'd first been introduced to Del's younger brother, Caddie had sensed Lon saw beneath her facade of assurance. She'd sometimes felt he was looking straight through her dress and corset and layers of petticoats, admiring her in a way he had no business doing.

Yes. Lon might recognize her vulnerability and try to exploit it. But what about the Yankee? Caddie had little doubt he'd put a bullet into Lon if push came to shove. Or was that just a ruse on his part? If so, Manning Forbes had nerves of iron and a poker face. Right now, Caddie was grateful for both.

"Have it your way," Lon snarled. Clearly, he wasn't

prepared to call the Yankee's bluff. "Lydene and I were talking about moving over to Hemlock Grove for the summer, anyhow. A few months trying to fend for yourself out in the country and you'll come begging me to take the place off your hands by fall."

With every word, Lon's easy confidence returned and slapped Caddie in the face. Pulling out another cigar, he gave it an appreciative sniff and grinned at his wife. "Go pack up what you need for tonight, sugar. We'll collect the rest in a day or so."

"But, Lon…"

"*Now,* Lydene. I'll go hitch the buggy." Lon gave Caddie and Manning Forbes a jaunty salute with his cigar and ambled toward the stables.

Lydene glared at Caddie, her ruddy complexion grown pale as skim milk. "We'll be back. Like the colored folks say, bottom rung's on top, now. You ain't the lady of the manor anymore, *Miz Caddie.*"

As she stood there with her children, waiting for Lon and Lydene to go, every sign of damage and neglect around the once proud plantation rose up to mock Caddie's dream of reviving it. Sabbath Hollow had once bred some of the finest stock in a state famed for its horseflesh. Who in Virginia was left with the money to buy pedigreed beauties like the Marshes had once produced? And if anyone did, how would Caddie raise the capital to get back into such a costly operation?

Would the sheer scope of Sabbath Hollow defeat her as the Yankees had failed to do?

Watching Lon Marsh's buggy trundle off down the lane, Manning sensed the tightly wound tension seeping out of his shoulders. His taut grip on the rifle stock eased. Unsure if he could have brought himself to shoot the Virginian,

Manning breathed a little easier since he hadn't had to find out.

His gaze came to rest on Caddie Marsh and the children. His muscles tightened again. Now that he'd served his purpose in getting rid of her unwanted in-laws, would she send him away with a flea in his ear, as she'd sent them?

Holding the gun out to Mrs. Marsh, he approached them. The little girl continued to regard him gravely, while the boy scuttled behind his mother. From the look on Caddie Marsh's face, Manning could tell she wanted to draw back from him, too. Perhaps for the benefit of the children, she held her ground and studied him with a determined gaze.

"Thank you for making my brother-in-law go, Mr. Forbes." Her words were a correct and proper expression of gratitude, but they lacked a single degree of warmth. "Now, if you'll excuse us, my children are hungry and tired from our trip."

He would like to have allowed her the luxury of settling in before he made his offer. A little time might have made her more receptive to the notion. But he could not ignore the subtle threat posed by Lon Marsh. It was against such threats Manning had sworn to defend her.

"We need to talk, Mrs. Marsh, ma'am. And I'm afraid it can't wait. I've known men like your brother-in-law. Smooth as cream when everything's going their way, but deny them what they want and you'd better watch your back."

She stiffened. "I'll thank you not to speak slightingly of our kin, Mr. Manning. I'm certain when he sees I mean to stay and make a go of this place, Lon will come around."

The turbulence in her eyes betrayed doubt. "As for talking to me, I have more pressing concerns just now. Good day, sir."

He wasn't going to get anywhere by forcing the issue, Manning realized. Opposition would only strengthen her contrary resolve. He needed to take a different tack and stall for time. Give Caddie Marsh an opportunity to change her mind.

"I apologize for upsetting you with my harsh assessment of your brother-in-law's character, ma'am." He wouldn't retract what he'd said, though, for it was the truth. "Let me make amends by stabling your horse and unloading your wagon."

When she looked ready to refuse, he laid the rifle at her feet. "If I wanted to steal anything, I'd just hold you at gunpoint and take it, ma'am. Why don't you go feed your children and put them to bed?"

The boy peeped out from behind his mother's skirts. "Can we eat, Mama? I'm awful hungry."

When the child ventured to look him in the face, Manning shaped his features into an encouraging smile. Winning this young fellow's trust would be as tricky a challenge as taming a yearling fawn—and perhaps just as rewarding.

Manning nodded toward his camp and addressed his offer to the boy. "I caught a pair of fine fat trout in your creek, so I guess they belong to you. Would you like fresh fish for supper?"

With a jerky movement like a wooden puppet, the boy nodded his head.

The little girl withdrew the thumb from her mouth and announced solemnly, "I like fish."

This time Manning did not have to *make* himself smile. "That settles it, then." He turned away before Caddie Marsh could refuse. "It'll go fetch you that trout and some cornmeal. Then I'll see to the horse and wagon while you folks eat."

"Mr. Forbes."

Her voice stopped him, but Manning couldn't bring himself to look back. "Yes?"

"Thank you." The words sounded less forced than the first time she'd uttered them. "You've been most kind."

Her gratitude hit him like a minié ball in the back. Manning's eyes stung. Without a word or gesture of acknowledgment, he began to walk again.

He didn't deserve Caddie Marsh's thanks. He owed her this simple meal and every other comfort he could provide for her and her children. He owed her the protection he'd extended them today. Now, and for as long as they needed it.

Expressions of gratitude did no more to assuage his guilt than carbolic acid soothed an open wound. But he dared not tell her that, or she would spurn his help. Then he would be left with no way to make amends.

Manning could not bear that thought.

Caddie struggled with her conscience as she returned to the dining room after tucking the children into bed.

For the first time in years, her little family had eaten more than their fill, yet a generous helping of fish remained on the plate. Her ears picked up the sound of Manning Forbes stowing her meager possessions in the entry hall. She'd expected him to invite himself to dine with them, but he hadn't.

Slowly, Caddie began to clear the table. A small, bandy-legged piece of furniture, it had once held pies to cool in a corner of the pantry. Caddie missed the magnificent creation of tastefully carved cherry wood that had occupied this grand room before the war. One that could sit two dozen for a hunt breakfast, if folks didn't mind rubbing elbows. One that a pair of house servants kept polished to a dark sheen. For Caddie, the Sabbath Hollow dining table was now a lost symbol of the whole congenial, hospitable way of life Southerners had once enjoyed.

Its absence tore at her heart.

She didn't know what had become of that table in the dark days since Fort Sumter. And she didn't want to know. It would only rile her up, and to no good purpose.

At last only a single plate remained to be cleared away. Part of Caddie insisted she cover the uneaten fish and put it down in a cool part of the cellar for the children's breakfast. If the Yankee wanted fish, he had the means to catch more.

Her early upbringing reproached her for such ill-bred selfishness. If the hard years in Richmond had made her mean and ungracious, then the Yankees had won a most distressing victory. She refused to concede it to them, even if it meant treating one of their number with greater courtesy than such people deserved. Battling her more practical inclinations, Caddie fetched a fork.

For a moment she stood in the doorway of the dining room, watching as Manning Forbes brought the last of her provisions in from the wagon. He carried a wooden box perched on one broad shoulder, steadied by large, long-fingered hands. The rough clothes hung loose on his lean-muscled frame. Blue trousers—Union army issue, no doubt, held up by leather suspenders. A white shirt, open at the neck.

Nothing about that garb should have stirred her memory of the well-tailored frock coat Delbert Marsh had worn to the Charleston cotillion on the first night they'd met. Smitten with admiration, Caddie had set her cap for Del…and lived to regret it. Now, heaven help her, a stray draft of foolishness breathed upon the cool ember of her long-ago fancy and made it glow again.

The Yankee looked up and caught her watching him. His sternly handsome face grew crimson, as though he could read every preposterous thought that flitted through her mind.

"You must be hungry after carrying in all this gear."

Her voice came out an octave higher than normal. Caddie coughed. "There's still some fish left, and a pone of fresh cornbread, if you'd care to eat."

A strange look came over his face, as though she'd done him an injury. Perhaps one of the new masters of the land would take offense at eating the leavings of folks they had conquered.

Caddie's pride savagely uprooted the tiny seed of interest she'd taken in Manning Forbes. "Of course, if you'd rather not—"

"No!" The word exploded from him. Then, as if shamed by his own eagerness, he added quietly, "I'd be glad of a bite to eat. Thank you, ma'am. I'll just go wash up first."

Before she could recover her composure enough to tell him where he might find a water pump, he had gone out the front door. Caddie wasn't certain what made her follow him.

Perhaps it was her fear he'd take too long hunting for the pump out behind the old smokehouse. Darkness had begun to gather on the eastern horizon and she didn't want to be entertaining a strange man—a strange Yankee—in her dining room after moonrise.

To her surprise, Manning Forbes strode the unlikely path to the smokehouse as though he knew the way by heart. He jerked the pump handle up and down several times until he got a good flow going. Then he rubbed his hands under the cold running water. A few more tugs on the lever and he thrust his head under, gasping at the water's chill.

He gasped again when he opened his eyes to find Caddie staring at him.

"You don't have to spy on me every minute, Mrs. Marsh." The Yankee raked long fingers back through his dark, wet hair.

The harshness of his voice went through Caddie like a winter wind, making the hairs on her neck stand on end and the tips of her breasts push out against her basque. She couldn't summon up a single word of reply.

"If I was going to steal from you or…anything else, I wouldn't need to sneak around."

Too flustered to contend that this was *her* house, and that she had a right to monitor the comings and goings of anyone on her property, Caddie sputtered, "H-how did you find this pump? Visitors always used to complain of it being hard to locate."

"The pump?" He gave a sort of shamefaced grin, like a little boy caught in mischief. "Why, I went looking for it when I needed to water your mare. You're right, it was tough to find. Easier the second time."

Heat smoldered in Caddie's cheeks. "The mare, of course. You should have come and asked. I'd have told you the way."

He shrugged. "You were busy getting that fish cooked for the children."

"The fish. I almost forgot. Do come and eat."

Without another word, Manning Forbes followed her back to the house. Every step of the way, Caddie sensed his intrusive presence behind her, even though he kept a respectful distance.

The light had dimmed enough by the time they reached the dining room that she was obliged to rummage through her precious hoard of supplies for a candle. Though it took her some time to find and light one, Mr. Forbes was still eating with slow, meticulous bites when she set the flickering taper on the table.

Caddie hesitated. Now that she had nothing else to occupy her, it seemed rude not to sit with her *guest* while he finished his meal. After months of scrambling at the beck and call of several Union officers at the boardinghouse she'd kept in Richmond, she'd vowed it would be a frosty day in Hades before she ever again broke bread with a Yankee.

It felt traitorous. Like everything else about her reaction to this man.

As if he sensed her indecision, Manning Forbes glanced up. He didn't smile. Caddie suspected he seldom did.

"I know you aren't anxious to hear what I've come to say, Mrs. Marsh." He turned the fork in his hand over and over as he spoke. "But since we have to pass the time for a few minutes anyhow, what can it ail you to listen?"

There was something grave, and perhaps a little shy, about his expression that put her in mind of her son. She could no more resist or deny it than she could resist or deny Templeton.

"Very well." Reluctantly, she lowered herself into the chair opposite him. "Speak your piece, since you seem determined to. Only don't expect to receive the answer you want."

He broke their gaze abruptly, concentrating instead on digging a delicate filament of bone from his fish. "You don't even know what I'm going to ask."

"No, but I can guess it won't be anything to my advantage."

"Don't be too sure, ma'am."

He glanced back up, unexpectedly. Piercing her with a steel-blue stare that seemed to ferret out all her secrets, while protecting his own. "I have a little capital. Not much, but it's in gold and greenbacks, so it'll go a ways here in the South. Your country's been destroyed by the war, ma'am, and I believe there's money to be made in fixing it back up again."

An angry retort rose to Caddie's lips, but hung there unuttered. In Richmond they had a term of derision for Yankees like Manning Forbes—men who flocked south to pick clean the rotting carcass of the Confederacy like carrion crows.

Carpetbaggers.

Because they came with all their worldly goods in a carpetbag, ready to turn around and skedaddle back up North once they'd wrung every dollar they could out of the conquered South.

An ache of disappointment throbbed at the back of Caddie's throat, making it impossible for her to hurl that damning insult. She couldn't understand her contrary feelings. Hadn't she expected something like this from the Yankee when he'd mentioned having a business matter to discuss with her?

For the sake of her children's future, she wasn't sure she dared dismiss him, as she longed to do. This man who reminded her so acutely of things she most wanted to forget.

In the face of Mrs. Marsh's hostile silence, Manning stubbornly pushed on. "You have a fine place here, with a lot of potential, but it's going to take hard work and some seed money to make it prosperous again."

She should be able to see that, shouldn't she? Would this woman let pride stand in the way of a future for her children?

"I'm offering to put myself and my capital at your disposal, Mrs. Marsh, to get Sabbath Hollow back on its feet again."

Why didn't she say something? Manning wondered. Was he meant to take her opposition for granted?

"On what terms would you extend me this assistance, sir?" She spoke in a hushed tone, as if blaspheming against the Confederate cause and fearful of invoking the wrath of a secessionist Divinity.

The possibility of her acceptance rocked Manning as the probability of her rejection had not.

Her features flushed to a rosy hue, heightened by the candlelight. "What made you choose me and Sabbath Hollow in the first place? There must be other plantations that offer greater opportunities for profit, with less work and lower risk."

Manning's mouth opened and closed in rapid convulsions, like the trout writhing and gasping for water on the creek bank after he'd fished them out.

"I—I, that is, I fought in battles not far from here and I saw firsthand what a mess they made of this beautiful country. I guess I want to do a little something to make amends." Close enough to the truth, but not too close. "I suppose that sounds like foolish fancy to you."

She seemed to weigh the sincerity of his words. "On the contrary, Mr. Forbes. It's the most sensible thing I've heard a Yank—*anyone* say in quite a spell."

Manning could tell she grudged him the compliment. Still, it provided him with enough encouragement to plow ahead. "I make only one condition on my offer, ma'am. That our partnership be both a business and personal one."

His tongue fumbled over the words. Surely there must be a more graceful way to ask? His ears felt like a pair of red-hot fire irons. "What I mean is, I'd like you to marry me, ma'am."

If he'd torn the front of her threadbare dress open from collar to hem and begun to take liberties with the tender flesh beneath, Manning doubted Caddie Marsh could have looked more outraged.

Her face suddenly pale as whitewash, with green flames blazing in her eyes, she sprang from her chair and pointed toward the door. "How dare you even suggest such a thing? Take your infamous proposition and get out of my house this instant, you no-account carpetbagger!"

Her outstretched finger vibrated with barely suppressed violence. She must want to slap his face some bad.

Strangely, Manning found her abuse easier to accept than the hospitality she'd shown him earlier. With all the mute dignity he could muster, he rose from the table and left the house. Part of him wanted to perform a jig of relief that Widow Marsh had refused him in such emphatic terms.

Another part, a tiny one, to be sure, grieved his lost opportunity.

Chapter Three

Soldiers marshaled on the field of battle. Bugle notes punctured the expectant air. In the distance, an officer bellowed the order to charge.

Now they were stampeding toward her, rifle barrels belching smoke and bullets. A chorus of eerie ululating shrieks and the staccato crack of gunfire filled Caddie's ears. She crouched behind queer breastworks made of scrub buckets, washboards and butter churns. Her hands ached from their straining grip on the rifle stock.

"Let 'em come," bade a voice of harsh authority. "Don't waste your ammunition until the first wave gets good and close."

Caddie's nerves quivered as minié balls whizzed by her, so close she could feel the lethal breeze of their passing. Soon the enemy would storm this vulnerable position and butcher her.

"Open fire!"

In one swift motion, Caddie rose, leveled her weapon and discharged a shot. It caught one of the oncoming soldiers square in the chest. His arms flailed out as he staggered backward, slowly falling. He would be dead before he hit the ground.

The man's mouth rounded in a circle of surprise and dismay. His gaze stabbed her like a bayonet, and Caddie saw that she had shot her own husband.

"Cock-a-doodle-do!"

The rooster's shrill crow woke Caddie with a start. Her pulse thundered and beads of sweat prickled on her hairline. She stifled a scream as she found herself crouched in front of the nursery door with a Union army issue rifle clutched in her hands.

Out by the deserted slave quarters, the rooster crowed again. Fighting her mind free from the terrifying thrall of her nightmare, Caddie remembered that she had brought the vocal old bird with her from Richmond. Along with a few scrawny hens, precious as gold.

She forced herself to recollect how she'd acquired the Yankee's gun. In fractured pieces it all came back to her. She remembered sitting in the pillaged dining room of Sabbath Hollow, listening to the carpetbagger offer her everything she'd need to restore the plantation and her children's future. Much as it had galled her to accept help from one of his ilk, she'd been ready to swallow her pride one more time for the sake of Tem and Varina.

Then Manning Forbes had made his fumbling, preposterous proposal of marriage, igniting the powder keg of her brooding hatred for an enemy who'd stolen the heritage and birthright of her children. The heat of her rage had frightened Caddie, for she sensed it sprang from more than her loathing of the Yankees.

Wariness, perhaps, of failing again where she'd failed before. Fear of becoming intimate with a man once more—arming him with the power to maim her heart.

Giddy from lack of sleep, Caddie laughed out loud at her own foolishness. That kind of dangerous potential only lay in a relationship fueled with vulnerable trust and armed with an explosive charge of passion. She wouldn't need to worry about entertaining those kinds of feelings for a Union man. No matter how strongly he reminded her of the husband she'd once loved, before long-festering grievances and the subtle venom of suspicion had poisoned their marriage.

A few minutes after she ordered the Yankee out of her house, he'd come knocking at the door to offer her his rifle. This time he'd refused to take no for an answer.

"Even if your brother-in-law has decided to bide his time, this isn't a safe place for a lone woman and small children. I'll leave my gun and some ammunition by the door for you to collect after I'm gone. Do you know how to load and shoot?"

"I do." Caddie had shuddered at hearing herself speak those words to the carpetbagger.

His warning had spooked her, though. An inspection of the house revealed broken locks on more than one door. So Caddie had dozed fitfully, sitting outside the room where her children slept, clutching a Union rifle much like the weapon that must have killed her husband.

Now, as if reluctantly wakened by the cock's persistent crowing, feeble rays of early-morning sunlight ventured in through the windows. The panes of glass that hadn't been shattered were caked with four years of grime. Finding the money, time and energy to fix and clean them would have to be low on her list of priorities. After her long trip and all but sleepless night, Caddie wasn't sure she could summon the ambition to make breakfast for her children, let alone tackle the countless problems of Sabbath Hollow.

Surrender was not an option, though, Caddie sternly reminded herself as she struggled to her feet, trying to ignore the protests of her aching bones. What she wouldn't give for a cup of morning coffee. Real coffee—not the bitter brew of hominy and parched corn that no amount of sorghum could sweeten. So intense was her longing for it that

Caddie almost fancied she could smell its dark, rich aroma on the morning air.

Pulling her shawl tight around her thin shoulders, she did her best to disregard the beguiling falsehood her nose was telling her. She removed the ammunition from Manning Forbes's rifle and took the empty weapon down to the kitchen, where she set it on top of a tall cupboard.

"I wonder if those worthless old hens have managed to lay an egg or two for the children's breakfast?" she mumbled to herself, shuffling out the kitchen door.

On the back step, the toe of her shoe collided with a spouted pot of battered tinware. If it had been empty, she might have kicked it over. But it wasn't empty. The heavenly fragrance of real coffee could no longer be denied.

Suddenly wary, Caddie glanced around at the outbuildings for Manning Forbes. She saw no sign of him. The notion that he'd been camped all night down by the creek, within earshot of the house, flooded her with a ridiculous sense of security.

She tried to resist the pot of coffee. Accepting it felt traitorously symbolic of a more significant consent. And wasn't it just like a Yankee to think she could be bribed into dishonor with small luxuries?

Caddie's noble self-denial lasted less than a minute. By the time the children began to stir, she had two cups of black coffee inside her, warming her belly and firing her ambition. She'd managed to collect four eggs and an armload of firewood to cook breakfast. As she hummed a chorus of "Dixie," the restoration of Sabbath Hollow no longer seemed quite so daunting.

"Where's the fish man?" demanded Varina awhile later, her chin yellow with soft-boiled egg yolk and crumbs of cornmeal. "Will he bring us more for dinner?"

"I don't imagine so, precious." Caddie wiped the child's face with a damp rag while Varina grimaced and squirmed.

"The creek is full of fish, free for the taking, though. Maybe Tem can rig up a line and catch us some."

Templeton pushed a long hank of hair off his brow, but kept his gaze fixed on his plate. "I don't know how to catch fish. Besides, there might be wild animals down by the creek."

"If there are, they'd be far smaller than you, dear." Caddie struggled to keep a sober face. There was nothing amusing about her son's timidity. Any eight-year-old who'd lived through as many frightening experiences as Templeton had a right to be cautious. "Quite a few of them are good eating, too. Roast quail—mmm."

"Do you think Mr. Forbes would teach me how to fish and shoot a gun, Mama?" Tem looked up just then, with a pointed gaze that made Caddie flinch.

"I don't believe Mr. Forbes will be staying around these parts much longer, Son." Though she tried to pass the remark off in a light, casual tone, the thought provoked strong conflicting feelings within her.

"That's too bad. He's nice—for a Yankee."

"I don't b'lieve he *is* a Yankee," declared Varina, as if that settled the matter.

"'Course he's a Yankee, puddin' head." Tem made a face at his sister. "Just not like the Yankee soldiers from Richmond, smoking and cussing and ordering folks around. There must be *some* good Yankees, mustn't there, Mama?"

A spiteful retort died on Caddie's tongue. No matter what her own feelings, she would not raise her children to hate. Not because the Yankees didn't deserve it, but because a mother's intuition warned her it would damage Tem and Varina to harbor such corrosive emotions in their young hearts.

"You must recollect what I've always told you, Templeton. There's good and bad in all of us, like vegetables and weeds in a garden. We need to tend to our virtues and root out our vices as best we can. Some folks let the weeds in their nature get away from them, until all the good is choked out.''

Catching her children in an exchange of meaningful glances, Caddie chuckled. The rusty sound surprised her. She could scarcely remember the last time she'd laughed.

''You didn't think I could let our first morning back at Sabbath Hollow get by without a moral, did you? Besides, you brought it up, Tem. I can't imagine why you two have taken such a shine to that carp—er, to Mr. Forbes.''

Why indeed? Could it be his likeness to their father? Caddie doubted it. Her one photograph of Del had disappeared forever in the flaming anarchy of Richmond's fall to General Grant. Varina had been just a baby on Del's last leave. And Templeton had never been close to his father.

The boy shrugged. ''I just wish he didn't have to go away.''

Varina nodded in solemn agreement. ''I like fish.''

It was going to take more than a mess of brook trout, a pot of coffee and the loan of a rifle to persuade Caddie Marsh he wasn't some kind of monster. Manning wasn't sure anything on earth could change that woman's mind once she'd made it up. While he admired such stubborn strength, he had to find some means to win her over.

Last night, after she'd given him his marching orders, Manning had wandered back to his camp by the creek in a daze of relief and defeat. He'd asked the woman and she'd said no; he would simply have to find another avenue to fulfil his vow.

Protect and provide.

He'd made a feeble stab at both commissions with the rifle and the fish. Yet his showdown with Alonzo Marsh had made Manning realize something. Unless he married

Caddie, he would have no authority to intervene on her account.

Retrieving a blanket from his camp, he had trudged back up to the gentle rise overlooking the plantation. There he'd propped himself up against the trunk of an old poplar tree and watched the house until dawn. The long empty hours of his vigil had given him plenty of time to think.

Too much time.

Perhaps he could try furnishing money and other aid to them from a distance, Manning decided, staring up at the pale, haunting face of the full spring moon. The notion appealed to him. He could keep his promise without constant reminders of his transgression chafing his conscience.

The moon's ghostly visage seemed to mock him. If only it could be that simple! What if the widow took it into her head to marry someone else, by and by? And what if that someone mistreated her or the children? Manning would have no right to take their part then, either. The thought of such impotence tied his belly in knots.

Vivid recollections of Caddie Marsh bedeviled other parts of his body, much to Manning's shame. The flickering caress of candlelight coaxing her hair to a coppery glow, softening the ravages of hardship from her features. The intensity of her gray-green gaze both times he'd caught her watching him. There had been a queer, mute intimacy in the looks they'd exchanged—almost like a touch.

No other woman had affected him so. That this one did made Manning want to fling himself in the saddle and ride north as if the three-headed hound of Hades was baying at his heels. But his pledge bound him to her, like it or not.

With dawn not far off, he'd brewed coffee to warm and wake himself. On a whim, he'd stolen down to the old mansion in the hollow and left a pot for Caddie Marsh to find. He'd half expected her to chase him off with his own rifle, but when he reached the back step unchallenged, worry snaked through his gut. He couldn't stay awake every night to keep watch over them.

So Manning had saddled up his horse and ridden into the nearest settlement, Mercer's Corner. Midmorning found him wending his way back down the lane to Sabbath Hollow, with his saddlebags bulging and a lean, ugly dog loping behind his horse on a tether. Sometime during the past restless night and fatigue-addled daybreak, he'd made up his mind to match the fair widow stubborn for stubborn until she agreed to his proposal.

She looked as intractable as ever when he first caught sight of her wrestling a big trunk out onto the verandah. She looked disturbingly fair, too, with rebellious tendrils of auburn hair escaping from their sedate, orderly arrangement to curl around her face. A face rosy from her exertions.

Manning braced himself to be ordered away and scolded for returning after last night.

Instead, Caddie Marsh approached him without a word, the pink hue of her face deepening. Hands fluttering as if she wasn't sure what to do with them. Eyes downcast, unwilling to meet his gaze.

Emboldened, Manning swung out of his saddle and doffed his hat. "Morning, ma'am. I trust you and your children weren't disturbed in the night."

No matter how badly she might want him gone, Southern gentility prevailed. "We're fine, Mr. Forbes, thank you. You've decided to move on, I see."

Did she sound just the tiniest bit regretful?

"I expect you've come to collect your rifle," she continued. "It was kind of you to give me the loan of it last night. I suppose I have you to thank for the coffee, as well."

It stuck in her craw, being beholden to a former enemy; Manning sensed it as plainly as if she'd screamed the words in his face. Somehow he must convince her that a business and personal partnership between them would be a favor from her to him, not the other way around.

Before he could tell her she was welcome for the rifle and the coffee, Caddie Marsh looked up. The green blaze in her eyes belied her modestly composed features. "I won't be bought."

"Bought?" The word spewed out of him. "Of course not! How can you think such a thing?"

"After Richmond fell, I saw plenty of women sell themselves to the Yankees, Mr. Forbes. They'd have rather died first, but they did it to keep their children alive. I was lucky enough to have a house still standing. With shelter at a premium, I only had to board Yankee officers, not bed them."

Was she trying to shock him into going away and leaving her alone? Manning felt the blood rise in his face until his cheeks tingled. God bless him, he must be the color of a pickled beet!

No wonder she'd turned down his marriage offer. He knew so clearly what he wanted from her that he'd assumed she must understand, too. Apparently she'd drawn different conclusions.

"I wasn't making *that* kind of bargain when I asked you to marry me, Mrs. Marsh." A quiver in his loins warned Manning that he wished he was.

"You weren't?" Her face betrayed surprise and bewilderment.

"Not now." He stifled a vision that rose in his mind of candlelight flickering over Caddie Marsh wearing only a lace-trimmed nightgown, her mahogany hair unbound in a cascade of curls down her back. "Not ever."

"I…" She scanned the ground at his feet as if searching there for the words she needed.

Manning gave her the opportunity to collect herself. "I need to marry you for legal reasons, ma'am, to protect my interest in Sabbath Hollow. Once I start fixing it up, I'd have to spend long hours out here. I expect you know how folks talk. I wouldn't want to compromise your reputation—especially now that I know all you had to do to preserve it.''

"I see. So you wouldn't expect me to—"

"I wouldn't." He cut her off rather than risk hearing her say aloud what he proposed to deny himself. "I'll take a bed wherever you can spare one in the house. It'll just be like taking in another boarder."

"And my children?"

"I won't be a husband to you, Mrs. Marsh, but I *will* do my best to be a good stepfather to them, if you'll give me leave." He sensed a subtle shift in her bearing that might bode well.

Manning decided to press his advantage. "I mean to come asking every day until you say yes, ma'am. I hope your reason will get the best of your resentment against the Union. You need a man around the place, and unless you've changed your mind about your brother-in-law's invitation, men aren't in very abundant supply around here."

"And whose fault is that?" Her abrupt question bit into him, like a willow switch.

Manning hung his head. "I didn't kill all of 'em, ma'am." Was he voicing his protest to her, or to himself?

He heard her suck in a breath. "Of course you didn't, Mr. Forbes. I can't picture you doing anyone violence."

Manning flinched as though he'd taken a second strike directly on top of the first.

"What's the fish man doing here?"

Manning almost burst into giddy laughter at the child's imperious query, for it extracted him from an unbearably awkward exchange with her mother.

"He's come courting Mama," replied her brother in a

tentative tone that left Manning unsure whether the boy approved or not.

Caddy Marsh whirled around. "Templeton and Varina Marsh, how long have you been eavesdropping? Now that we're back home, I'm going to have to polish your manners, I can see that."

"What's courting?" demanded Varina.

Templeton nudged his sister to be quiet. "We haven't been here long, Mama, honest. I thought you'd hear us coming."

"*What's* courting?"

Mrs. Marsh relented in the face of her son's chagrin. "Next time, make a noise or call out from a distance before you can hear what folks are saying. That's what a gentleman would do."

"*What's courting!*"

Manning fought back a grin. Dropping to his haunches, he looked at the little mite eye-to-eye. Something about her steely gaze put him in mind of General Sherman. "Courting means I've asked your mama to marry me, Miss Varina."

"What's marry?"

Before Manning could reply, Templeton spoke. "Shucks, Rina, don't be such a baby. Marry means he'd live with us and be our new pa." The boy's tone sounded anxious, but whether from fear or eagerness, Manning couldn't tell for certain.

"And we'd have fish for supper every night?"

"Varina Virginia Marsh!" cried her mother.

Surrendering to his own amusement, Manning chuckled. By the sound of it, he had a potential ally in his campaign to make Caddie Marsh his wife. An ally of considerable determination.

"I can't promise fish *every* night, Miss Varina. You

might get sick of it if I did. But I can hunt possum and quail. Maybe buy a sow to raise shoats for barbecue.''

"What's barbecue?''

"Something you'll enjoy, unless I miss my guess.''

Abandoning her interrogation for the moment, the child looked up at her mother. "Did you tell him *yes,* Mama?''

"I—I have to study on it, Varina.'' Caddie's cheeks pinkened and she cast Manning a glance that might have held bashfulness or resentment. Possibly a compound of both. "A lady shouldn't accept a gentleman's proposal right off. That'd be too forward.''

Manning almost chuckled again. The woman made it sound like he was some sort of gallant beau and she a blushing debutante culminating their lengthy courtship.

"Your mama's right, Miss Varina. Marriage is a big step folks oughtn't to rush into.'' He straightened from his crouch. "I'm content to bide my time until she makes up her mind.''

From behind his sister, Templeton spoke in a quiet, wistful tone. "That's a nice dog you got there, sir.''

Manning glanced back. Though the poor beast was anything but handsome, it had behaved well during his talk with Mrs. Marsh. Perhaps he'd tuckered it out trotting back from town. It lay in the shadow of his horse, panting softly.

"He's not mine, Son. I brought him for you folks. An out-of-the-way plantation like this needs a good watchdog.''

With wary incredulity, the boy looked from Manning to the scarecrow mongrel.

"I think he's hot and thirsty,'' said Manning. "Would you and your sister do me a favor and take him to get a drink?''

"All right.'' Varina answered for her brother, but it was Templeton who lunged forward to take the rope tether from Manning's hand.

Caddie Marsh watched her children as they walked away with the dog—Templeton holding on to the end of the rope, Varina's sturdy fingers fisted through the loop around the animal's neck. The dog's tail picked up momentum with each step, wagging from side to side. It seemed pitifully grateful to have found a home.

Manning envied that scruffy old mutt with all his heart.

"That was very thoughtful of you, Mr. Forbes." Mrs. Marsh nodded after Tem and Varina. "Templeton's always wanted a dog of his own, and I'd feel a good deal safer with a watchdog around the place. But I'm going to have trouble keeping the children and myself fed. That poor creature needs a master who can afford to take proper care of him."

"I'll furnish whatever he needs, Mrs. Marsh. With the Sergeant on guard duty, I can get some sleep at nights."

The carpetbagger's words rocked Caddie back on her heels. "You stayed awake all last night keeping watch on the house?"

"Yes, ma'am." Manning Forbes turned his hat round and round by the brim, looking for all the world like a petty criminal confessing his misdeed to the justice.

"That makes two of us." Caddie yawned just thinking about it.

Though he struggled to suppress it, a yawn overtook the Yankee, too.

Perhaps that exhaustion had sapped her will, making her too tired to resist. Too tired to hate.

By herself, she'd barely be able to scratch out a living at Sabbath Hollow for her children. Manning Forbes had the wherewithal to make it *something* again. Tem and Varina needed a man in their lives—a soft-spoken, generous man to make them forget the Yankee officers in Richmond.

The kind of marriage he offered was one she might succeed at. One uncomplicated by double-sided emotions like love and passion. As she grew more familiar with Manning Forbes, surely his bewildering likeness to Del would fade and her unsettling fascination for him would dim.

Manning Forbes admitted another good deed. ''I took the liberty of bringing a few things from town that I thought you might need, ma'am. You're welcome to them whether you say yes or no to my proposal.''

He appeared bent on putting her in his debt. For pride's sake and for Tem and Varina's future, she must repay him with the only currency left to her.

''Yes,'' gasped Caddie before she lost her nerve.

He didn't seem to understand what she was telling him. ''I'll just shift these supplies into your kitchen, then, shall I, ma'am?''

''Yes!''

He turned to his horse and began unloading his saddlebags.

''Yes, Mr. Forbes. Yes, I'll marry you. If you're stubborn enough to keep asking until I agree, I'm smart enough not to delay the inevitable.''

He froze with his back to her. When he turned again, his face had paled to the gray-white of ash. A barb of disappointment snagged Caddie's heart. Despite his protestations that their marriage would be for the sake of business and propriety only, she'd expected him to greet her answer a bit more eagerly. If only so he wouldn't have to spend another night sleeping out-of-doors.

''That's fine then.'' His voice sounded hollow. Haunted. ''If you want to break the news to your children, I'll harness the mare so we can all ride into town and hunt up a preacher.''

An hour later, Caddie found herself standing before the Methodist parson in Mercer's Corner making promises she'd sworn never to make again. She tried to steel herself for the stares she'd get when her neighbors discovered she'd wed a Yankee carpetbagger.

By contrast, she could hardly wait to see the look on her brother-in-law's face when he heard about her marriage.

Chapter Four

"Caddie's gone and done *what?*" As Alonzo Marsh glared at Manning, the muscles of his aristocratic jaw stretched so tight they looked ready to twitch.

On the way home from their hasty wedding, Manning and his new family had stopped by Hemlock Grove to drop off the rest of Lon and Lydene's belongings.

Manning resisted a nagging urge to grin over the drawling Virginian's obvious agitation. "I'll say it again, louder, if your hearing's poor, Mr. Marsh."

He raised his voice, exaggerating each word. "Your sister-in-law and I got married in Mercer's Corner half an hour ago."

"I heard you the first time, Yankee!" Lon ground his heel onto the faintly smoking length of cigar that had fallen from his mouth. "I don't know what kind of tricks or threats you used to drag that fool gal in front of a parson, but I warn you, you're going to regret meddling with my family and my property."

"*My* family, now." Saying those words made Manning almost dizzy. Yet they tasted so sweet on his tongue, he could not resist saying them again. "My family and my wife's property. Meddle with either and *you'll* have cause to regret it.''

Lon's pale eyes narrowed. His nostrils flared, as if they couldn't drag enough air in to stoke the furnace of his fury.

''You don't know who you're messing with, Yankee.'' His voice was quiet, but harsh with hate. Manning knew better than to underestimate the danger this man might pose.

''Neither do you, Marsh. So why don't we agree to stay clear of each other? I can't speak for you, but I've just about had my fill of fighting.''

The Virginian's mouth turned up at the corners, but no one would be fool enough to mistake it for a smile. ''I'm just getting warmed up, Yankee.''

Over Manning's shoulder, he called to the children in the wagon. ''If this carpetbagger here treats you bad, you two just light out to your uncle Lon, you hear? You'll always have a good home waiting for you with me and Lydene.''

Not once during the war, when it had been his duty to shoot and kill his fellow Americans, had Manning Forbes wanted so desperately to do another man injury. His hands balled into hard, tight fists at his sides. They trembled with his yearning to batter Lon Marsh's handsome, contemptuous face. Clinging to his self-control, Manning forced himself to turn his back on the Virginian and stalk off to the buckboard.

He glanced at Caddie's ashen face as he vaulted onto the wagon seat, then flicked the reins over the mare's skinny rump. Had Lon's words spawned greater doubts about the wisdom of wedding him? Surely she hadn't paid any heed to that venomous slander about him mistreating the children?

''What's a carpetbagger?'' asked Varina as the buckboard rattled away from her uncle's place. She perched on her mother's lap, while Templeton sat wedged between the adults, with the dog huddled at his feet.

"It's a very nasty word," replied Caddie before Manning could collect himself to reply. "I'll wash your mouths out with soap if I ever hear you or Templeton repeat it. Is that understood, Varina Marsh?"

From behind them, Lon hollered, "At least have the sense to keep him out of your bed, Caddie! Then you'll be able to get out of this fool marriage when you come to your senses. Have you thought what Del would say if he knew you'd brought a Yankee to live under his roof?"

"Ya!" Manning urged the old horse to greater speed, fleeing Lon's barrage of poisoned missiles.

Was it his sensitive imagination, or did he feel Templeton edging away from him? The boy's hand passed over and over the back of the dog in a rhythm perhaps intended to soothe himself.

Almost too quietly to be heard, the little fellow murmured, "You won't treat Varina and me bad, will you, sir?"

"Templeton Randolph Marsh!" cried his mother. "You apologize this minute for asking such a question."

Beneath the scrupulous Southern civility, Manning heard a faint note of doubt in her voice. Nothing Alonzo Marsh could say would have the power to wound him like this mute shadow of uneasiness from Caddie.

"Don't scold the boy, ma'am." Manning wondered if he'd ever bring himself to speak her Christian name. He certainly couldn't call her *Mrs. Marsh* anymore. And *Mrs. Forbes* would sound vaguely blasphemous to him. "It's an important question and he has a right to know the answer."

"So do I," insisted Varina.

For the first time since they'd driven onto Lon Marsh's property, Manning felt his brooding ill-temper begin to lift. He had no experience of little girls, yet he sensed this one was out of the common. He was pretty sure he liked the difference.

"You do, Miss Varina. You both do." Manning took a deep breath. He didn't want to give them unrealistic expectations. Perhaps it wasn't in him to be a father, or even a second-rate substitute for one.

"I can't promise you'll always like what I say or do, but I swear I'll try to be as good to you as your own pa would if he was here. Your uncle Lon doesn't know me very well, and—"

"He thinks you're mean on account of you shot at his toes," Varina explained with exaggerated patience, as if illuminating a great mystery.

Manning glanced at Caddie over the top of her daughter's head. She raised her eyes heavenward as if to ask *What am I going to do with this child?*

He ventured a brief smile, hoping to let her know that whatever she'd done so far was just fine.

To Varina he replied, "I guess I'll have to be on my best behavior for a while. To show your uncle I don't go around shooting at folks as a rule."

They drove the rest of the way home in silence. Off in the distance Manning glimpsed fine old houses scourged by the tide of war. If his plans for Sabbath Hollow took shape as he wanted them to, Manning hoped it might be a catalyst to revive this whole section of the county.

Now that he and Caddie were married, he would have to get busy putting his plan into effect. After the previous night's tense vigil and the momentous events of the day, however, all Manning wanted to do was throw himself onto some excuse for a bed and sleep long and deeply.

"Ham and grits for supper," announced Caddie when the buckboard pulled up at Sabbath Hollow. "Tem, take your sister and go collect me some kindling for the fire."

"Can we take Sergeant with us, sir?" the boy asked Manning.

"That's what he's here for, Son. To go around with you two and look out for you."

Manning jumped from the wagon and hurried around to help the womenfolk down. When Caddie's hand, coarsened by work but still slender and graceful, made contact with his, a queer sensation traveled all the way up his arm.

He let go abruptly and turned to speak to the boy. "He's your dog now, Templeton. You don't have to call him Sergeant if you have another name you like better."

Remembering what Caddie had told him about boarding Union officers in Richmond, Manning doubted that anything military would have pleasant associations for her children. "I just called him that on account of my sergeant used to have a beard about the color of this fellow's coat."

"Sergeant's a good name."

The dog swiped his tongue over Templeton's fingers as though acknowledging the compliment.

Tem chuckled. "He's like a soldier, standing guard over us. Come on, Rina, let's get the wood for Mama to cook supper."

"Ham and grits and ham and grits, ham and grits, ham and grits…" sang Varina as she marched off with her brother.

She was still singing it more than an hour later when they sat down to eat and later still when it came time for bed.

Templeton gazed at Sergeant with wistful eyes when his mother forbade him taking the animal to sleep in his room.

"He needs to stay outside so he can keep watch, Tem." Caddie pointed her son toward the stairs.

"Then can I sleep outside with him?" Before his mother could answer, Tem turned to Manning. "Can I, sir?"

Manning glanced from the boy's hopeful face to his

mother's. "Would it be so terrible if Sergeant slept at the foot of the boy's bed for this one night? It's the children I bought him to guard in the first place."

"Yahoo! Thanks, sir. Come on, Sarge." Flashing Manning a grateful grin, Templeton raced up the stairs as fast as his skinny legs would carry him.

The dog scrambled after his master, paws scratching against the bare wood of the stairs.

Before Manning could properly savor his stepson's felicity, Caddie swept past him. Her tight-lipped glare made him feel like some vermin who'd invaded her house.

He frowned back. Was it such a crime to have made the boy happy? The house was a mess, anyway. A whole pack of dogs running loose couldn't have made it a whit worse. Besides, this might go a ways to allaying any fears Templeton might harbor about the treatment he could expect from his stepfather.

Thrusting the whole incident to the back of his mind, Manning busied himself with a few small repair jobs around the house while Caddie put the children to bed. Sabbath Hollow would need a lot of labor and care to make it anything like it had once been. The only way to get there would be one job at a time in every minute he could spare.

By the time Caddie came back downstairs, Manning was losing the struggle to keep his eyes open.

"I made up a bed for you." She spoke in a frost-crusted voice, staring steadily at some object just behind him. "Third door on the left at the top of the stairs. I got the linen out of an old trunk in the attic. It smells awful musty, I'm afraid, but I'll wash it tomorrow."

Manning turned toward the stairs. "It has to beat an old army blanket and a tree trunk. Thank you for making the bed up—you needn't have gone to any trouble."

He had not climbed far when Caddie's voice stalled him. "Is it true what Lon said?"

His head rocked with weariness and his body ached in strange ways from being so close to her. The day's events had roused his emotions to a pitch he usually took care to avoid. He was tired of being called and thought a *Yankee* and a *carpetbagger*.

As Manning spun around and thundered back down the stairs to face his unclaimed bride, his anger flashed like a photographer's phosphorous.

"Did you not listen to what I told the children, or did you think I was lying to them? I've given you no reason to think I'd ever mistreat Templeton and Varina. Just because I wasn't born in the South doesn't mean I'm some kind of criminal!"

"No, no!" She clapped a hand to her lips and moved toward Manning, stopping so close to him he could have reached out and touched her.

If he'd dared.

Her slender fingers fluttered down her lips, coming to rest on her chin. "I didn't mean about the children. It's the other. About getting out of our marriage if I didn't...if we didn't..."

"Oh, that." Manning's anger ebbed, but the strange agitation lingered.

Her nearness disturbed him. The queer look in her eye, half frightened, half curious, disturbed him. The subject of her question disturbed him most of all.

"I can't claim much knowledge of these matters." He stepped back from her. "But I don't think your brother-in-law is lying. An unconsummated marriage can be dissolved."

"Then must we...?" She hugged her arms tightly around herself, as if protecting her bosom.

Manning didn't want to think about her bosom.

She tried again. "You said we wouldn't need to..."

"And you think because I'm a Yankee I must have bamboozled you into wedding with false promises?'' Manning shook his head. ''I haven't. Nobody needs to know our...sleeping arrangements but us. This can be a kind of insurance policy for you, if you decide I'm more trouble than I'm worth to keep around.''

''You mean it?'' She seemed to sway on her feet, but whether from relief or exhaustion, Manning wasn't sure.

''I do.'' It was the second time he'd spoken those words to her in the last several hours.

Would he be able to keep from blurting them out a third time if she asked him one short, simple question?

Do you want me?

It wasn't as though she wanted a Yankee carpetbagger in her bed, Caddie told herself as she tossed and turned on her musty sheets. So why had her flutter of panic been accompanied by another flutter in that secret spot, deeper than the pit of her belly? Why had her sigh of relief also quivered with a faint note of regret?

Because he reminds you of Del, reason informed her, like a schoolmarm impatient with the class dunce. *You're back in Del's home with Del's children, married to a man who bears a strong resemblance to him.*

Of course. Caddie chuckled softly to herself as she rolled over again. Considered in that light, it was only natural she'd think about the things a husband and wife did together in the dark, private moments before sleep.

But to think of them with a tremble of longing? Caddie lay on her back and stared at the ceiling, where shadowy moonbeams danced. She'd never taken much pleasure from those hasty, demanding marital encounters with Del. She was pretty certain proper-bred ladies weren't supposed to.

A few times she had sensed the potential for enjoyment in Del's probing caresses of her bare skin, in his hurried thrusting between her legs. Before it could develop into anything more than a vague pulse in her loins, Del had always made one last grunting jab into her and rolled off, snoring.

One of the most painful shards of memory from the day she'd caught Del and Lydene in bed together was the sound of that vulgar creature. Giggling, purring and panting—obviously relishing Del's carnal attentions. More shameful still, Del had sounded as though he was enjoying himself far better than he ever had in his lawful marriage bed.

How Caddie wished she could forget about it all and go to sleep!

Thanks to the man resting peacefully in the next room, she couldn't forget. Like a toothache, those sordid, painful memories gnawed at her until nearly dawn. And when that strutting old he-creature of a rooster began to trumpet the rising sun, Caddie very nearly ran outside to ring his neck. To blazes with what he cost and how much they needed him to start a brood of chicks!

Squeezing her eyes shut, she tried to extract a few moments of true rest from the night. Then the dog barked from the nursery. Caddie jammed the lumpy, threadbare pillow over her head to shut out the noise and almost suffocated from the dank odor. When she came up gasping for air, the dog had quieted, but her new husband was stirring in the room next door.

"Is there some kind of male conspiracy afoot to deprive me of a decent night's rest?" Caddie grumbled to herself as she rose and dressed.

She stripped the musty linens from her bed, then marched out the door. There she collided with Mr. Forbes, who had just emerged from *his* room.

"Oh, glory be!" Caddie stumbled over one of his long feet.

Manning caught her. The cloth of her dress had grown

so flimsy, she could feel the heat of his large, strong hands through it. Where he touched her, it burned.

Or did it itch?

Manning Forbes might be a stranger, but he was also her husband. If he made up his mind to lay hands on her, he'd be well within his rights. She had only his word that their connubial arrangement stopped short of the bedroom door.

The word of a Yankee. Caddie had never expected to see the day when she'd be prepared to rely on that. Was Lon right? Had she lost her mind, agreeing to this marriage?

"Pardon me!"

"My fault. I should have been watching...."

They fumbled apart. Both blushing. Neither making more than fleeting eye contact.

This arrangement had sounded so easy and practical when Mr. Forbes had advanced it yesterday. In the intimate light of early morning, Caddie realized it would be anything but. In fact, she suspected it was going to be mighty awkward. Today and for a long time to come.

"You slept well, I hope." She plastered herself back against the wall, the bundle of bedding held like a shield in front of her.

"Fine." The shadows under his eyes told a different story. "And you?"

"Very well, thanks." If he could lie about it, so could she.

"I'll get some coffee from my pack and brew us a pot, shall I?" Manning asked as they descended the stairs.

"You fetch the coffee. I'll make it." Eager as she was for a cup, somehow the notion of a Yankee blundering around in her kitchen didn't sit right with her. "Then I'll go check if the hens have laid."

"I can do that for you." Manning Forbes passed Caddie a small sack of coffee beans, then headed for the door.

"No!"

The questioning, anxious look on the Yankee's face reproached her in a way no words could have done. She didn't mean to sound ungrateful, but she'd already accepted more of his help than her pride could tolerate.

"I'll see to breakfast." Caddie struggled to blunt the sharpness that crept into her voice. "In the meantime, could I prevail upon you to chop me some firewood?"

"Yes, of course." His whole bearing radiated eagerness to be of service. "I'll get Templeton to help me."

An anxious whimper rose unbidden from Caddie's throat.

"Yes?" Manning Forbes shot her a swift glance.

It galled her to admit weakness in herself or her kin, especially to a Yankee. Concern for her little boy did battle with her pride and left it a bloody wreck.

"Don't expect too much of Templeton, please. He never was a very forward child and he had a hard time growing up through the war. So many frights. So many worries. Varina never knew anything else, so she took it all as a matter of course. She'll sleep like a log anywhere and eat what doesn't eat her first."

Manning chuckled as he headed out the back door. "She seems a very self-reliant little mite."

"Oh, she's all of that. And it was a blessing while we were in Richmond. I don't know how I could have managed with *two* highstrung children." Caddie had no intention of confiding in a Yankee, but somehow she couldn't help herself. "It's going to be uphill work making a proper lady of her, though."

Manning found out just what Caddie meant later that morning when he and Templeton were scavenging for deadwood to split.

They had pulled a fallen maple trunk clear of some underbrush when a series of piercing shrieks rent the air. Manning had heard nothing like them since the battlefield amputations at Antietam. Sergeant began to bark wildly.

Had an intruder broken into the house and attacked Caddie and Varina? Manning dropped his hatchet.

"Stay here, Son!" He glanced at Templeton, then bolted for the house.

Strangely, the boy did not look a bit perturbed.

"Mr. Forbes, sir," Templeton called out, barely audible over the screaming and the barking. He didn't sound perturbed, either. "That's prob'ly just Rina getting her hair combed."

Manning slowed his desperate scramble and looked back at the boy. "Are you sure?"

Templeton nodded, petting the dog to calm it. "She takes on like this every time Mama combs her hair."

The ferocity of the caterwauling had not abated. Manning found it hard to believe the child wasn't being butchered with a dull meat ax.

"I'll just go see if I can help any."

The boy looked dubious. "I'd stay clear if I was you."

Manning kept walking toward the house, though his gut tightened way down deep, a sensation he recalled from the tense hours before battle.

He found Caddie and her daughter in a large room that must have once been a fine parlor. At some time before or during the war, it had been stripped of furnishings right down to the curtains. Once likely spread with luxurious rugs, the hardwood floor now hid its proud face under a carpet of grime many layers thick.

In the corner beside an impressive fireplace, Caddie had managed to corral her daughter. Now she held the struggling child tightly around the waist, while her other hand raked a comb through Varina's rusty mane. Manning winced as he watched the little girl's sturdy heel collide with her mother's knee. Wrestling a yearling hog would have been easier.

Varina's raucous vocal protests echoed off the bare expanses of wall, ceiling and floor, making them sound even louder.

If he had any sense, he'd heed Templeton's warning and steal away again. But he couldn't bear to let any opportunity to help escape him.

Manning sucked in a deep breath, and when the child paused briefly for air, he bellowed, "That's quite enough, young lady!"

Thanks to battlefield promotions, he'd mustered out of the army a captain. He'd had to learn how to put the fear of God into his subordinates when necessary. Now he put on his sternest face of command. "*What* is the meaning of all this commotion? I thought someone was being murdered!"

Mother and child froze in a comic tableau, their eyes wide and mouths round.

Caddie recovered her wits first. "Don't pay any mind. Varina always takes on like this when I comb her hair— and near as bad when I wash her face. I don't care how our family fortunes have fallen, I won't have my child traipsing around like some little cracker gal!"

She seemed to be addressing this last part to the child, but the resentment in her voice suggested that he, being the nearest Yankee at hand, was personally responsible for her daughter's deficiencies in grooming.

Varina thrust out her lower lip and scowled. "I bet Aunt Lydene wouldn't comb my hair or wash my face."

"You are not too big to paddle, young lady!"

"Combs hurt!"

"If you wouldn't squirm so, I could take my time and be gentle. Besides, you never take a scrap of notice when you fall and bloody your knee."

"No call to cry after it's over."

Manning almost choked on suppressed laughter. By will, he dragged down the corners of his mouth. "Ladies, ladies. That'll be quite enough. Templeton and I could use your help gathering wood, Varina, but if your hair is flying wild it'll get caught in the twigs. That'll hurt worse than your mother's comb."

The child's pout grudgingly twisted into a grin.

"May I have the comb, please?" Manning held out his hand.

"I'm fully capable of dressing my own daughter's hair, sir."

"Not without raising the roof in the process." His palm remained where it was.

Caddie looked ready to protest again, but instead she handed over the comb. Her wry look asked if he was man enough to tackle the job he'd set himself.

Though he tried to appear confident, deep down Manning had his doubts. What if he bungled the whole thing? What if he made such a mess of it that Varina took it into her determined little head to run off to her uncle?

As his hand closed over the comb, his fingers suddenly felt like enormous sausages, far too big and clumsy to assay the delicate operation of grooming a little girl. He might not have any experience with children, Manning conceded, but he'd once owned a wildly spirited mare who'd resented being curried.

Perhaps the situations were not so different.

"Now, you want to help Templeton and me, don't you?" he asked.

Varina gave an emphatic nod, sending her rusty mane into a wild tangle about her head.

"Then turn around and stay still. I promise I'll stop if you tell me it's hurting you."

He moved the comb up and down, not actually making

contact with Varina's untidy tresses. "That doesn't hurt, does it?"

"No." She sounded surprised and a little suspicious.

Gradually Manning worked the comb deeper and deeper, always pulling back just before he sensed Varina was about to protest.

"How does that look?" he asked Caddie awhile later.

She stared at him as if he'd just withdrawn his head, unbloodied, from the jaws of a lion. "I—I reckon I can braid it now."

When he passed the comb back to her, she handled it like some magical artifact of frightening power.

Manning tried to keep his chest from puffing out like the old rooster's. Light-headed with satisfaction, he even dared to offer a suggestion. "Maybe if her hair was cut shorter, it'd be easier to keep."

"Maybe." Caddie sounded dazed as she plaited her daughter's hair into a neat braid. "Run along now, precious. And be good."

Varina strode over to Manning and grabbed his hand. "Let's go see about that firewood."

As she dragged him out of the parlor, Manning heard Caddie call softly behind him. "Mr. Forbes?"

He only had time to glance back and raise an eyebrow.

Caddie's forehead furrowed in a look of intense curiosity, and perhaps a shade of fear. "Are you sure you've never had children of your own?"

The question could easily be taken as a compliment, and that warmed Manning. But he heard something else in Caddie's tone that he couldn't quite fathom.

And it sent a chill through him.

Chapter Five

Who was this husband of hers? Where had he come from? Who were his people? What did his past hold?

These and many other questions plagued Caddie as she stirred the bed linens in a cauldron of hot, soapy water.

She'd been raised in a society that set great store by a person's lineage. It needn't to be terribly exalted, just so you knew where they came from and how they fit into the great interconnected community of the South.

Before she'd danced a single reel with Delbert Marsh, she'd known he belonged to a distinguished Virginia family of spotless pedigree. That, as much as anything, had led her to set her cap for him. Back then her family'd called her "La Princesse" and she'd had a bevy of beaux that included scions of most every good family in the Sand Hills, and many from the Low Country, too.

Del had caught her eye right away. Throughout the South, Virginians were noted for their pride, and Delbert Decatur Marsh had merited the reputation in full measure. With more than her fair share of that quality, Caddie had always admired men of distinction and presence who didn't underestimate themselves. Too late, she'd discovered how difficult it could be for two proud people to make a marriage work.

She and Del had both been accustomed to getting their way. As the man of the family, her husband had the full weight of Southern tradition empowering him to continue doing so. Unused to coming second to anyone, Caddie had let her nose get out of joint at the slightest provocation.

Proud folks didn't stoop to ill-bred bickering. They behaved correctly but coldly. If Del had been surprised or even hurt by the change in manner of his formerly adoring bride, he'd been too proud to ask what was wrong. And if he had asked she'd likely have been too proud to tell him.

Stirred from her bitter musings, Caddie looked around her. What cause for pride did she have left? Not her looks, that was certain. The state of her hands and complexion would have scandalized the rigorous mammy of her girlhood. Caddie's station in life was no longer anything to boast about. These days she worked as hard as any house slave before the war, while eating less and dressing worse.

She was proud of her children, though. Proud of having survived the war and its aftermath with some dignity intact. Proud of her Southern heritage.

Yet she'd married a man about whom she knew nothing.

Caddie rinsed the sheets, wrung them out and hung them to dry. Hopefully a day of April breezes and sunshine would make them fit to sleep on.

Once she'd done the laundry, Caddie tackled the dirt-encrusted parlor floor. With each swipe of the scrub brush, she brooded over all the things she *didn't* know about her new husband. Her alarm mounted by the minute.

How old was he? Around the age Del would have been, Caddie guessed. Since soldiering put years on a man's face, she couldn't be sure. What schooling did he have? His conversation wasn't peppered with slang or cussing, like many of the Yankees she'd known in Richmond. That suggested some kind of decent upbringing and education.

Had he been married previously? Was it possible he still had a wife up North to whom he might return after he'd made his fortune in Virginia? That would explain why he hadn't been anxious to consummate their marriage.

What if he had a criminal record in one or more of the Northern states? The thought clouted Caddie like a physical blow. Scrambling up from her knees, she skidded across the still-wet floor to one of the windows. She meant to holler at Tem and Varina to come inside. After all, what mother wanted her children consorting with a man she knew so little about?

Even if she had been reckless enough to marry him.

The words died on her lips as the sound of children's laughter wafted in on the fresh spring air. She couldn't recall the last time she'd heard Tem or Varina laugh. Her son was so timid and sensitive, her daughter so willful. And there hadn't been much to laugh about in the wake of Richmond's fall.

Caddie stood at the open window, soaking in the sound and the sun's golden rays. Almost against her will, both warmed her.

She couldn't help resenting the carpetbagger for hitting it off so well with her son and daughter. He'd had no business allowing Tem to keep that dog in the nursery at nights, not to mention meddling in her management of Varina. Some rebel spark of fairness compelled Caddie to admit that she wouldn't have minded the Yankee's interference so much if he hadn't possessed such a rare knack for handling her children.

For the moment, though, the tight fist of suspicion and bitterness unclenched from around her heart. It gave a queer flutter, like an uncaged bird suddenly spreading its wings. The sensation felt strangely akin to a quiver of fear.

* * *

Manning sat at the supper table mopping up the last morsel of baked beans with a slab of corn bread and basking in the unfamiliar warmth of family. He had to reach far back into his past to retrieve the memory of a day as pleasant as the one he'd just spent. Hearing Tem and Varina tell Caddie of their adventures, Manning felt his heart resonate with a faint, precious echo of their glee.

"The rooster tried to peck Varina." Merriment danced in Templeton's soft brown eyes. "But she waved her arms and hollered, 'Boo!' You should have seen him run off squawking."

"Catch that old buzzard try to peck me again." Varina looked well pleased with her victory as she held out her plate. "More beans."

"May I have more beans, *please*," Caddie reminded her daughter, ladling second helpings from the crock.

Noticing Manning's empty plate, she refilled it, too.

"I hope you behaved yourself and didn't get in Mr.—er, in the way."

For some reason her fumble over his name relaxed Manning further. Apparently he was not the only one ill at ease with their new domestic arrangements. "They were both a big help to me. We managed to gather enough deadwood to keep the stove fueled for a while."

"May I be excused, Mama?" Templeton pushed away from the table. "I'd like to feed Sergeant and have a play with him before bed."

"Go on, Son. Don't stray too far from the house, though."

"Me, too!" Varina bolted her second helping of beans, then scrambled down from her chair, swiping the back of her sleeve across her mouth.

Before her mother could deliver a sermon on manners, the child had darted away after her brother.

Caddie shook her head. "How am I ever going to make a proper young lady out of that child? If only Templeton could be more like her and she more like him."

"You've done a fine job raising them all by yourself," said Manning. "Especially with the war and all. They're both smart, willing and good-natured. The rest'll sort itself out."

Caddie made no reply, but two bright spots flamed in her cheeks.

With the distraction of the children gone, they finished their supper in awkward silence. Once they were done, Caddie stacked the plates and cutlery, then carried them out to the washtub in the kitchen. Manning followed with the bean crock. He watched Caddie pour scalding water over the dishes from a heavy kettle simmering on the fire, followed by cool well water from a bucket on the floor. Unbuttoning the cuffs of her sleeves, she rolled them up past her elbows and began to wash the dishes.

"Can I get you some coffee?" she asked Manning.

"No, thank you. It would likely keep me awake."

That and imagining her asleep in the room next to his. Manning hoped he'd soon get used to it. He desperately needed some rest. His tired mind was entertaining too many dangerous fancies.

He considered excusing himself from the kitchen to go keep an eye on the children. But there were matters he and Caddie needed to sort out so he could get on with his mission. Reluctantly, he rummaged around the dimly lit room and found a length of homespun cotton Caddie had been using for a dish towel. He'd rather have kept his distance from her, but he couldn't sit idle while she worked.

"We need to talk about my plans for Sabbath Hollow." Picking up a plate still warm from the wash water, he began to dry it.

She glanced at him with a queer expression on her face,

as though he was the most peculiar object she'd ever beheld. Her cheeks were flushed from the heat of the dishwater, and a faint sheen of perspiration moistened her nose and hairline.

As if in answer, beads of sweat broke out on Manning's brow.

"What are you doing?" she asked.

Wisps of her fiery hair had pulled free of the tightly pinned knot on the back of her head. They framed her face like a copper halo. The creamy sweep of her forearms tapered with delicate grace to a pair of absurdly fragile wrists.

Giant invisible hands seemed to clench around Manning's throat. "Drying the dishes," he croaked. "Is there something wrong with that? I promise I won't break any."

She tapped a plate of the cheapest tinware against the side of the washtub. "You'd have to work hard to break these. I've just never seen a man take a hand in house chores before."

Manning shrugged. "Nothing like the army for teaching a fellow to look after himself. I learned how to cook and wash clothes, too, if you ever need me to pitch in there."

"I can manage the chores on my own." She released him from the power of her silvery-emerald gaze, turning her attention back to the dishwater. "Were you in the army long?"

"Since First Manassas."

The plate in Caddie's hand dropped back into the water with a splash. "I thought up North folks called it Bull Run?"

Manning felt the heat stinging in his face. What *had* made him refer to that battle by its rebel name? Was he just trying desperately to fit into a world where he'd always be an outsider?

"I guess whoever wins a fight should get to name it." Manning didn't need to remind his rebel wife that Confederate armies had beaten Union ones both times they'd clashed over that creek in northern Virginia.

"I reckon so." She didn't sound convinced by his explanation. "What kind of work did you do before joining the army, Mr. Forbes? Whereabouts up North do you come from?"

If she'd demanded his answers over the barrel of a cocked pistol Manning could not have felt more threatened.

"What difference does it make?" he snapped. "The past's gone and nothing this side of heaven can change it. It's the present and the future that matter. Let's talk about Sabbath Hollow and what we need to do to make it prosperous again."

"You needn't get so riled up over a couple of innocent questions." Caddie collected the dishes he had dried and began to put them away, making considerable noise in the process. "I just thought that since we're…married, I ought to know a little more about you. Folks are bound to ask me, and it'll look mighty peculiar if I can't tell them."

"Of course. You're entitled to know, I guess." Evading her questions was apt to make her more suspicious, not less. "Nothing very interesting to tell, is all. I was a woodworker before I enlisted. Lived in Pennsylvania, not too far north of here. Anything else you want to know?"

"As a matter of fact, there is." She glanced toward him, but refused to meet his eyes.

Not that Manning really wanted her to. He had an uncanny feeling she could see right inside him and read all his secrets.

Fetching a broom from the corner, Caddie began to sweep the floor. Manning braced himself for her interrogation.

"Did you leave any folks behind in Pennsylvania?" Caddie seemed to concentrate on her sweeping, tossing off the question as if just making small talk.

Something about the way she cocked her head, and a certain tension in her posture, told Manning his answer mattered to her. Mattered very much.

"Parents?" she prompted when he didn't answer at once. "Children? A wife?"

That's what had her worried! Manning almost laughed with relief. "I swear you're my first and only wife, ma'am, and my folks have passed on. Part of the reason I came to Virginia was because there was nothing left for me up North."

Silently he prayed Caddie wouldn't ask him the other part of what had drawn him to Sabbath Hollow.

Fortunately, she didn't.

"I reckon you're right about putting the past behind us. That may be easier for the victor than the…vanquished." She seemed to gag on that word. "Let's talk about the future of Sabbath Hollow. Getting hold of good breeding stock won't be easy or cheap. We might buy a few brood-mares from Kentucky."

Manning shook his head. "Even if it were possible to breed horses again, nobody around here could afford to buy them. Besides, I barely know a horse's withers from its fetlock."

"Then I reckon you'd better learn." Her long-fingered hands clenched around the broom handle. The face that had looked so soft and appealing only a few minutes ago turned hard as her fine brows tensed and her delicate jaw clenched. "You promised to help me restore this plantation. I took that to mean you'd return Sabbath Hollow to the way it was before the war."

"I promised I'd do everything in my power to make it prosperous again," Manning corrected her. "Horse breeding isn't the way to do that."

His vow to protect and provide for the family didn't include indulging a woman who foolishly clung to the old and familiar, no matter how ill-suited to a changed world.

Caddie thrust her slender shoulders back, holding the rough corn broom as though it was a royal scepter. "There are things in this world more important than financial prosperity, sir. Heritage. Traditions. Not that I'd expect a man when he's come to Virginia with no higher purpose than to chase a dollar to understand such ideals."

Though her words dealt his spirit a harsh blow, Manning knew he dared not protest. Better Caddie think him a grasping exploiter than for her to guess his true intent. Some of the hurt he tried to mask must have shown on his face, though.

Caddie's stiff, imperious manner thawed by several degrees. "I beg your pardon, Mr. Forbes. I must sound like an ungrateful shrew. You put yourself at the disposal of me and my children. It's not my place to impose restrictions on your efforts."

Staring into the distance as if gazing back in time, she sighed. "Only, I did want Templeton to be able to carry on the gentlemanly enterprise of his forefathers."

Damnation! Manning almost gagged on that unuttered curse. Caddie arrogant and contemptuous, he could have resisted without a qualm. But Caddie gracious and wistful outgunned his bristling defenses and took his honor hostage.

"The Marsh family didn't always breed horses, did they?" Did he dare challenge her on her own territory— family tradition? "When I scouted the property in this area, I discovered an abandoned sawmill. Doesn't look like it's been used in a while, but I believe with a few repairs we could get it operating again. Folks are going to need lumber to rebuild. We'd be providing a needed service."

"The old mill," Caddie murmured, more to herself than to him. "Somebody must've used it once upon a time."

"Heaven knows there's plenty of woodland around these parts." Manning gestured toward the window and the stand of mature hardwood visible through it. "We could buy timber from the folks hereabouts and help *them* get back on their feet, too."

As he waited in silence for her answer, the children ran past, shouting and laughing, with Sergeant barking at their heels.

Manning ventured one last appeal. "This place belongs to your boy. The final say is yours. I'd like us to have a fighting chance to make a go of it, though."

Tentatively, perhaps reluctantly, Caddie nodded. "If we make a decent profit from the mill, perhaps we could purchase some breeding stock. Get back into it, gradual like."

"That sounds like a fine idea." Somehow Manning found himself happier with this honorable compromise than if Caddie had agreed to his plan right away. "I'll give the mill a good close inspection tomorrow, to see what repairs t'll need. If I have time afterward, I'll ride into Mercer's Corner and post some notices for a crew to run the mill and others to let folks know we'll soon be looking to buy wood."

The direction of their future settled, Manning headed off to tackle a few more small repairs around the house before sundown. Once Caddie had gone to bed, he would lock up the house and turn in. The last thing he wanted was another embarrassing encounter like this morning.

He'd gone a few steps up the back stairs when another thought struck him. "While I'm in town," he called down to Caddie, "I'll see if I can hire you some help for around the house."

"Can we afford that?" She sounded almost offended by the suggestion. "I'm quite capable of managing on my own."

Was she talking about a hired girl, Manning wondered or about him?

She'd been forced to accept his help, but she resented the necessity—that much was clear. When it came to Varina's stubbornness, Manning didn't think that little crabapple had fallen far from the maternal tree.

He turned and looked back at Caddie—tattered, overworked, but somehow still regal. Her fierce pride and bullheaded independence would not make it easy for him to fulfil his vow. He couldn't let it stop him, no matter how much he admired those qualities.

"We all need help now and then, ma'am. There's no shame in accepting it."

Chapter Six

"You're a fine one to talk about accepting help with good grace, Mr. Forbes." Caddie's voice echoed in the bare entry hall. She shot Manning a challenging look as she donned her bonnet.

A full week had passed since their negotiated agreement to reopen the old sawmill, yet they still hadn't engaged a single worker. Despite the notices Manning had put up all over Mercer's Corner no lumber contracts had been forthcoming and no girls from the neighborhood had inquired about the housekeeping job. Caddie intended to find out why.

"Give it a little more time." Manning raked long fingers through his dark hair.

Stiffened with sweat, it stood on end like the bristles of a corn broom. It shouldn't have looked the least bit attractive to a fastidious woman like Caddie.

But it did—damn it.

"Your neighbors probably don't get into town that often," Manning protested. "Word'll find its way around in time."

"It certainly will." Caddie spoke in a brisk tone as she pulled on her last decent pair of gloves. "For I intend to spread it myself. You need a crew of good workmen to finish the repairs on that mill. Mark my words, if you keep trying to do everything by yourself, you're going to wind up injured. Or else get yourself run down until you fall ill. I've lost one husband, sir. I can't afford to lose another.''

Was it her imagination, or did Manning's complexion suddenly take on a grayish pallor? The stormy look in his steel-blue eyes was surely more than her fancy. Could the man be that set on working himself to death? Or was it something more?

He jammed his hands in his pockets. "I don't like you having to go cap in hand to your neighbors on my account."

Neither did she, but Caddie wasn't about to let that stop her. Having discovered something she could *do* to speed the rehabilitation of Sabbath Hollow, she wouldn't have let General Grant and his entire Army of the Potomac stand in her way.

Manning had been working so hard. Too hard.

Though she wouldn't have let him guess it for the world, genuine concern lay beneath her offhand talk of losing another husband. Every morning, that ornery old rooster had barely finished crowing when Manning took a corn pone and a piece of cold meat for his breakfast, then trudged up the hill and through the woods to the mill. Awhile after the sun had set behind the Blue Ridge Mountains, he dragged himself back to Sabbath Hollow for a late supper.

Every evening Caddie noticed some new injury—a gash on his forehead, a blackened thumbnail, a slight limp. And every evening Manning appeared more exhausted from his day's labor. Last night he'd fallen asleep at the supper table before he could even finish his meal. When no amount of calling succeeded in rousing him, Caddie had been obliged to shake his shoulder.

But not before the sight of his peaceful, unguarded features had tempted her to graze her fingertips down the side of his face to rest for a furtive, tender moment on his jutting chin. Many hours later, the memory of that stolen touch fueled a scorching blush in her own face.

She turned away from Manning, hoping he wouldn't notice. "It's not as though I'll be begging for handouts. I'll just pay a few social calls on my neighbors, to let them know the children and I are home. If I happen to mention the sawmill in conversation, where's the harm in that?"

Before Manning could tell her what harm there might be, she walked over to the bottom of the stairs and called up. "Varina, Templeton, come on, now. I'm pretty near ready to go."

With a deafening clatter quite out of proportion to her small feet, Varina charged down the staircase. Templeton dawdled quietly along behind her with his faithful canine shadow. Though Caddie saw the brindle-colored mongrel dozens of times a day, his homeliness never failed to jar her. During the past week, the dog's faithful devotion to Tem had begun to win her heart in spite of his appearance.

Varina dashed straight at Manning. Perhaps to keep from being barreled over, he bent and scooped her up into his arms. Though he tried hard to hide it, Caddie saw him wince. Her daughter was a sturdy little armful, especially for a man with so many injuries.

"Do I look pretty?" As usual, Varina didn't ask a question so much as demand an answer.

Before Caddie could exclaim in outrage at such forwardness, Manning nodded. "Pretty as a picture."

"Pretty as Mama?"

"Varina Marsh!" Though Caddie tried to force her gaze away from Manning, it flew right to him.

Their eyes met and locked. Caddie doubted she'd blushed as often during all her debutante days as she had in the past fortnight. Many years had passed since she'd

been so intensely conscious of herself as a woman, or cared
if a man noticed how she looked.

She didn't *want* to give a fig what Manning Forbes
thought of her. Any more than she wanted the sound of his
footsteps on the porch to set her heart skipping like a flat
stone across a still pond. He'd turned her world upside
down. Did he have to thaw out her long-frozen emotions
and set them all topsy-turvy, too?

"Pretty as Mama?" Varina's question jolted Manning
so hard that he almost dropped the child on her sturdy little
backside.

In spite of his futile resistance, Caddie lured his gaze to
her. Manning saw what he'd been running from for the past
week—a woman who grew more beautiful and desirable by
the day.

Through the shock of that realization, he managed to
choke out a diplomatic answer to Varina's question. "I'm
sure you will be once you're a grown-up lady. If you keep
your hair combed and your face clean, that is."

The child wrinkled up her nose as if at a bad smell.
"Then I reckon being pretty ain't worth the bother."

Caddie shook her head and gazed heavenward. Manning
chuckled as the brittle tension between them shattered into
tiny harmless pieces. He nuzzled Varina's plump cheek
coaxing her into a fit of giggles.

"I wager you'll change your tune in about a dozen years,
young lady." He swung her down onto her feet. "For today, I'm sure you'll charm all the neighbors."

"Not if she goes fishing for compliments, she won't."
Caddie beckoned to her daughter.

"What kind of fish is that? I want to learn to catch 'em."

"Not a fish you eat, Rina." Templeton spoke up from
his perch on the bottom step as he petted the dog. "When
folks fish for compliments it means they ask if they're

clever or if they look pretty. Fishing for compliments is bad manners.''

Perhaps figuring she'd as soon be hanged for a sheep as a goat, Varina spun around and stuck her tongue out at her brother.

The muscles in Manning's face ached from his strenuous effort not to grin.

''That'll be quite enough of that, missy.'' Caddie brushed a smudge of dust off Varina's skirt and straightened her hair bow. ''If you can't behave nicely, I won't be able to take you along.''

A small lower lip thrust out. ''Suits me. I'd sooner go up to the mill with Manning.''

He had visions of his whole week's labor undone in an hour.

''Me, too, Mama.'' Templeton spouted his little sister's favorite phrase.

Caddie looked from one of her children to the other, motherly exasperation written plainly on her face.

Manning suspected a little of it extended to him, as well. For the life of him he couldn't figure why. The woman didn't seem to need any better reason than his presence in her house to be provoked.

Taking Varina's hand in a firm grip, Caddie motioned for Tem to join them. ''I declare, you two. The poor man has his hands full enough at that mill without playing mammy to both of you for the afternoon. You'll come with me and you'll behave nicely, or we will have words. Is that understood?''

The dispirited tone of Tem and Varina's ''Yes, Mama'' chorus tugged at Manning.

''Ah...ma'am?''

Caddie lifted a finely arched brow to inquire what he wanted.

''I...well, the fact is, I could use the boy's help up at

the mill for a few hours, if you'd oblige me by letting him stay.''

The transparent mixture of happiness and gratitude on Templeton's face gladdened Manning more than anything in a long time. Caddie's look of horror cast him back down again in the space of a heartbeat. My, but that woman had a talent for putting a worm in a fellow's apple!

"I'm sorry to *dis*oblige you, sir. The mill's too dangerous a place for my son. If anything should happen to him—"

Manning cut her off. "I wouldn't *let* anything happen to him. I'm talking about simple jobs like holding a board steady for me to nail so as I don't hammer any more of my fingers.''

"I could do that, Mama. Please.''

Varina yanked on her mother's arm. "Me, too, Mama!''

Now look what you've done. Caddie's glare said it plainer than words.

A quick stride took Manning to the little girl. He dropped to his haunches before her. "Your mama needs you with her even more than I do, Varina. I tell you what, though. If you go along and behave yourself real well, I promise I'll take you fishing tomorrow. Tem, too, if your mama needs him to go.''

"Fishing—yahoo!'' Varina jumped up and down in most unladylike excitement.

Tem hung his head.

As Caddie's eyes rested on her son for an instant, Manning sensed her struggle between a mother's natural protectiveness and an intense desire to make the boy happy.

"I *suppose* Templeton can lend you a hand for the afternoon, if you both promise me you'll be very careful.''

"Yes, ma'am.'' Manning and Templeton replied together, exchanging a look of triumphant allies.

When Manning rose to his feet, he caught Caddie regarding him with a very different expression. He'd seen one like it on the face of a Union general whose battlefield blunder had been remedied by the quick thinking of a junior officer.

The look had not been one of gratitude.

She should be grateful to the man, a feeble voice of prewar gentility protested in Caddie's mind as she and Varina drove off to pay their calls around the neighborhood.

Thanks to his providence, she and her children were eating better than they had in years. She didn't have to endure the humiliation of staying at Sabbath Hollow as *guests* of Lon and Lydene. In large measure, she'd been able to shift the heavy burden of reviving the plantation onto Manning's broad shoulders. But didn't the Yankees owe her at least that much for all they'd stolen? The caustic bile of bitterness stung in Caddie's throat. If not for Manning Forbes and hundreds of thousands just like him, her family's fortunes wouldn't need restoring. Sabbath Hollow would still be gracious and prosperous. Her children would never have known a moment's hunger or fear. And they wouldn't need a stepfather, kind or otherwise, for their own pa would still be living.

A shiver ran up Caddie's back and the contents of her stomach curdled to think what her married life would be like if the war had not intervened. Not for an instant would she credit Del's death as a favor on the part of the Yankees. Though the tensions and ill will in their marriage had festered as acutely as those between North and South on the eve of Fort Sumter, Caddie had never wished her husband dead.

Had she?

"Where're we going, Mama?"

Her daughter's question rescued Caddie from having to face the impossibly painful inquisition of her conscience.

"Several places, dear. Willowvale, Gordon Manor, Oak Hill."

Just saying the names lightened her mood, bringing back fond memories of parties, hunts and racing meets. Dressing up pretty and dancing, gossiping with the women and flirting innocently with the men.

"Which one first?" Below the hem of Varina's skirts, two sturdy pantalet-clad legs swung back and forth in time to the jingle of the horse's harness.

"The Pratt place, Willowvale." Caddie tugged on the reins to urge their old mare off the road and down the Pratts' long lane. "They're a fine old family. Mrs. Pratt was your grandma Marsh's dearest friend and her husband once sat in the General Assembly."

"Anybody there to play with?" Varina didn't sound much impressed by the Pratt family pedigree.

"I don't reckon so. Mrs. Pratt's family are all grown. Some of them might be married and have young'uns, though."

Varina craned her neck and raised a hand to shade her eyes as she peered toward the plantation house. "I see somebody!"

The child's eagerness made Caddie wonder if bringing Varina along had been such a wise idea.

She cast her daughter a sidelong glance. "You recollect what you were told about behaving yourself, young lady. Mrs. Pratt always was most particular about good children being seen and not heard. If you want to go fishing tomorrow, you'll have to make sure you only speak when you're spoken to and then give a nice, respectful answer. Is that understood?"

Heaving a dramatic sigh, Varina clasped her hands primly in her lap. "Yes, ma'am."

Thank goodness for Manning's blatant bribe. An impulse of unforced gratitude gripped Caddie's heart.

Reining the buckboard to a halt, she glanced at the Pratts'
sprawling plantation house of cream-colored brick. The
place looked to be in worse shape than Sabbath Hollow.
The whole roof of the east wing had collapsed and most of
the windows had been clumsily boarded up. When the
Yankees had first marched through this part of Virginia,
had the Pratts refugeed elsewhere, never to return?

As if to dispel Caddie's doubts, the front door flew open
and a young woman in a black dress rushed out. Sleeves
that should have fit snugly on slender arms hung painfully
loose on hers.

She called back to an older woman who had stepped onto
the porch. "Visitors, Mother. Isn't this a treat? We've had
more company the past week than we got all winter. I
reckon the worst of hard times are behind us."

"I hope they are, Ann." Caddie climbed down from the
buckboard and greeted the young woman with a smile.
"It's good to see you again."

Ann Pratt jerked to a halt, like a greyhound curbed hard
by an invisible leash. Her half eager, half anxious smile
vanished. "Caddie? What are you doing here?"

Turning to the buckboard, Caddie lifted Varina down.
She forced herself to overlook Ann's uncivil greeting. Folks
weren't accustomed to receiving visitors like they'd once
been—Ann had said as much, herself. No doubt Mrs. Pratt
would correct her daughter's manners as Caddie would
have corrected Varina.

"I apologize for taking so long to get around and call
on everyone, ladies." She raised her voice to include Mrs.
Pratt in the conversation. "The children and I came home
from Richmond a little over a fortnight ago, but we've been
busy getting settled back in at Sabbath Hollow. I can't stay
long. I just wanted to give everyone our regards and catch
up on all the news."

From the porch, Mrs. Pratt spoke. "We heard you were

back.'' Her tone left Caddie no doubt that those tidings hadn't cheered Willowvale. ''We also heard you'd remarried in some haste.''

Tilting her chin defiantly, Caddie clutched Varina's hand a little tighter. ''I have remarried.''

''I'm surprised you had the face to call on folks,'' said the older woman, as her daughter continued to stare at Caddie in mild horror. ''If you're brazen enough to come, I reckon I'm curious enough to let you set a spell. Though no further than the porch, mind. The devil take it if I'll entertain a Yankee carpetbagger's wh—'' she broke off, then amended ''—*wife* in my home. Ann, fetch us some chairs.''

Ann backed toward the house as though she didn't dare risk turning away from their less-than-welcome guests.

For a moment Caddie toyed with the notion of telling Mrs. Pratt the devil *could* take her, then driving away with her nose in the air.

But reason prevailed.

What had she expected? it asked Caddie in a wry voice strangely reminiscent of Manning's. Had she entertained some impossibly optimistic notion that the neighbors, isolated on their plantations, struggling to put food on the table, hadn't heard about her remarriage? She should have known better. This kind of gossip spread faster than measles in an army camp.

Towing Varina by the hand, Caddie picked her way over rutted ground and past overgrown shrubs to the Pratts' front porch. Alienating the neighbors wouldn't get the sawmill operating. And it sure wouldn't put any logs in the millpond.

Ann reappeared with a rocking chair for her mother to sit on. Caddie pretended not to notice the gaping hole in its cane seat. The footstool Ann offered her had seen better days, too.

Off in one of the fields, Caddie could see a man and a boy walking hand in hand. Why was Jeff Pratt strolling around his acres instead of planting them? Why hadn't he or Josh or Willie thought to take unbroken panes of glass from some windows to repair the most important ones, as Manning had done at Sabbath Hollow? Why couldn't he have spared a few minutes to tack a slab of cut lumber on the seat of his old mother's rocking chair? The place even smelled of wood rot and mildew.

Had decades of owning slaves made Southern folks too shiftless to look after themselves decently? Hard as Caddie tried to stifle that treasonous thought, it would not go away.

The creak of Mrs. Pratt's rocking chair filled the awkward silence as she stared off in the same direction as Caddie.

"Well, well," she said at last, shaking her head. "What do you reckon poor Delbert Marsh would say about his widow bringing a Yankee carpetbagger to live under his roof?"

What indeed? And what would Del say if he caught her watching that carpetbagger with a strange hunger in her eyes? Or caressing his stubbled cheek while he slept?

Though shame burned in her belly like a white-hot coal, Caddie did her best to answer Mrs. Pratt with calm civility…as Manning would have done. "I reckon Del might say he's glad his children are getting plenty to eat."

Mrs. Pratt gave a sniff of derision. "You're mortgaging your children's birthright for a mess of Yankee pottage, missy. And stabbing their kinfolk in the back, while you're about it. Mark my words, this carpetbagger of yours will hang around just long enough to wring every dime out of Sabbath Hollow, then he'll skedaddle back up North where he belongs. When that happens, don't think you'll be able to turn to your neighbors for help."

The word *kinfolk* echoed in Caddie's ears. "You've been

listening to Lon, haven't you? Well, let me tell you something, Mrs. Pratt. I'd trust Mr. Forbes with my children and my property any day ahead of a no-account schemer like Alonzo Marsh. Likely Del would have, too. Mr. Forbes can't help where he was born. He may be a Yankee, but he's decent and kind and trustworthy.''

Even as she spoke the words, Caddie couldn't figure where all her praise for Manning was coming from. She'd *thought* things about him every bit as bad as Mrs. Pratt had *said*. Yet Caddie found she could no more let the woman run him down than she could have sat silent while someone insulted Tem or Varina. In some strange way, whether Caddie wanted him or not, Manning now belonged to her, and she'd defend him to outsiders with her last breath.

She cast a pointed look around at the boarded windows of Willowvale's once-imposing facade and at several broken floorboards on the porch. ''My husband works harder than most menfolk around these parts, I reckon. He's fixing up the old sawmill on Sabbath Creek and looking for a crew to work it. He'll bargain wood contracts with anyone industrious enough to float a boom of logs down the creek. Might your boys be interested in undertaking either of those?''

Mrs. Pratt's tiny mouth stretched into a thin, taut line and her face blanched to the same gray-white shade as her hair.

''No, I don't reckon they would.'' She spoke the words in a tight, vicious whisper. ''Now clear off my porch and off my property, missy. You're no better than that vile carpetbagger husband of yours.''

During this conversation with Mrs. Pratt, Varina had remained so unnaturally quiet, Caddie'd almost forgotten the child was there. Rising from the footstool, she reached for her daughter's hand. Whatever had possessed her to bring the child? Some cowardly assurance that folks would keep civil tongues in their heads in front of a four-year-old?

Another coal of shame took fire in Caddie's belly. Varina *liked* Manning. Only the powerful inducement of a fishing trip could have made her listen to so many ugly slanders against him without rebuttal.

Shaking off her mother's grip, Varina marched over to Mrs. Pratt's rocking chair. The old lady seemed to relent for a moment. Perhaps in her bitterness, she had forgotten that little pitchers had big ears.

"What's your name, precious?"

"Varina Virginia Marsh."

"After your grandmother, of course." Mrs. Pratt looked the child over with a fond, sad smile. "Varina, you seem like a real smart little mite. For the sake of your grandma's dearest friend, will you tell your mother what you think of her betraying your blessed papa's memory by marrying a Yankee carpetbagger?"

Before Caddie could gasp her indignation and whisk Varina away from Willowvale, the child spoke. "*Carpetbagger*'s a nasty word. You need your mouth washed out with soap for saying it."

As Mrs. Pratt's face paled even whiter and her mouth opened and closed, Varina turned and walked back over to Caddie.

"Can we leave now, Mama? I don't like this place." Louder, she added, "It smells bad."

Caddie hustled her daughter back to the buckboard before the child provoked Mrs. Pratt into a seizure of some kind.

Not a word passed between them as they drove back up the lane at a bone-rattling clip.

Finally, when they pulled in sight of Sabbath Hollow, Varina asked, "Where are we going next?"

"Home." Caddie blinked furiously to dispel a fine mist

that fogged her vision. Their visit to the Pratts had been one of the most humiliating experiences of her life. She couldn't face repeating it right away.

"When will you go to the other places?"

"Tomorrow, maybe."

Now that she'd had a foretaste of what to expect, she dreaded the prospect, but that didn't matter. The mill needed workers and wood. If facing down the neighbors and countering the lies Lon had spread might help, she would do it. She just needed a little time to mend the tattered shreds of her self-respect.

"Do I have to come with you?"

Transferring the reins to her left hand, Caddie patted Varina's small knee with her right. "No, dear. I believe it would be better if you stayed home and went fishing."

"I *can* go? Even though I talked disrespectful and made that old lady mad?"

Caddie had spent nearly four years trying to teach her daughter proper manners. Rewarding decorous behavior, punishing impertinence. With the fortunes of the Confederacy falling, she'd sensed it might be the only lasting legacy she could bestow on her children. What she was about to do could render all those painstaking lessons useless.

"Some things are more important than manners, dearest."

"They are?" Varina turned and stared at her mother as though she'd grown a tail or her face had turned blue.

Caddie nodded. "Like sticking up for your friends when folks say mean things about them that aren't true. I'm proud of you for doing that, Varina." The words almost refused to pass her lips.

"*But,*" she added in case her daughter should draw the wrong moral from what had happened, "I'd have been even prouder if you could have found a more respectful way to say what you had to."

"Yes, ma'am." The child sounded impatient with the frequently repeated admonition, but also a bit relieved that one constant in her world hadn't shifted too dramatically.

"Mama?"

"Yes, dear?"

"I was proud of you, too."

Chapter Seven

"You gotta take me fishing tomorrow! Mama said!" Bellowing her good news, Varina raced toward Manning and Tem as they emerged from the wooded path that led to the old mill.

The child grabbed Manning's hand in hers and swung it in a wide, exuberant arc between them. A hearty grin spread between her plump cheeks. For a moment Manning felt his hurts ease and the weight of weariness lift from his shoulders and eyelids.

He still had so much work ahead to make the neglected sawmill fit to operate. His goal to protect and provide for the family spurred him to keep at it every available minute. And yet...

Didn't he owe them something more? As a child, he'd been fed, clothed and schooled. Never known danger or harsh physical punishment. Looking back, Manning realized he'd have willingly taken a few licks, gone hungry or ragged now and then in return for a little more fun and affection in his life.

"Fishing sounds like a fine way to spend the day." As he looked first at the little girl and then at the boy, Manning

elt the muscles of his face stretch, curve and warm in ways
hey never had before.

His heart felt as if it was being stretched and warmed,
oo. "If you were as well behaved and as big a help to
our ma this afternoon as Tem was to me, I guess you both
leserve a treat."

As Manning's gaze lingered on the boy, a smile flickered
cross Tem's face and he seemed to hold his slender frame
little straighter.

"I figgered Mama wouldn't 'llow me to go fishing after
sassed that old lady." Varina sounded a little suspicious
f her good fortune. "But I didn't care. She had it com-
ng."

Manning ran a hand through his hair, puzzling why Cad-
ie would reward the child for impertinence. Though she
avished plenty of affection on Tem and Varina, their
nother was a stickler for good behavior—manners espe-
ially.

"You know, a proper young lady respects her elders,
'arina." To his surprise, Manning heard himself parroting
'addie. "I hope you apologized."

Varina shook her head so hard her rusty braids swung
vildly. "Nope. Won't neither till she 'pologizes for run-
ing you down."

The back of Manning's throat tightened and his eyes felt
ke they'd been bitten by a swarm of blackflies. What had
e ever done to merit such a stalwart little champion?

He gave the child's dimpled hand a squeeze. "You
eedn't have got yourself in trouble sticking up for an old
'ankee." Hoarse with emotion, his voice sounded gruff.

Cheerfully indifferent to his tone, Varina skipped along
t Manning's side as they neared the house. "Mama stuck
p for you, too. She told Mrs. Pratt you're kind, and dust-
orthy."

A high, wet squeal drew Manning's gaze to the hand

pump, where Caddie was filling a bucket with water. Thei
eyes met, then instantly averted. In that briefest exchange
of glances, he could tell she'd overheard her daughter.

Manning knew he shouldn't ask—shouldn't care abou
the answer. But he couldn't help himself on either count
"You said that?"

Letting go of Varina's hand, he hefted the water bucket
The rope handle bit into his palm. He risked another quick
glance at Caddie.

If he'd caught her committing a crime, he doubted she
could have looked more thoroughly unsettled. Her hands
fluttered like a pair of small, pale birds. One rose to her
face, pushing back a strand of rich, mahogany hair.

Her lips parted, then clamped together again, as if wag
ing a struggle over what words they would permit to es
cape. After a couple of false starts, her answer forced it
way out.

"Of course I did. How can we expect folks to do busi
ness with our mill if I'm not willing to tell them the pro
prietor is honest and trustworthy?"

Trustworthy? Though he knew he should feel flattered
the word rang in Manning's ears like an indictment. Would
Caddie consider him trustworthy if she knew the secret
he'd been keeping or his true motive for coming to Sabbat
Hollow?

"My *dear* brother-in-law's behind all this." Caddie'
brisk words splashed over Manning like icy well wate
from the bucket he carried.

"How do you mean?" He welcomed the diversion.

Caddie turned to the children. "You two run along an
play until suppertime."

"Can we go dig up some worms for fishing tomorrow?"
Varina looked from Caddie to Manning as if weighin
which of them would be most likely to give consent, an
who'd have the final say.

Manning held his peace.

After a moment's consideration, Caddie nodded. "Try
ot to get *too* dirty."

When Varina ran off without answering, Templeton
alled back, "I'll do all the digging, Mama. Rina'll just
old the can I put the worms into."

Shaking her head as if to say she'd believe that when
he saw it, Caddie held open the kitchen door for Manning
) tote in the bucket of water.

"I didn't want to say what I think of Lon in front of the
hildren," she muttered. "The scoundrel *is* their kin, even
f he hasn't acted much like it lately."

"Has he done something to hurt Tem or Varina?" Man-
ing dropped his bucket, not caring that a good deal of the
vater sloshed out onto the kitchen floor.

Rage thundered through him like a cavalry charge. This
verwhelming urge to protect the Marsh children went far
eeper than the demands of his promise. That shook him.

Caddie looked from the spilled water to Manning's face,
er brow puckered in annoyance. "No need to get so riled
p. Of course Lon hasn't hurt the children...except by try-
ig to prevent us earning a living."

"How's he doing that?" Unnerved by the relief that
wamped him, Manning fetched the mop and swiped it over
ie floor.

Caddie emptied the remaining water into a pair of pots
n the stove. "By going around to the neighbors and
preading all kinds of stories about us. Making folks think
's their patriotic Southern duty not to have any dealings
rith a Yankee-owned sawmill."

She sat down at the table and began breaking a mess of
arly green beans into smaller pieces for the cooking pot.

Manning leaned on his mop. "Sounds like you and Va-
na didn't have a very pleasant visit this afternoon."

He'd worried that Caddie might not receive too warm a

welcome. Lon's gossip spreading could only have made worse.

Silence fell in the kitchen, punctured by the juicy sna of the beans and the soft thud of them dropping into th pot. Caddie kept her eyes cast down, as if the mindles chore demanded her total concentration.

It looked like his plan to make life easier for the Marshe had misfired badly. "I'm sorry if I've made you and th children outcasts in the community."

"It's not your fault." Her voice sounded as though had squeezed out of a tight opening. "I hate to think wha a pass we'd be in by now if you hadn't come along. Som folks just have a knack of saying the most hurtful thing body can hear. Unfortunately, old Mrs. Pratt has alway, been one of them. I don't know what possessed me to ca on her first off."

Though reason cautioned him to keep his distance, Mar ning propped his mop against the doorjamb and took a ste toward Caddie. "What did she say that was so hurtful?"

He didn't really expect Caddie to answer, but he had t ask just the same. It caught him by surprise when she l out a shuddering sigh and began to speak.

"Nothing I don't know in my heart to be true. That' what makes it hurtful, I reckon. Nobody wants folks tellin them the things they can't bear to admit to themselves."

He understood far too well. Perhaps that was wha dragged him another step closer to her. He sensed her re luctance to say any more, and he shared her obvious astor ishment when something forced her to continue.

"Mrs. Pratt says I'm selling my children's birthright fo a mess of Yankee pottage."

Manning winced. He knew how deep those words mu: have cut. She'd only agreed to marry him for the children' sake. Now she was being denounced for harming them wit her desperate sacrifice. Caddie had been right about Mr

Pratt's talent for striking at her opponent's gravest vulnerability.

A direct order from General Grant himself couldn't have made Manning take one step closer. But when Caddie dashed the back of her hand across her eyes and swallowed a stillborn sob, his feet turned renegade, carrying him to her. Before reason could protest, he dropped to his knees beside her chair and gathered her into his arms.

He didn't tell her to hush, for some intuition warned him it would do her good to cry. He'd come to know her well enough to be certain she didn't often allow herself the luxury of a moment's weakness.

Denouncing Lon Marsh or Mrs. Pratt probably wasn't a good idea. Caddie seemed to resent him speaking ill of any Southerner. Manning longed to croon some foolish endearment, but he didn't know any. Nothing in his past life had taught him words like that.

Not knowing what to say, he kept quiet. He just held Caddie in a firm but gentle embrace, willing mute sympathy to radiate from his heart. He kept expecting her to pull away from him at any second, but she didn't. Not even after her sobs subsided to a sniffle now and then.

As those seconds stretched into minutes, feelings he'd been evading for over a week suddenly ambushed Manning and took no prisoners. He fought a desperate rearguard skirmish against desire, but it overpowered the ragged forces of his will to rage through his body.

Caddie fit into his arms so perfectly, like the snuggest dovetail joint that hardly needed glue or peg to hold it in place. Her fragrant feminine softness promised to fill a gaping void he'd refused to acknowledge in his life. Her nearness roused him and tempted him to venture even closer.

If she felt this good sitting on an old kitchen chair, fully clothed and with her hair pinned up… His imagination caught fever as he pictured Caddie sprawled naked on a feather bed. Manning's mouth went dry and every inch of his flesh smoldered. The kiss he didn't dare give her burned on his lips.

If he held on to her much longer, Manning suspected his sense, his honor, even his fear might be incinerated to useless ashes. They wouldn't provide any kind of barrier to prevent him making the second worst mistake of his life.

With an awkwardness born of forcing himself to do the opposite of what he wanted, he let Caddie go and scrambled to his feet.

"If I can't get men to work, or wood to mill, it doesn't make much sense for us to stay around these parts." He spoke the first suitable words that came into his head. "I've got enough saved to let us make a fresh start somewhere else. Out west in the border states, maybe."

When Caddie tensed and her tear-streaked features stiffened, Manning knew he'd blundered yet again.

"Leave Sabbath Hollow? Not while I have breath in my body. This is my children's home and I mean to see it thriving again by the time Templeton's old enough to claim it in his own right."

She snatched the pot of beans from the table and slammed it onto the stove, cheap tin clashing with futile defiance against thick black iron. "No sneaking scoundrel of a brother-in-law and no shiftless, gossipy neighbors are going to stop me, either!"

Had she meant to add *no Yankee carpetbagger husband* to that list? Manning wondered. He'd been a fool to think Caddie had softened her attitude toward him on the basis of a moment's weakness and a few words in his defense hurled at old Mrs. Pratt.

Before he could demand to know how they'd make a success of the mill without the grudging cooperation of the community, Caddie spoke again.

"While you keep the children occupied fishing tomorrow, I plan to call on the rest of the neighbors and make sure they know what's what. If they aren't willing to help themselves, I'd sooner you brought in a crew of Yankees to run the mill than let Lon get his clutches on Sabbath Hollow.''

Verdant fire fairly crackled in her eyes—the most attractive show of defiance Manning had ever witnessed. He knew better than to gainsay her decision. Did he like her best soft and vulnerable, weeping in his arms, or proud and gallant, a tigress ready to battle the world on behalf of her cubs? Both, he decided at last.

Both. Far too much for his own good.

For all her bravado before Manning, Caddie drove down the Gordons' lane with a sinking sensation in the pit of her belly. Please let them give her a more cordial reception than the one she'd received from Mrs. Pratt, she prayed.

She had some hopes of it. Before the war, she'd been good friends with Mrs. Gordon, a genial lady who also hailed from South Carolina.

If her pride did take another mauling today, Caddie vowed not to seek sympathy in the arms of a Yankee this time. She cringed at the memory. Somehow those few chaste moments weeping on Manning's shoulder felt more disloyal to Del than if she'd committed flagrant adultery while he was still alive.

As Caddie pulled up outside Gordon Hall, a slender girl hurried out to greet her. All Southern girls looked slender these days, Caddie reflected bitterly, remembering the withered wraith Ann Pratt had become. They no longer needed punishing corsets to achieve a fashionably tiny waist.

The thought of Ann made Caddie brace for a frosty welcome, but this young woman's tone sounded much more agreeable—apologetic, even.

"Mrs. Marsh, we heard you'd come back. It's kind of

you to call when you must have so much to do settling in again. I'm afraid Mama's indisposed today and not up to receiving guests.''

"Dora?'' Caddie could scarcely believe it. The last time she'd seen Dora Gordon, the girl hadn't been much older than Templeton was now. "Why, you're all grown up, dear.''

Grown up too fast, under harsh conditions. Like her own children. Caddie caught herself wishing damnation on all Yankees when she remembered Manning and her errand.

"I'm sorry to hear your ma's feeling poorly.'' Was it the truth, or just Mrs. Gordon's polite excuse not to receive a woman of dubious reputation? "I reckon I've picked a bad time to call on folks. Mrs. Pratt wasn't anxious to visit with me yesterday, either.'' This gentle rebuff hurt almost as much as the harsher one she'd received at Willowvale.

A slight flush brightened Dora's pinched face. "You've been to the Pratts? You didn't happen to see Jeff while you were there?''

Was Dora sweet on young Jeff Pratt? If Caddie recollected right, Jeff had been a boon companion of Dora's brother, Monroe. For a tender passing moment the intervening years, with their blighted harvest of loss and defeat, seemed to evaporate. Caddie fancied herself the mistress of a thriving plantation with no weightier responsibilities than matchmaking among the young folks of the neighborhood.

"I only spied Jeff from a distance—at least I think it might have been him.'' Necessity forced Caddie back to the present, much as she resented it. "If you're talking to Jeff, would you mention that we're fixing up the old mill at Sabbath Hollow and looking for men to work? We'll pay wages in cash, plus cut lumber if he needs any for fixing up Willowvale.''

What ailed Dora? Every word Caddie spoke seemed to bite into the girl. By the time she finished, Caddie could have sworn she saw a film of tears in Dora's misty gray eyes.

"I…don't believe he'd be interested, Mrs. Marsh."

After what she'd seen at Willowvale the previous day, Dora's stiff words riled Caddie. Did Master Jeff consider himself too good to work for the likes of Manning and her?

"My name is Mrs. Forbes now, in case you haven't heard. And if Jefferson Pratt would rather sit idle while Willowvale rots to pieces than soil his hands to earn an honest dollar, that's his business, I'm sure."

Dora flinched again, then recovered her composure and shot Caddie a defiant glare. "I don't imagine he wants to sit idle, *Mrs. Forbes.*"

The girl's tone reminded Caddie of someone else. An instant's reflection told it was her own voice when she'd defended Manning to Mrs. Pratt.

"But Jeff doesn't have much choice about it, seeing as he's been blind since Sharpesburg!"

This time Caddie flinched. "Oh, I'm sorry, Dora. I hadn't heard. No wonder Mrs. Pratt sent me away with a flea in my ear yesterday. What about Willie and Josh?"

Staring at the ground, the girl shook her head in reply.

So Mrs. Pratt had lost two of her boys. Caddie hardly dared ask, "Monroe?"

The tremor in Dora's shoulders told her more than she wanted to know. It reminded her of the old Bible story about the Lord striking down the firstborn of every Egyptian family. The prosperous people of Egypt hadn't been anxious to part with their slaves, either. Was it possible that Del, Monroe, the Pratt boys had fought and sacrificed their lives in an unrighteous cause?

Caddie expelled the treasonous notion from her mind. Just because she'd married a Yankee didn't mean she had to think like one.

"I'm sorry for your family's loss, Dora. I'll come back

tomorrow with some game broth and egg custard for your ma. In the meantime, tell her I was asking after her, will you?''

She had barely climbed back onto her wagon when a man rode up the lane on a horse that looked to have seen better days. Not recognizing the rider, Caddie swung the buckboard around and waved goodbye to Dora.

If she didn't know him, the horseman appeared to know her. "Caddie," he called, "Lon said you'd come home. Claims you married some Yankee carpetbagger who ran him off Sabbath Hollow."

At last Caddie recognized the voice. "Dr. Mercer?"

It hardly seemed possible this could be the same man who had delivered Templeton. Dr. Mercer had always been quite stout. Now his clothes billowed over a shrunken frame and the once-ample flesh of his face hung in folds like a hound dog's.

"So you do remember me, missy?" The doctor cracked a sour grin as he dismounted. "Living on weevily hardtack for four years helped me regain my girlish figure. Might as well get used to it—I won't be waxing fat off my practice anytime soon."

Doc Mercer had always been something of a wag, yet Caddie didn't feel much like laughing at his caustic quip. Fortunately, he turned his attention to Dora, inquiring about her mother.

"She's much the same, sir. Still pining for Pa and Monroe. Maybe if we had better food to give her, but she just turns up her nose at what we've got."

So Mrs. Gordon's indisposition hadn't only been an excuse to keep from seeing her. The thought comforted Caddie a little. Then, hearing the frustration and fear in Dora's voice, she told herself to quit being so selfish. Better to have May Belle Gordon snubbing her in good health than wasting away of a broken heart, and fretting her daughters like this.

"There, there, child." Doc Mercer patted Dora's hand. "You and the girls have been doing the best you can for her under the circumstances. I've brought a tonic, if we can coax her to take it. I'll see if I can rile her up some. Folks need fight in them to stay alive during hard times."

Dora replied with a vigorous nod. "She was ever so much better the other day. After you told her she mustn't give the Yankees the satisfaction of having killed off another Gordon."

"Cheap medicine." The doctor shrugged. "All I can afford to dispense these days." He turned on Caddie, as if his troubles and those of his patients were all on account of her.

"Don't waste your time calling on me if that fancy Yankee husband of yours gets you in the family way, missy, for I won't attend you. I don't imagine the pair of you will last long here. Lon's made sure folks know what's what. They'll *eat* their wood before they bring it to your mill and they'll starve before they work to make another carpetbagger rich."

Unsettled by the thought of Manning getting her with child, Caddie shrank before Doc Mercer's anger. But hearing Lon's name kindled her own. "You're a fine one to go on about Mrs. Gordon pining away on account of the Yankees, sir. If folks around here don't work to make a decent future for their young'uns, won't that be just as much a victory for the Yankees? I'll tell you what I told Mrs. Pratt—my husband is a good man and he means well even if he is a Yankee. Lon's just stirring up trouble to get rid of us. Then he can get his hands on Sabbath Hollow."

Her late mother would have been scandalized to hear Caddie talking back to one of her elders. Mammy Dulcie would have washed her mouth out with soap.

"Now see here, young lady—'' growled the doctor.

Thirty years of soft-spoken propriety threatened to gag Caddie, but she fought against it. "No. You *see here*. Other folks can starve if they choose, and let their plantations fall to rack and ruin before they'll have dealings with a Yankee. I might, too, if I didn't have children to provide for. But I won't make Tem and Varina pay for troubles that aren't of their making. Now, if you'll excuse me, I plan to call on everyone in the neighborhood and tell them what I've just told you."

As the doctor glared at her and looked like he was fixing to explode, Caddie addressed Dora. "I can use a good, willing chore gal if you or Charlotte or Alice would like the job. I'll pay cash, too, so you can buy the kind of vittles that might tempt your ma's appetite."

"I—I'll think about it." Dora didn't look like she meant to give the idea very serious consideration.

"Good. You know where to find me." With a curt nod of parting, Caddie clicked her tongue at the horse and jogged the reins. As she drove down the twisty lane, she could almost feel the eyes of Dora Gordon and Dr. Mercer boring into her back.

Let them look. Let them talk. Let the whole neighborhood talk. If they wanted to cling to the past and allow the war's old wounds to fester, they could go right ahead. They'd better not expect to pull her and her children down with them, though.

The afternoon had almost ebbed away by the time Caddie turned the buckboard toward Sabbath Hollow again. A light drizzle had begun to fall, cooling her temper and dampening her zeal. At least a few folks had given her a fair hearing. Some had nodded grudgingly when she urged them to put the past behind them and move on with their lives.

The sounds of laughter, barking and splashing drew her

gaze toward the creek and made her smile in spite of herself. She'd struck a devil's bargain with Manning Forbes. One that didn't include restoring Tem and Varina's lost childhood. She'd had nothing worth bartering for so precious a boon.

Instead he'd made them a gift of it.

Her conscience smarted at the thought of every unkind word she'd ever spoken to the man. How sincere was *she* about looking ahead to the future, it demanded, instead of always back over her shoulder?

Chapter Eight

"**M**anning?" Caddie glanced up suddenly from her last few bites of supper and caught him squarely in her sights. "I've been thinking about the mill."

The sound of his given name on her lips for the first time made a queer hot shiver run through him, as though she'd touched him in some intimate place.

"What about it?" He scowled and dropped his gaze to his plate, hoping she wouldn't notice the fierce blush spreading up from his too-tight collar.

Instantly, he felt ashamed of himself for snapping at Caddie. After all, it wasn't *her* fault he'd been gaping at her like some calf-eyed adolescent.

Manning gentled his voice, though he still couldn't bring himself to meet her eyes. "Whatever you said to the neighbors last week must have worked. I've managed to hire a decent crew to work the mill since then, and we have a couple of contracts for wood in hand."

"That's good."

From outside came the sounds of the children and the dog at play. Though Manning had savored this compound of noises for the past three weeks, it hadn't lost its power to tickle him. If he lived to be a hundred, their jolly afternoon of fishing would stand out as one of the happiest of his life.

Caddie took a deep breath and continued. "It wasn't only Lon's troublemaking that kept folks away, you know."

"Oh?" Jolted from his pleasant thoughts, he braced for her to point out something he'd done wrong.

"There just aren't many able-bodied men left around these parts who can work at a sawmill or cut lumber." Caddie shook her head, and wistful sorrow infused her voice. "Jeff Pratt's blind. Bobbie Stevens lost both legs at Antietam. Mrs. Gordon only has her three girls left."

Every shot he'd ever fired in battle seemed to ricochet back on Manning, riddling his heart. What could be wrong with him? Other men who'd fought in the war didn't seem to take personal responsibility for the destruction their armies had wrought.

Why must he?

If Caddie expected him to reply, she gave no sign of it— almost as though she was thinking aloud. "When I took the Gordons some fish cakes this afternoon, I asked Dora again about coming to help me around the house. I know she wants to, if she can just find the gumption to stand up to her ma."

And humble her pride if she had any left, Manning thought. For a young lady brought up with wealth and privilege, stooping to domestic service would be a bitter pill to swallow.

Perhaps the same notion had occurred to Caddie. Her brow furrowed. "I wish we could start some kind of business that'd make it possible for women and wounded men to earn a dollar. *They're* the ones struggling to support families these days."

Her words anointed his wounds with healing balm.

"Caddie, you're a genius!" In the grip of his idea, Manning scarcely noticed that he'd called his wife by her first name.

Before he could stop himself, he reached across the table and enfolded her hand in both of his. "We can take some of the lumber we mill and start a sideline building furniture—plain, serviceable chairs and tables."

With his own background in woodworking, the plan immediately felt right to him. "Most of the finish work could be done by women. I'll bet that fellow who lost his legs can still operate a lathe or drive a team. As for Jeff Pratt…" Manning shrugged. "There's got to be something he could do. Learn to weave rattan cane or sea grass for chair seats, maybe?"

"That would be perfect!" Her face lit in a way Manning had never seen it, Caddie brought her free hand up to squeeze his.

Perhaps it was only wishful thinking, but he suspected if the table had not formed a barrier between them, she might have thrown her arms around his neck. It scared him almost nauseous to realize how much he yearned for one fleeting, impulsive embrace. That weak moment when he'd taken Caddie in his arms had whetted his appetite for forbidden fruit.

Determined to resist his growing attraction, he pulled his hands away from hers with such force that he knocked over a glass tumbler—one of a precious few that had survived the war. One look at Caddie's face told him he'd done something inexcusable.

Pushing back his chair, he cursed under his breath. "We shouldn't be using these for everyday. They ought to be locked up for special occasions!"

Before Caddie could summon any words of rebuke, he stalked off to the sawmill, where he worked feverishly on some final repairs. The chores occupied his hands and part of his mind.

Not all of it, though.

He was doing what he needed to do—what he'd promised to do. Manning had hoped that might buy him a little peace, and it had. But only a little. Something else gnawed at him now.

He'd lied to himself by pretending marriage to Caddie Marsh was the only way to repay his debt. He could have found a less personal means, if he'd given it some hard, honest thought.

Instead, he'd surrendered to his bone-deep longing for a family, using the Marshes' desperate situation to foist himself upon them. In the days since, Templeton and Varina had burrowed their way into his guarded, empty heart. Somehow, they had tapped a wellspring of spontaneous affection and fatherly intuition Manning had never suspected in his nature. With a swiftness that terrified him, the children were becoming as essential to his existence as water and air.

If he should ever lose them... Manning pictured a fish writhing on the creek bank, its gills straining against the dry air that could not sustain its life.

As he tightened the mill's belts for the third time, Manning's renegade thoughts turned to Caddie. From one minute to the next, his feelings for her reeled between intense wariness and equally intense attraction. Like the lethal push and pull of a jagged saw blade. There were times like tonight, when she'd clutched his hands across the narrow table, that he feared it would cut him in two.

For his own peace of mind, he must go one way or the other, and the only reasonable course was to fight the relentless pull she exercised upon him. He had no right to her, after all. Besides, she was so dangerously inquisitive with her subtle but persistent questions about his past. If she ever guessed his true motive for coming to Sabbath Hollow—and there were times Manning was convinced she must *know*—she would turn him out, depriving him of the only real family he might ever have.

One that grew more precious to him by the hour.

With the familiar, comforting aromas of old timber and fresh sawdust filling his nostrils, Manning made a vow to keep his bride at arm's length or farther, and to fight the powerful grip she'd begun to exert upon him.

Already he felt like an exhausted trout trying to swim up the millrace.

Several days later, Caddie glanced out at the laundry she'd hung to dry and bit back a cuss word.

May had blown in like the lion that belonged to early March. The children loved this windy weather, for Manning had helped them build kites out of brown paper and slender strips of strapping from the mill.

Caddie hated the unseasonable gales. Doors blowing open, startling her half to death. A hundred drafts whistling in the boarded and broken windows of Sabbath Hollow. Not to mention the havoc wreaked on her clothesline.

Sheets knotted around the long rope. Undergarments blasted off, sprawling on the grass in lewd positions. Stray twigs and pine needles besmirching the laundry she'd labored so hard to wash clean. Lately Caddie felt like a sheet on the clothesline of life, blown and twisted by fickle, powerful winds.

Some days her spirits soared higher than the children's kites. After her years in Richmond, struggling to care for Tem and Varina on her own, it was such a blessed relief to have help feeding, clothing and loving them. With that wearying weight lifted from her shoulders, her whole disposition felt buoyed, until she found herself smiling and laughing for no reason at all.

Except that it felt so damnably good to be alive again.

She had a new dress for the first time in years, and for

the first time in years she found herself taking an interest in her appearance. Just the other night, when she had caught Manning in a rare appreciative glance, her heart had wafted up to a dizzying altitude. Though she'd steeled herself against it, she couldn't help admiring the man, even liking him a little.

He was so solicitous of her and the children. He helped out with the house chores, took a firm but fond hand with Tem and Varina, and never failed to return from town with some small luxury for them. He seemed to draw nourishment from the simple labors of family life, absorbing them almost greedily.

Then some searing reminder of the war and its aftermath would dash Caddie painfully to earth again. She'd recollect that Manning Forbes was a Yankee, a member of the race she'd sworn to condemn with her last breath. No matter how hard he tried to ingratiate himself with her family, the fact remained that he had come south with the sole purpose of making his fortune. When he had done that, there was every danger he might leave—inflicting a loss on Tem and Varina more memorable and personal than the death of a father neither of them could recall.

Like a mercurial weathervane, Caddie's manner toward her husband shifted as it was blown first by a warm zephyr, then by a frigid Arctic blast. Not that he seemed to notice or care most of the time. Manning's transparent affection for the children contrasted sharply with his often gruff indifference to her.

Though she tried to convince herself it was just the way she wanted him to behave, in her secret soul it rankled. Clearly, she must lack the power to captivate a man. Hadn't Del's indiscretion with Lydene convinced her of that?

Bang! Caddie jumped at the sound of the front door blowing open yet again.

"Mama!" Varina hollered at the top of her lungs from the entry. "A lady's come calling to see you!"

Caddie's stomach twisted up tight. This was the first time any of the neighbors had paid a visit to Sabbath Hollow. Had they decided to quit shunning her at last?

Hiking up her skirts, she raced to the top of the stairs, then gulped a deep breath before gliding down the steps with no trace of ill-bred haste. She smiled at the sight of Dora Gordon. The girl wore a look of furtive guilt, as though she'd just crossed the threshold of some house of ill repute.

"Varina, dear." Caddie gave her daughter *the look.* "When you announce a caller, you're supposed to come find Mama and tell her in a nice quiet voice."

"Yes, ma'am." Varina swiped a stray rusty-red curl out of her eyes. Her tone proclaimed that such niceties were a waste of valuable time, but she had better things to do than argue the point. "I have to go get my kite out of the maple tree."

"Be careful, now. Tem can—"

The front door slammed shut behind the child. This time Caddie knew better than to blame the wind.

She gave an exasperated shake of her head, then held out her hands to Dora. "It's good to see you again, dear. I hope your mother hasn't taken a turn for the worse."

"No, Mrs. Forbes, ma'am." The girl spoke Caddie's married name in the hushed tone usually reserved for blasphemy. "Ma seems to be rallying. I reckon Doc Mercer was right about needing to rile her up. The food you've brought has helped, too."

"I'm glad to hear it." Caddie wondered if she might also be the cause of Mrs. Gordon's agitation. "I'd invite you into the parlor, but we haven't a decent stick of furniture in it. Would you mind taking a cup of tea with me in the kitchen?"

"Real tea?" whispered Dora.

"Isn't it a treat?" Caddie led her guest to the back of the house. "My, er, husband brought some back the last time he went into town."

The girl murmured a reply that Caddie didn't quite catch.

"I beg your pardon, dear? I must be getting old, though I feel years younger since we've come back to Sabbath Hollow."

Dora giggled. "I didn't mean to say anything, ma'am. It just popped about." She seemed to weigh Caddie's ability to take a joke. "I wondered if Mr. Forbes might have a younger brother who was looking for a wife."

"I guarantee *that* would rile your ma into robust health." Caddie counterfeited a laugh so Dora would not think her offended.

In fact, the innocent jest stung her pride like a burr. Was that what the neighbors thought of her marriage? That she'd latched on to a Yankee carpetbagger who could lavish her with all the luxuries she'd missed during the war? Couldn't they see it had been a matter of survival for her and her children?

Had it? queried Caddie's conscience as she brewed the tea and made polite conversation with Dora. She and the children *could* have moved in with Lon and Lydene, extending their stay indefinitely. They *could* have gone home to her brother Gideon in South Carolina. Marrying Manning Forbes had simply been the least humiliating option available to her.

She'd put her own sinful pride before Southern loyalty.

As she poured the dark, steaming tea into Dora's cup, Caddie tried to scour her mind of that damning conclusion. Like a stubborn stain, it would not go away.

"Have you thought about coming to work at Sabbath Hollow?" She forced herself to concentrate on trying to hire Dora. Anything to distract her thoughts. "Don't be daunted by the size of the house. I wouldn't expect you to keep it up to the standards we were once used to. In fact, there are several of the rooms we've closed for a while. I don't plan to sit back and play the lady of leisure, either.''

Dora closed her eyes and breathed in the aromatic steam rising from her cup. Perhaps the smell fortified her resolve, for she replied, ''I've given it plenty of thought, Mrs. Forbes. I'd like to come work here provided I don't have to live in. I promise I'll be here good and early every morning to start the fires. It's no distance from our place to yours if I cut through our back pasture.''

''Very well.'' Caddie let her held breath ease out. ''You're hired. I plan to take care of upstairs myself, if you'll see to the downstairs and kitchen chores.''

She wasn't sure she wanted anyone else poking around the bedrooms, discovering the family's sleeping arrangements.

They talked about hours and wages. Finally Dora savored her last mouthful of tea. ''If it's all right with you, ma'am, I'll start first thing tomorrow morning.''

''I'll look forward to it.'' She would, too, Caddie realized.

It had been such a long time since she'd had another woman around to talk to over a cup of tea, midmorning or before starting supper. With less of her time occupied by mundane chores, perhaps her mind wouldn't so easily fall prey to futile regrets and even more futile fantasies.

A thick ledger book in his hands, Manning waited at the foot of the stairs as Caddie came down after putting the children to bed. ''I'd like to ask a favor of you, ma'am.''

''Favor?'' Caddie stared at the book.

''Now that you've got the Gordon girl to keep house, I wondered if you could lend me a hand with the business. Seeing as we're supposed to be partners and all.''

She glanced back up again. Her eyes sparkled with interest, but her puckered brow looked guarded. "You know I'll be glad to help out if I can. What is it you need me to do?"

Manning's Adam's apple bobbed wildly in his throat. He'd been trying so hard to keep both physical and emotional distance from Caddie. But the further he pulled away, the tighter some invisible cord between them stretched, until he feared it would wrench him off his feet and propel him forcefully into her arms.

"I need somebody to keep the books, and I think you'd be good at it." He gestured to indicate the entry hall, unfurnished but immaculate. "You're so methodical. Even before Miss Gordon came, you always kept the house neat as a pin. Everything in the kitchen has its place. I marveled at how you packed so much onto that old buckboard for your trip from Richmond."

Caddie looked flustered, but a trifle flattered, too. For a wild moment Manning mistook her for eighteen instead of twenty-eight.

"You're very observant, sir. Not everyone considers my craving for order a virtue, I'm afraid." She pulled a droll face. "My daughter, for instance."

He couldn't help but chuckle. Nor could he stop himself from meeting her gaze. "Well, I do."

The laughter froze in Manning's throat, yet he had to clamp his lips tight to imprison a torrent of words that threatened to gush out of him. He longed to tell Caddie of all her other special qualities he'd noticed. Some he'd sensed from the beginning, like her strength of will and her devotion to her children. Others, like her concern for anyone in trouble and her appreciation of the smallest kindness, had taken him by surprise as he'd come to know her better.

Caddie's gaze faltered before his, falling once again to the ledger in his hands. "I—I've never kept accounts before, other than the household money. What if I made a mistake?''

His face suddenly felt cold, as if all the blood had leached out of it. ''Everybody makes mistakes, Caddie.''

He certainly had. Was he making a big one right now? Putting forward a plan that would force the two of them into more frequent contact. Standing so close to her without the distracting presence of Tem and Varina. Close enough that he might reach out and graze her hair with his fingertips, if his shaky self-control slipped for an instant.

Perhaps it wasn't too late to correct his mistake. ''If you'd rather not—''

At the very moment he pulled the ledger up to shield his chest, Caddie raised her hand to rest on the book's green cover. Its movement towed her a step closer to Manning and brought her fingertips to rest against the base of his neck. The lightest of touches, yet it threatened to cut off his air.

Caddie wrenched her hand away and took a step backward. ''I didn't say I wouldn't do it. I only meant…I'd need your…help.'' She made it sound like a shameful admission.

''It…isn't so difficult.'' A good deal easier than catching his breath. ''You just keep track of the money coming in on one side of the ledger and the money going out on the other side. Whatever's left over at the end of each month is our profit.''

''I reckon I could manage that.'' One corner of Caddie's mouth curved upward, coaxing just the hint of a dimple where her face had begun to fill out.

Manning caught himself inhaling deeply, to draw as much of her scent into his lungs as they would hold. It reminded him of the fresh sweet aroma of an orchard after a spring rain.

His hands clamped down on the ledger to keep them

from trembling. More desperately than he'd fought at Gettysburg, Manning battled his urge to drop the book and seize his wife instead. Feasting on her lips and glutting his nostrils on her fragrance, he might find the nourishment he craved.

But at what cost?

"I—I'd like you to pay out the wages at the end of each week, as well." Manning's voice rasped in his ears as he struggled to keep it steady. He thrust the heavy book at Caddie, then jammed his hands into his pockets to keep them from reaching for her. "I know a lot of the folks on our payroll would rather not work for a Yankee if they had any choice. If you give them their wages instead of me, it mightn't bother them so much."

He turned and headed for the door. The Stevens boy had put the old lathe to use, turning a few decorative balusters to match the broken ones that marred the elegance of Sabbath Hollow's front porch. Might as well get started replacing them while he still had a bit of daylight. More importantly, he wanted to get away from Caddie before he did something foolish.

Hardly aware that he was speaking aloud, he muttered, "Besides, if you keep the accounts you won't need to worry that I'm cheating you."

He pulled the door shut behind him and proceeded to attack the broken posts with a crowbar. The strenuous chore gave him a safe outlet for his overwrought emotions. As he repaired the broken railings, Manning struggled to shore up the rickety barricade he'd raised around his heart to keep Caddie out.

Every day, without half trying, she tore fresh holes in it. Heaven help him if she should ever decide to lay siege in earnest.

Chapter Nine

"Dora, can you keep an eye on the children while I take the payroll up to the mill?"

As Caddie tied her bonnet strings, she resisted an urge to glance in the cheap little decorative mirror Manning had recently purchased. Folks would be too busy counting their modest earnings to care what she looked like.

Don't go lying to yourself, Caddie. It isn't the workers you're gussying up for—it's their boss.

She peeked in the mirror, after all. Just long enough to stick her tongue out at herself...and to twist a loose strand of hair around her finger until it curled.

Varina barreled into the entry hall. "I want to go."

Gazing at the child, Caddie stifled a sigh. "You most certainly cannot. I'll be busy giving folks their wages and I won't be able to keep an eye on you. Heaven knows what scrapes you'd get into among all the machinery and sharp tools."

"Manning wouldn't let me get hurt."

For a foolish instant, Caddie wished she could make that boast. Hard as she tried not to care, she found herself elated by his smallest attention and stung by his persistent coolness.

"Manning will be busy working. He won't be able to spare the time to keep you out of harm's way."

Whether or not he could spare the time, Caddie knew he'd cheerfully watch Varina if she decided to bring the child.

"But, Mama…"

"Varina Virginia Marsh, I said no and that's my final word."

The little girl heaved a martyred sigh. "Yes, ma'am."

In the face of her daughter's disappointment, Caddie relented a little. "If you go clean yourself up, perhaps you could help Dora make doughnuts."

"I s'pose." Varina cast a critical look over her hands, as if trying to figure how little washing they could get away with. "That's still not as much fun as going to the mill."

Caddie pulled on her gloves, then retrieved her ledger and cash box from the stairs where she'd set them.

"I'll speak to Manning about it. Perhaps you and Tem can come with me next week."

"Bet he'll say yes." Varina hopped from foot to foot.

"Don't go counting your chickens before they hatch, now." Caddie pressed a finger to her daughter's button nose.

"Will you give Manning something from me?"

Caddie thought of the "treasures" Varina had brought her stepfather in recent days. Stones with *gold* in them. Fishing worms of impressive dimensions. "That depends on what it is."

"This." Seizing Caddie's hand, Varina hauled her mother down to plant a moist, noisy kiss on her cheek.

Caddie dismissed the ridiculous rush of heat to her face and the giddy tightness in her stomach. "Why don't you wait and give it to him yourself at suppertime?"

He'll like it a good deal more coming from you than from me.

Before Varina could reply, Dora called to her from the kitchen and she raced away.

Caddie shook her head at her own foolishness as she left the house and set off up the wooded path that led to the mill. Blustery winds of May had mellowed to playful June breezes, fragrant with the scent of wildflowers. A honey-gold sun had coaxed the Virginia countryside to blossom out in its most brilliant colors. Birds chirped a saucy chorus from the eaves of the surrounding woodland. Off to the west, a bank of malicious dark clouds skulked behind the distant Blue Ridge Mountains.

How long had it been since she'd looked around her and found the world beautiful? Caddie wondered. Her feet wanted to break into a skipping, waltzing step unsuited to a sober matron rapidly approaching thirty. A sprightly little tune ran through her mind, and if she wasn't careful, she'd catch herself humming it.

Recalling how quickly such fragile bubbles of happiness could shatter into jagged shards of pain, she didn't dare give in to them. Much as she longed to on a day like this. Blast Manning Forbes for setting in motion this civil war between her head and her heart!

Caddie heard and smelled the mill before she saw it. The enormous wooden wheel creaked as it turned, bearing each load of water down to splash free at rhythmic intervals. Together with the rasp of the saw and pounding of hammers, it made a kind of robust music. The resinous tang of freshly sawed lumber smelled like energy and optimism.

Perhaps the folks who worked here found it so, too. When Caddie stepped into the mill clearing she discovered the place bustling with activity. A young woman wearing leather gloves and a thick canvas apron over her dress toted bundles of lathe-turned wood to a nearby shed that Manning had converted into a woodwright's shop. Two lanky boys carried long boards of cut lumber out of the mill and stacked them to dry.

Bobbie Stevens hobbled from the shop into the mill. A single stout cane had replaced the crutches Caddie'd seen him using only a fortnight ago.

Catching sight of her, the young man waved. "Afternoon, Miz Caddie. Shall I go tell the boss you're here?"

"If you can tell me where I might find Mr. Forbes, I don't mind hunting him up for myself." She glanced around to make sure no one else was within earshot. "How are you feeling these days, Bobbie? The work around here isn't too much for your constitution, I hope."

"Better too much work than too little, ma'am." He flashed a rueful grin. "Never reckoned how good it would feel to earn a week's pay."

For the first time since she'd met him during her honeymoon with Del, the boyish young fellow looked like a grown man.

"I'm glad to hear it. That's why I've come, as a matter of fact." Caddie glanced down at the ledger and strongbox. "To pay everyone their wages."

She didn't mention her nagging worry about finances. Since taking over the bookkeeping, Caddie had come to wonder if they'd hired more folks to work than they needed. Would the business turn a profit before they exhausted Manning's resources?

Bobbie's grin stretched wider. "I'd better not hold you up, then, or I won't be too popular around here. You'll find Mr. Forbes in the shop yonder, doing some joining work on a batch of chairs."

She must have spoken a few polite words of parting to the young man, but afterward Caddie couldn't remember. Nor did she recall Bobbie Stevens walking off to the mill. For she turned toward the woodwright shop and caught sight of Manning. The shop, the mill and everything else around her seemed to melt away, leaving only the solid, focused figure of that one man.

Absorbed in his work, he paid her no heed, but carefully fixed a caned seat to a chair frame. Rays of bright June sunlight pierced the leafy canopy of lofty elms and dappled the clearing below. Through the wide door of the shop, they shimmered over his crisp profile and his large, deft hands.

With strength, skill and patience, those hands had refashioned a life for Caddie and her children. As she watched her husband's hands move over the wood in a kind of caress, a strange pleasant warmth rippled through her flesh. Her imagination stirred with fancies of his long brown fingers tangled in her unbound hair or whispering over her bare skin.

He glanced up and their eyes met. The air between them fairly crackled, the way a comb pulled through wool threw off tiny sparks and shocks on a winter night.

Their marriage was nothing but a business arrangement to him, Caddie sternly reminded herself. If she had a particle of sense or pride, she'd want to keep it just that way.

She'd always possessed a generous measure of sense and rather too much pride. They came to her rescue now, stiffening limbs that wanted to melt like butter in the sun. Infusing her slack, dreamy features with brisk reality. She forced herself to approach him with calm, sedate steps.

"I hope this isn't a bad time to do the payroll?" Caddie willed a cool, businesslike tone into her voice when it threatened to turn soft and breathless.

"No. It's fine. Just fine." The tension of his stance and the stiff, grave set of his expression contradicted Manning's words. "Would you mind sitting outside if I bring a chair and a table for you? Better light out there, and you won't end up with sawdust all over your clothes."

If he wanted her out from underfoot, why didn't he just say so? "Very well. Outside it is."

Manning disappeared into the shop, returning a moment later with a chair like the one she'd watched him assemble. Forgetting the contrary feelings that pulled her heart like a mess of warm taffy, Caddie reached out and ran her hand down the long, clean line of it.

"Where did you find this design? It looks good and sturdy, but not too heavy." The chair's clean, spare frame had an elegant simplicity. "I like it."

"I came up with the design myself." Manning sounded as though he expected her to change her mind on that account. "It's cheap and easy to build. The cane seat makes it comfortable to sit on and lighter to transport."

Thoroughly practical, just like its designer. Yet anything but ordinary.

"Where did you learn to build furniture like this?"

Manning didn't answer.

Perhaps he hadn't heard her as he concentrated on finding a likely spot for her to set up.

"Somewhere the breeze is calm," he muttered to himself. "Don't want papers or money blowing away."

He set the chair in a brightly lit spot, then glanced at Caddie and pulled it back into the shade. "Don't want you getting sunstroke. You look a little flushed already."

That wasn't the sun's fault, Caddie decided as Manning returned to the shop to fetch her a table.

At least that's what she assumed he meant to do. When several minutes passed with no sign of him coming back, Caddie set her ledger and strongbox beneath the chair and wandered over to a part of the clearing where she could see the big water wheel turning.

Leaning against the trunk of a tall elm, Caddie closed her eyes and drank in the peaceful murmur of the river. Gradually she became aware of two male voices in conversation. Something in their tone drew her closer to the mill and made her listen more carefully.

"Recognized him the minute he visited our place asking after his wife and the children," said a voice that sounded like Bobbie Stevens's. "When Ma came back into the house from talking to him, I asked why she hadn't invited him to stay for supper. She told me he'd been killed back in '64."

"I'll take your word they *look* the same," replied another man, possibly Jeff Pratt. "And you can take mine that they aren't. Don't sound a thing alike."

They were talking about Del and Manning. Caddie's insides commenced to churn the way they had when she'd first laid eyes on Manning Forbes. Like Bobbie, she'd been so certain the man was her husband, mysteriously risen from the grave. In the weeks that followed, their physical likeness had struck her at odd moments. As she'd gotten to know Manning Forbes, however, she'd ceased to see the resemblance.

"'Course he doesn't sound the same, what with putting on the Yankee talk," Bobbie protested. "He wouldn't be the first soldier who got reported dead when he wasn't. I heard tell of a fellow down Danville way who came home to find his family'd put up a tombstone with his name on it."

"Plain foolishness, that is. Why in creation would he pretend to be a Yankee?"

Caddie strained to hear Bobbie's reply.

After a pause that stretched her nerves taut, the answer finally came. "I never met a man who liked to win quite as bad as he did. Maybe this is just his way of landing on the winning side. Seems to be working, if you ask me."

As Caddie struggled to make sense of Bobbie's preposterous suggestion, Jeff spoke again. "Whoever that man is, he *isn't* Del Marsh. I'll tell you something else for free. We both know another fellow who likes to win just as bad as Del did."

"And who might that be?"

"Del's brother. Lon."

Jeff's words sent a shiver through her.

"Sorry to take so long fetching you the table," Manning called to Caddie.

At his words, she started. When she spun around to face him, a look of furtive guilt blazed on her features, as though he'd caught her in the commission of some shameful deed.

Did she think he begrudged her a moment of peace and quiet?

"There's no rush." He set a small table in front of her chair.

Once he got a little time, he wanted to build Caddie a proper desk for bookkeeping. At the moment, he needed to concentrate on producing furniture for sale.

Slowly, Caddie approached, her eyes trained on his face as if searching it for something. He'd caught her watching him earlier, but somehow that had felt different. For a daft instant Manning had imagined her gaze simmered with desire. Or had he only seen a reflection of the hunger that brooded inside of him?

In the full, uncompromising glare of June sunlight, Manning couldn't fool himself about the way Caddie looked at him. Her gaze fairly crackled with interest, but not the carnal type. The wariness that had bristled from her when he'd first arrived at Sabbath Hollow had returned in full force, joined by suspicion and a flicker of fear she tried hard to mask.

She knows.

The certainty of it slammed into Manning like an artillery barrage at close range.

Caddie stooped to retrieve the ledger and cash box from beneath the chair. "You didn't answer my question, before."

"Question?" Manning heaped his tone with gruffness,

praying it would camouflage the guilt. "I don't recollect any question."

With deliberate care, Caddie arranged the ledger and cash box on the table, then settled herself on the chair. "Perhaps you didn't hear me."

She ran her hand down one of the subtly tapered legs of the table, and Manning felt a prickling sensation down his own leg, as if she'd stroked it, instead.

"I asked where you'd learned to make furniture like this."

An innocent enough query, but with this woman one question had an insidious way of leading to another.

"Awhile back I told you I was a woodworker before I enlisted. Did you think I was lying?" He slapped at the top of the table—hard. "Here's the proof I was telling the truth. Maybe now you can believe me and quit digging into my past."

As Caddie flinched from his outburst, Manning felt like a fool and a bully. He didn't want his thwarted attraction festering into hostility, but he couldn't seem to help himself. Staying on an even keel with this woman required the skill of a lumberjack rolling a wet, slippery log beneath his feet.

Though tricky and dangerous at times, it made him feel more alive than he could ever remember.

Caddie began to sputter in protest, but he cut her off. "I'll start sending folks out to collect their wages." Manning consciously softened his voice in a tacit apology. "I'd better get back to work if I want to have anything to pay them with next week."

Marching back into the shop, he sent a couple of young women out to get paid. Once Caddie was fully occupied with them, Manning blew out a shaky breath. He needed to put some distance between him and Caddie. Shore up is self-control. Remind himself of what he had at stake. A chance at redemption that he couldn't afford to lose.

Administering the payroll kept Caddie's thoughts productively engaged until quitting time, for which she was grateful. The force of Manning's outburst, and the all-too-familiar look on his face, had added fresh fuel to the glowing embers of doubt Jeff and Bobbie's conversation had stirred up. In anger, Manning looked most like Del as she remembered him.

But he couldn't be! Caddie slammed the lid of the cash box closed, as if to imprison her suspicions with the dwindling pile of silver and greenbacks. Watching the workers take their leave and Manning lock up for the weekend, she clung to Jeff Pratt's certainty when her own faltered.

Bobbie Stevens's speculations were too preposterous to entertain. Weren't they?

The hollow sensation deep in her belly told Caddie otherwise. She remembered how Del had often put on a Yankee accent to mock their undeclared enemies in those tense years prior to the war.

Suddenly afraid of Manning in a way she never had been when she believed him a perfect stranger, Caddie didn't wait for him, but headed back to the house on her own. When the soft pad of footsteps and rustle of branches told her he'd caught up, her pulse quickened.

Behind her, Manning cleared his throat. Did he plan to apologize for snapping at her? Del wouldn't. Anytime he'd done something sure to anger or offend her, he'd simply picked up and gone away for a few days.

Hunting with some of his cronies. Visiting a cousin in Westchester. Taking a stallion to service a mare down in Charlottesville. Returning only when he'd calculated that enough time had passed to cool her temper. It would have cooled, all right. Congealed into another hard layer of resentment that encased and smothered whatever love she'd once felt for him.

"I have to go away for a little while." Manning's quiet words thundered in Caddie's ears.

She wanted to turn on him and demand an explanation but she couldn't bring herself to do it. What if the scales of self-delusion fell from her eyes and she could no longer pretend not to recognize Del?

"I'll put young Stevens in charge while I'm gone," he continued. "I told him to clear any important decisions with you first."

"How long do you expect to be away?" Caddie tossed the question back over her shoulder, all the while telling herself it shouldn't matter.

"Can't say for sure. I need to find a market for the lumber and furniture we're producing. I'll try Washington first. Move on to Baltimore if I have to."

When Caddie couldn't find her voice to say anything more, Manning overtook her in a couple of long loping strides. "Getting this place back on its feet is costing more than I figured. We can keep afloat for a while, but the business is going to have to start paying some of its own expenses."

His reasoning made perfect sense. Why, then, did she get such a strong sense he was telling her less than the whole truth?

"I don't imagine you'll have much trouble finding buyers for the furniture—it's so well crafted." Caddie risked a quick sidelong glance at Manning. "Besides, I never intended you to support Sabbath Hollow as a charity."

For a carpetbagger, he'd put far more money into the plantation than he could expect to get back out anytime soon. If she hadn't known better, Caddie would have sworn he'd envisioned their business as a charitable scheme to rehabilitate the veterans and dependants of Mercer's Corner.

But that didn't tally. Nothing about Manning Forbes tallied with what she expected. She was tired of trying to solve a riddle she couldn't even put into words.

Their path emerged from the woods onto the sweeping meadow that sloped down behind the house. Off in the distance, Caddie could see Tem and Varina at play. The children wobbled around on pairs of stilts Manning had made for them. Where he'd found the time, Caddie couldn't guess.

Varina must have spied them coming, for she leaped off her stilts, letting the poles fall where they might, and raced up the hill to meet Manning and Caddie. Tem and his faithful Sergeant followed not far behind.

The tightness in Caddie's chest eased, and the knot deep in her belly began to untie itself. What else in the world mattered, so long as her children were happy?

Varina pelted up to them, gasping for breath, a triumphant smile glowing on her small flushed face. Seeing Caddie's arms loaded with her ledger and cash box, the child threw herself at Manning instead. He swung her up onto his shoulder while she squealed and giggled.

"Mama, Papa," she crowed. "Guess how many steps I can go on my stilts without falling down?"

Caddie wasn't sure what possessed her to reply as she did. Perhaps she needed to refute out loud the ridiculous suspicion that her first husband and her second might be the same man. Or maybe it was guilt that a Yankee carpetbagger could make her blood heat and her loins ache in a way the loyal Confederate father of her children never had.

"Varina Marsh, that man is not your father! You know very well some Yankee killed your real pa."

Those poisoned words had scarcely left her mouth before

Caddie wished she could suck them back in again. Even if they sickened her almost to death.

A look of hurt displaced Varina's bright smile, fused with righteous indignation, as though she'd been harshly and unjustly punished. Manning's eyes held nothing but hurt—a bottomless ocean of it. Like a dog whipped and told he was bad for the hundredth time in as many days.

Never in her proud life had Caddie felt so ashamed.

Chapter Ten

First light came early with the approach of summer, but Manning woke even earlier. After the tense, brittle silence of last night's supper, he couldn't bear to face an awkward parting this morning. If the children questioned when he'd be coming back, Manning wasn't certain he'd have any answers to give them. Looking into their small faces, he might end up making promises he didn't dare keep.

With quiet movements he collected his few belongings and stuffed them into a sturdy canvas rucksack. At the very bottom he placed a small latched box containing his papers. On his wedding night, he'd removed a certain letter from his shirt pocket and placed it in the box for safekeeping.

He hadn't wanted to risk Caddie or Miss Gordon finding it among his laundry, but he couldn't bring himself to destroy it, either. Though it had served its purpose in helping him track the Marsh family to Sabbath Hollow, perhaps he needed it to remind him of his debt and his promise.

As he tiptoed past the children's room, Manning almost gave in to the temptation to push their door ajar and…do what? Stand beside their beds, feasting his hungry eyes on Tem and Varina while they slept? He'd barely have enough light to make out their shapes under the quilts. Blow a kiss or whisper a word of goodbye they might hear in their dreams? The dog would probably start barking and wake everyone.

With only a slight hesitation in his step, Manning kept going down the stairs and out the door. Across the newly repaired porch and back to the stable, where he harnessed his gelding and Caddie's old mare to the buckboard.

Birds piped and trilled in the cool half-light and beads of dew glistened on the grass as Manning drove around to the mill. There he loaded samples of cut lumber and furniture, then headed east to peddle his wares.

How often, Manning asked himself as he drove toward Washington, did two of the best and worst moments of a person's life crowd together in the space of a minute?

When Varina had called him Papa, pride and happiness had swelled so rapidly in his heart it had pained him. In those few sweet seconds, he'd guessed how a fledgling bird must feel the first time it abandoned its safe, dull perch and soared skyward.

Then Caddie had taken aim and shot him down. His spirits had plummeted back to the hard ground of real life. If his body had done the same, breaking every single bone, he doubted it could have hurt worse.

Ever since he'd come to Sabbath Hollow, he'd been able to distract himself from unwelcome thoughts and feelings by keeping busy. Concentrating on practical matters over which he exercised some control. Fixing up the house, restoring the old mill, hiring workers, supervising the day-to-day operations. On a long wagon ride like the one he was taking this morning, what could a fellow do *but* think?

All the secrets, fears, regrets, doubts and yearnings he'd been running from caught up with him on the road to Washington that day. Perhaps the chase had made them stronger, or the energy he'd spent trying to outrun them had exhausted his defenses. Either way, he was no match for them.

He'd been a damned fool, he decided, to let himself get so intimately mixed up in the lives of Caddie Marsh and her children. It had been such a long time since he'd cared about another person that he hadn't been prepared for Tem and Varina to take immediate possession of his heart.

And their mother? She excited such a seething stew of emotions within him. Some good, some bad, but all far too intense for his liking.

Long ago he'd learned that caring about folks gave them the power to hurt him. In the long, empty years since his boyhood, he'd forgotten that harsh lesson. Until yesterday, when Caddie had given him a remedial course.

Promise or no promise, he wondered if they all might be better off if he didn't return to Sabbath Hollow.

Himself most of all.

"Face facts, Caddie-girl. You've seen the last of that carpetbagger." Lon Marsh looked over the bustling mill and woodwright's shop with the air of a fond parent indulging his children in a game far beyond their ability. "What a shame you didn't heed my warning about him."

Caddie's fingers tingled, wanting to slap the gloating grin off her brother-in-law's face. Perhaps his words wouldn't have aggravated her to the same degree if they hadn't so closely mirrored her own worst fears.

Not for an instant would she give Lon the satisfaction of knowing it, though. "I declare, I don't know who you're talking about. We don't have any truck with carpetbaggers around here."

"I'd say marrying one is pretty good truck." Flicking the ashes from his cigar, Lon called out, "Wouldn't you say so, Bobbie?"

Bobbie Stevens walked toward Lon and Caddie. "I'd be

obliged if you'd put that cigar out, sir. Sawmills and fire don't mix real well."

For an instant, Lon's mask of affability slipped. The mocking twinkle in his blue eyes hardened, like the surface of a pond in January. If Lon had his way, it proclaimed, Bobbie Stevens would regret that polite but firm request and all it implied about the young man's loyalties.

Caddie suppressed a shudder. Her instincts about Lon had been right on the mark. What would happen to her and the children if Manning *didn't* return, and she had to stand against this man on her own?

In less time than he needed to take a deep draw on his cigar, Lon Marsh became his old too-charming self. "Trouble with sawmills and fire, Bobbie—" He chuckled and let the smoking brown cylinder fall to the ground, where it set a few blades of grass alight "—they mix too dang well."

Stamping out the tiny blaze with fierce vigor, Caddie couldn't decide if she was glad or sorry not to have a gun in her hand. "Bobbie, could I trouble you to fetch a little water and douse this bit of ground?"

"Surely, Miz Caddie."

She held Lon's gaze as she listened to the retreat of Bobbie's uneven gait. When she decided the young man was no longer within earshot, she pointed to Lon's horse. "If you've got nothing better to do than stir up trouble, I suggest you go do it somewhere else. Folks here are busy preparing to fill the orders *my husband* will bring back from his travels."

Her brother-in-law smirked as if she'd just told him a particularly amusing joke. "As a matter of fact, I came by to offer you and the young'uns my advice and support. Seemed the least I could do, as head of the family. We both know that Yankee's skedaddled right back where he belongs, once he found out this place wasn't goin' to make him a millionaire overnight."

Caddie didn't dare let herself believe that. "I—I know no such—"

His smirk became an outright leer as Lon's gaze roved over her. "Or maybe he found out a good-lookin' woman can still be cold as creek water when you get her in bed?"

If he'd struck her hard across the face, the man could not have shaken her worse. All Caddie's bewildering feelings about Manning and Del threatened to overwhelm her, along with her crippling doubts about herself as a woman and a wife.

She countered with the only ammunition she possessed. "You've got no right to Sabbath Hollow, Lon Marsh, and you're never going to get it."

As Caddie turned to stalk away, she nearly barreled into Bobbie Stevens, returning with a pail of water. Snatching it from his hands, she pitched its contents over the small circle of blackened grass. And Lon's handsomely buffed boots.

He jumped back, cussing.

Caddie passed the bucket back to Bobbie. "If Mr. Marsh doesn't leave peaceably, send a couple of boys to escort him off the property. At the point of a pitchfork if need be."

"Yes, ma'am."

"I can find my way," Lon growled. "You're making a big mistake, Caddie. Don't say I never gave you the chance to mend fences. You're soon going to need a friend like me, but I won't be there."

She walked away without another word. Head held high and back straight in the regal bearing her mother had taught her.

Let Lon taunt and threaten. Even if Manning didn't come back, she'd be able to hold on to Sabbath Hollow now that the mill was operating.

And the children? she asked herself that evening as the three of them ate supper in silence. Again.

Tem and Varina would manage just fine without a Yankee stepfather, her pride insisted. He'd kept so busy at the mill and making repairs to the house, they'd hardly notice his absence.

Her son soon disabused her of that hopeful notion.

"When's Manning coming home, Mama?" asked Templeton, as Caddie tucked him in for the night.

"I can't say for certain, dearest." She tried to sound matter-of-fact, and more confident than she felt. "It all depends on how long it takes him to find folks willing to buy our wood and furniture. No telling how long that might be."

"A week?" It wasn't like Tem to persist in questioning once she'd given him an answer, no matter how vague. "Two?"

Caddie sensed a vigilant attention from the unmoving form beneath the quilt on Varina's bed. Her daughter hadn't spoken a word to her all day.

"It could easily take as much as two weeks, if he has to go on to Baltimore." She ran a hand over her son's hair and pressed a kiss on his puckered forehead. "I know you'll miss Sergeant sleeping at the foot of your bed, but while Manning's gone we need the dog to keep watch outside. You're old enough to understand that, aren't you?"

"Yes, ma'am." The boy's words didn't carry much conviction.

"Good." She didn't need enthusiasm—just obedience. "Good night, dear."

Caddie planted a kiss on Varina's forehead, too, while the child squeezed her eyes shut tight in an unconvincing pretense of sleep.

Closing the nursery door behind her, Caddie wandered to the end of the hall and hovered outside Manning's room.

Since the early hours of that morning, when she'd woken to find him gone, a bilious ache had lodged in her stomach. In spite of her defiant words to Lon, nothing she'd done all day had been able to ease that nagging uneasiness.

Now, with the house quiet and nothing else to occupy her, it intensified. Would Manning return to Virginia, as she'd assured the children and insisted to their uncle? Or would he keep right on riding north and never come back— driven away by her suspicion and ingratitude?

With the heightened caution of a spy venturing into enemy territory, she stole through the open doorway and stood by Manning's bed.

Some unspoken compact had kept her from entering this room since the day he'd taken possession of it. He made his own bed every morning, depositing clothes and linen outside the door on laundry day. Perhaps she should give the place a thorough dusting and airing before he came back.

If he came back.

The possibility seemed less and less likely as Caddie stared at the empty coat hooks beside the door, slid open the bureau drawers and peeked beneath Manning's bed. He'd taken every blessed thing he owned.

With no brother-in-law around to oppose and no children to reassure, Caddie sank onto the bed, feeling more empty and forlorn than when she'd heard the news of General Lee's surrender. More twisted with guilt than when she'd seen Del's name on the list of casualties after his last battle.

As she rested her head on Manning's pillow, inhaling the faint aroma of his shaving soap, Caddie acknowledged that she'd felt more guilt than grief on learning of her husband's death. Del had joined the Army of Northern Virginia to escape the unspoken hostilities of their marriage. She had driven him to take up arms, which made her as responsible for his death as the faceless soldier who'd killed him in combat.

Had she nursed her deep bitterness against the Yankees because she couldn't bear to lay the blame at her own doorstep, where it belonged?

Caddie wasn't sure she had the courage to answer that question honestly.

One possibility she could not escape. In her guilt and misplaced spite, she had driven a far better man out of her children's lives. If some miracle should bring Manning Forbes back to Sabbath Hollow, Caddie vowed, she'd find a way to keep him there.

"A man came by today and left this for you, Mrs. Forbes." Dora handed Caddie an envelope when she returned from the mill at suppertime. "Yankee fellow, by the sound of him."

Manning? The name whipped through Caddie's thoughts as she tore open the envelope. Of course it couldn't be, she realized, even before she had time to unfold the paper inside. Dora knew Manning by sight. The girl would have said it had been him.

Perhaps he'd sent a message by way of a friend, though.

Caddie wished she'd been at home, to invite the stranger in. Over a cup of coffee or a drop of spirits, she might have learned a little more about her husband's past than he'd been willing to divulge.

Expecting some account of Manning's trip or a message to say when he'd be returning, she had to read the words on the paper several times before she could make sense of them.

"Bad news, ma'am?" Dora turned from the stove, a big wooden spoon in her hand.

"It—" Caddie shook her head, holding out the document. "It's a bill for back taxes on Sabbath Hollow."

Sinking onto the nearest available kitchen chair, she re-read the sum demanded. "We can't pay *this*. And we have more resources than most folks hereabouts. Are they fixing to evict the whole county?"

"Jeff Pratt told me about this when I called on Ann the night before last." Dora moved to where she could scan the paper over Caddie's shoulder. "He says they're only billing folks they reckon can pay. Or folks who have property some scallywag wants to buy up cheap after it's seized for taxes."

Something in a pot on the stove began to boil over. Dora scurried across the kitchen, lifted the lid and gave it a stir. "Gracious me, I hope none of 'em has an eye on our place. If we sold every blessed thing we have left, we couldn't begin to raise a tenth of what they're trying to levy on you."

"Don't go borrowing trouble, Dora. I don't reckon anybody has designs on Gordon Manor, but I see my brother-in-law's hand in *this* plain enough."

Caddie crumpled the paper in her fist. "If Lon Marsh thinks he and his trashy wife are going to run me and my children off this land, he'd better think again."

"Surely Mr. Marsh can't have anything to do with this." Dora shook her head. "Him such a well-spoken gentleman and all. What would he want with this place when he's got Hemlock Grove? Not as much acreage, but I hear tell the house is in fine shape."

What *did* Lon want with Sabbath Hollow? Caught up in her own compelling reasons for wanting to hold on to the place, Caddie had never given his a whole lot of thought. If she hoped to stay a step ahead of him, maybe she'd better start.

"Don't you go fretting yourself, ma'am." Dora pulled a pan of beaten biscuits out of the oven. "Mr. Forbes will be back soon with a pile of orders for wood and chairs.

Cash in hand for some of them, most likely. Then he'll go talk to that old tax collector, one Yankee to anoth—that is, he'll talk some sense to the man...."

Were Southern girls born with the knack of putting the best face on the worst situation? Caddie wondered as Dora's optimistic predictions went in one ear and out the other. Or did they learn the skill at their mother's knee? Even as President Davis and his cabinet had caught the last train out of Richmond, her sewing circle had insisted to one another that a Confederate victory was not only still possible, but very likely. They had temporarily managed to convince each other it was true.

The flaming apocalypse that followed Grant's ransack of the gracious Confederate capital, and the hungry, humiliating months thereafter, hadn't fully cured Caddie of the tendency to put the best face on a bleak situation.

"I reckon you're right, dear." No sense worrying Dora that she might soon be out of a job...unless the girl wanted to stay on and work for Lydene. Caddie almost made a face just thinking of it. "Mr. Forbes'll take care of all this when he gets back."

Except that Manning wasn't coming back. She'd better quit trying to fool herself on that score and face the truth.

How much longer could she go on pretending to the folks at the mill that they'd better work hard to prepare for the orders Manning was sure to bring? Running breathless to the porch every time the dog barked or the children claimed to see a wagon on the road? Assuring Tem and Varina, every night at bedtime, that his return was a day closer than it had been the night before?

"Would you mind calling the children for supper?" Caddie asked Dora. "Then you'd better head off home. Didn't I hear something about a prayer meeting in Mercer's Corner tonight?"

Dora gave a pensive nod. "Bobbie Stevens got his old

wagon fixed up and he offered to fetch a bunch of us into town.''

"Jeff going, too?'' Caddie smoothed the crumpled tax bill.

"He might be.''

Folding the paper, Caddie slipped it into her apron pocket. "You enjoy yourself tonight, dear. And don't worry about getting here too early tomorrow morning.''

"Yes, ma'am. Thank you.''

Dora was halfway out the door when Caddie called to her.

"Ma'am?'' Only a slight catch in Dora's voice betrayed a hint of impatience.

"While you're praying tonight, I'd be obliged if you said a little one for me.''

"Of course I will. I plan to thank the good Lord for how you and Mr. Forbes have been helping folks around here get back on their feet again.''

"That's kind of you, dear.'' As Tem and Varina filed in the kitchen door, Caddie couldn't bring herself to admit she really needed a prayer of intercession—a whole churchful of them, as a matter of fact.

Fortunately, the children didn't pester her with a lot of questions while they ate. Templeton picked at his pork and greens in anxious silence, while Varina consumed her supper with almost defiant concentration. Caddie had plenty of opportunity to fret about their future.

She wouldn't give in to Lon without the fight of her life. But barring a minor miracle, like finding the lost Marsh silver, Caddie much didn't fancy her chances of winning.

The Marsh silver! Could that be part of the reason Lon wanted to get his hands on Sabbath Hollow?

During General McClellan's first foray into Virginia, Caddie's father-in-law had moved his family to the comparative safety of Richmond. Before leaving, Mr. Marsh had hidden the family silver and some valuable pieces of jewelry.

Caddie'd assumed her father-in-law had confided the location to both his sons. But after he'd died suddenly of a stroke, Lon had arrived at the house in Richmond and turned the place upside down with no explanation. Shortly after that, Del had been reported dead in battle, and Caddie's world had begun a rapid descent into darkness. She hadn't dared let herself dwell on the fate of the Marsh silver, in case regret or wistful dreams paralysed her.

If the treasure still rested undisturbed, waiting to restore the family fortunes, Caddie knew better than to hope she might find it. Del's father had been a clever, some might say devious, man. Any hiding place she could imagine, he probably had, too, and discarded it for that very reason.

What about Lon, though? Had he been responsible for some of the ravages to Sabbath Hollow she'd blamed on the Yankees?

Caddie glanced up at Tem and Varina. "After you two round up the chickens, you can play for a spell before bedtime." She shook her head over Templeton's barely touched plate. "Are you sure you can't eat a little more, Son?"

Templeton worried down the mouthful he'd been chewing. "I just don't feel too hungry, Mama."

"Reckon *I'm* the onliest one with a appetite." Varina shot an accusing stare at her mother's plate.

Glancing down, Caddie was astonished to discover she'd hardly touched a bite. A sharp rebuke rose to her lips, but she held it back, wishing Manning was there to ease the volatile relations between her and Varina.

"You do seem to be the *only* one with *an* appetite. Which means you should have plenty of energy to coax those hens into the coop. Mind you don't chase them, now, or they won't lay."

"Yes, ma'am." Varina sounded disappointed not to get a fight she'd been spoiling for. "Come on, Tem."

The children left and the kitchen fell quiet.

Caddie tried to think more about the tax bill and the Marsh silver. Instead she found herself missing Manning's presence during these few minutes of the day they'd often spent together in the past three months. Savoring a cup of tea and a bit of placid ease after the children had gone to do their evening chores.

If she and Manning had exchanged words at all, they'd been about practical, everyday matters. Did she need anything particular from town the next time he went? What repair job should he undertake next? They'd cut so many board feet at the mill that day—a new record. Varina had come out with the funniest little saying.

Sometimes they hadn't talked at all, just sat in the dim warm kitchen and kept each other company.

A single salty tear inched its moist trail down Caddie's cheek. The last time she'd wept in this kitchen, on the broad shoulder of a reticent Yankee, she'd felt better for it—strangely liberated.

Now she just felt empty, and she had no one to blame but herself.

She woke, hours later, from a familiar nightmare.

Something had been chasing her. Something faceless and nameless, but all the more terrifying for its mystery. She'd tried to run, only to find her feet weighed down. Which had been worse—the fear of pursuit, or the suffocating frustration of a body that would not obey her?

So often, back in Richmond, this dream had robbed her of desperately needed sleep. Since she'd returned to Sabbath Hollow, it had come less and less often. Tonight it had overtaken her with a vengeance.

Caddie jolted fully awake.

In the warm darkness of a brief summer night, a fine

mist of sweat hovered on her brow and the nape of her neck. Her breath came in rapid, uneven little gasps. For an instant she relished the relief of waking.

Then she heard the dog bark.

Chapter Eleven

When Sergeant started to bark and a light flickered on in the house, Manning cursed under his breath. Of course it made sense that Caddie would leave the dog outside at night to keep watch. He should have known she'd do that.

Or had he let it slip his mind on purpose?

"Hush, now, Sarge," he called softly to the dog. "No need to wake everybody out of a sound sleep. Tem's mama won't thank you for it."

Would Tem's mama thank *him* for coming back to Sabbath Hollow if she caught him? Manning wondered.

By the time he'd reached Washington, he'd firmly decided against returning. After this he'd keep an eye on the family from a distance, provide assistance whenever Caddie or the children needed it, but not entangle himself in their daily lives. It had worried him a little that Caddie might one day dissolve their paper marriage. Perhaps he should have persuaded her to consummate their relationship, after all.

Too late now.

Each day away from Sabbath Hollow had eroded his resolve, like a steady rain on rootless soil.

As he took orders for lumber and furniture, Manning

decided he would have to talk face-to-face with Bobbie Stevens before he went away. Besides, he couldn't keep the horse and buckboard that belonged to Caddie.

At last he'd reached a compromise with himself. He would return the mare and wagon during the night, then saddle up his gelding and ride over to the mill. After he discussed business with Bobbie the next morning, he'd decide on his next move.

Only he hadn't reckoned on one vigilant, noisy dog.

"Come on, boy. Pipe down." When his pleas had no effect, Manning reined in the horses and climbed down from the wagon. "You know me. I'm not going to hurt your precious family."

As a warm wet tongue swiped across his fingers to the intermittent accompaniment of more loud woofs, Manning understood that he wasn't being challenged or warned away.

He was being welcomed home.

How many folks passed their thirtieth birthday without ever having experienced that simple but profound pleasure? And who cared if the welcome committee was only an ugly brindle-colored mutt without sense enough to keep quiet in the middle of the night?

Manning fell to the ground under Sergeant's rapturous assault. The beast wasn't wagging just his tail, but his whole body.

Fleet padding footsteps sounded on the porch. "Who's there? Don't move!"

Manning's heart gave a queer lurch at the sound of Caddie's voice. Then his gut contracted at the snap of a gun being readied to fire.

"Don't shoot! It's only me." He heard himself laughing like a lunatic as the dog's slobbery tongue tickled his face.

"M-Manning?" Her voice sounded strange. Was something wrong?

"That's right." He tried to push Sergeant away so he could get to his feet, but he couldn't manage more than a token effort. "Sorry I woke you."

He wondered if Caddie might shoot anyway, even knowing it was him. After he'd gone off without a word and stayed away longer than she could have expected. Then to arrive back in the middle of the night, waking her from a sound sleep, and likely scaring her silly in the process.

Looking at it that way, he could hardly blame her if she winged him.

"You came back." Caddie sounded as though she was talking in her sleep. Her voice drew closer with every word. "You really came back."

When he felt her arms go around him as he lurched to his feet, Manning wondered if *he'd* fallen asleep and dreamed this whole thing. When her hand fumbled its way to his whisker-stubbled cheek and rested there in a welcoming caress, he knew he couldn't be conscious. And when her lips somehow found his, he vowed to shoot any man fool enough to wake him up.

Her kiss tasted like sugar pie to a fellow who'd lived for years on beans and hardtack. Soft. Sweet. Comforting.

And every mouthful making him hunger for more.

"What's going on out here?" demanded a small voice, hoarse with sleep.

From out of the darkness, Templeton called, "Are you all right, Mama?"

The dog took to barking again as it ran toward the house. Caddie started and drew back from Manning in a way that told him their kiss had come as much of a surprise to her as to him.

Perhaps he should have resented the children for interrupting, but he couldn't. The sound of their voices made his throat tighten and his eyes sting. Somehow he knew that consulting Bobbie Stevens and returning the buckboard had been mere excuses to propel him back to Sabbath Hollow.

Because he'd left a piece of his heart behind.

"Everything's fine, dear." The quaver in Caddie's voice contradicted her assurance to the children. "Manning's home."

Would he ever hear two sweeter words?

A junior version of the rebel battle yell erupted from the direction of the house and hurtled toward him on a stampede of young, eager feet. Manning barely had time to hunch forward and stretch his arms wide to capture them.

Varina hit him like a warm cannonball. Her stout little arms went around his neck and squeezed so hard his head spun. Templeton gave him a less violent welcome, but no less affectionate, wedging his bony shoulder under Manning's left arm.

A warm breeze wafted the aroma of ripe clover. High overhead, friendly stars winked in the soft, dark sky. Manning was glad he'd come back to Sabbath Hollow at this ungodly hour, when protective shadows could veil the intensity of his emotions and a secret tear might fall to earth unmarked.

Caddie wrapped the night around her like a quilt as she scrambled to collect the patches of her tattered composure and piece them back together.

Never in her life had she thrown herself at a man the way she'd just done. A proper-bred Southern lady, she'd mastered the art of encouraging a favored gentleman to tender certain tokens of esteem. Offering an arm to clasp. Requesting the honor of a waltz. Perhaps begging for the liberty of a quick kiss.

Even after she'd married, Del had been the one to make his approaches, while she had submitted or discouraged him according to her inclination. When he'd stopped soliciting her favors, it would have been unthinkable to press her attentions upon him. And he'd been a husband to her in more than name.

Manning Forbes had never shown more than the faintest, most guarded interest in her as a woman. What must he think of her behavior tonight? Grabbing hold of him. Pushing her lips against his, like some paint-faced hussy soliciting her carnal business.

Caddie could only hope the exuberant welcome he was getting from the children and the dog would drive her brazen indiscretion from his mind. Or perhaps he'd excuse it on the grounds of her overwhelming relief to find he was not some dangerous intruder.

Surely to goodness that *had* been what prompted her to drop the gun and bolt into his arms.

What shocked and frightened Caddie was how much she'd enjoyed those sweet, too-brief moments. Why, if the children hadn't called out, she might still be standing there, her lips tangling with Manning's and only a threadbare cotton nightdress between his deft, purposeful hands and her supplicant body.

She didn't dare let herself dwell on that thought.

"Come on now, you two!" she called to Tem and Varina. Frustration sharpened her voice more than she intended. "If you carry on like this you'll tear the poor man to pieces, not to mention wake everybody from here to Mercer's Corner. Tem, make that dog hush!"

The dog quieted to a soft whimper that told Caddie he was ready to bark his head off again at a moment's notice. She didn't need to see her son's face to know her rebuke had soured a little of his delight over his stepfather's return.

"I'm sorry for waking all of you in the middle of the night," said Manning. "I forgot the Sergeant would be on guard duty. You have to admit, he makes a fine watchdog."

Caddie nodded. The sound of Manning's voice had

somehow stolen hers. Why, until this moment, had she never appreciated the simple pleasure of listening to him speak?

Maybe his accent did lack the easy, melodic Dixie cadence, but his voice had a deep, soothing resonance that reminded her of rain on a shingled roof. When he got riled, it could boom like thunder—which, in some curious way, added to its appeal.

"Well..." Manning cleared his throat. "I guess...you children ought to get back to bed...maybe...."

At Tem's and Varina's noises of protest, Caddie recovered her voice again. It only seemed to fail her when she tried to talk directly to Manning. "That's right. If the pair of you stay up any longer, you'll be cranky and quarrelsome tomorrow."

"Mama...?"

She didn't need to hear the question. "Yes, Tem, you *may* bring the dog to sleep in your room for the rest of the night."

"Woof!"

If she hadn't known better, Caddie would have sworn the beast understood what she'd said.

"Good night," Manning called after them. "I'll be in as soon as I stable the horses."

Her voice still wasn't anxious to cooperate, but Caddie forced it. "When did you eat last?"

"I—that is—"

"Come by the kitchen before you go to bed. I'll fix you something. A body can't sleep decently on an empty stomach."

"To tell the truth, I could eat a horse and chase the driver." He chuckled—a sound like the wind through a pile of crackly autumn leaves. "Thanks."

Eating, sleeping, tending the animals—mundane, practical matters they'd so often talked about. Just as though that baffling kiss hadn't taken them both by storm.

Which was just how she wanted to keep relations between them, Caddie told herself as she herded the children and the dog back into the house. She was grateful to Manning for not making a fuss about her singular lapse of self-control.

Still, a perverse streak of nature made her wish he'd betrayed some subtle sign that the rash intimacy had shaken him half as violently as it had shaken her.

Manning's hands shook as he removed the harness from the horses and turned them loose to graze.

How could a man perform such commonplace chores after Caddie had kissed him? He felt as though some powerful force had smashed him to pieces, then put him back together wrong. Suddenly he had to get reacquainted with an unfamiliar body, strange new thoughts and even stranger feelings.

True, he'd considered Caddie a very attractive woman from the moment he'd first laid eyes on her. Sometimes her attitudes and reactions had exasperated him, and he hadn't been certain if it was because she was a Southerner or because she was a woman.

In time he'd discovered many admirable qualities about her, and found himself anxious to win her approval. But never had he thought of her running into his arms and planting that kind of kiss on him. Now he couldn't seem to think of much else.

What had made her do it? He could hardly guess.

How had she felt about it once the whirlwind moment had passed? The answer to that seemed a little more obvious. Everything about her actions, her words and her tone of voice had told him she regretted it. Wanted to forget about it and pretend it had never happened.

If that's what she wanted, he could pretend with the best of them. But he knew it was no use trying to forget or regret that kiss.

He delayed going into the house as long as he dared, so Caddie would have time to prepare him a bite to eat, then go back to bed. The longer an interval passed before they had to look each other in the eyes, the easier it would be to behave as if nothing had changed between them.

Acting on a hunch, he groped around the ground at the base of the dogwood bushes and found his gun where Caddie had dropped it. A wonder it hadn't gone off, compounding the commotion of his return.

He sauntered back to the pump, where he washed his hands and soaked his head in an effort to keep awake long enough to eat. Finally, when he'd given Caddie time enough to cook up a five-course dinner, he hefted his gun and his rucksack and entered the candlelit kitchen through the back door.

When he heard Caddie's voice, he nearly jumped out of his boots.

"I was afraid you'd changed your mind and gone back to Washington again."

She sat at the table, across from a place set for him, her hands wrapped around a tin mug. A thick chestnut braid hung over one shoulder, the closest Manning had come to seeing her hair unbound. She'd wrapped a shawl over her nightdress, though she surely didn't need it for warmth on a night like this.

"If I'd known you were waiting on me, I'd have come sooner." Though Manning doubted his own words, he couldn't very well tell Caddie the truth. "You shouldn't have stayed up."

As he approached the table with hesitant steps, he raked his fingers through his wet hair, then let them slide down over his unshaved cheek. If Caddie wasn't already sorry for that kiss, she would be once she got a good look at him.

She rose from her chair and retreated to the stove. "I fried you up a mess of bacon and warmed over some grits. Now that you're here, I'll toss in a couple of eggs."

"That sounds good." The hollow ache in his stomach sharpened as she named the foods. His mouth had already begun to water at the savory smell of the bacon.

Or was it the shadow of Caddie's shapely legs he glimpsed through her nightdress? Manning tried to deflect his thoughts, only to find them shockingly resistant to his control.

Caddie cracked two eggs into the frying pan. They popped and hissed in the hot bacon fat. Lifting the blue enameled coffeepot from the back of the stove, she returned to the table and poured a dark, steaming stream into Manning's cup.

It was half-full when she abruptly tipped the pot back. "I hope this won't keep you from sleeping. Perhaps you'd rather have something else to drink."

Manning assured her the coffee would not prevent him from sleeping. Since he couldn't say the same for the sight of her slender bare feet, he avoided mentioning them at all. Though he couldn't keep from looking...and admiring.

When she set the plate of hot, delicious-smelling food on the table in front of him, he insisted, "Get back to bed now. Don't feel you have to sit up and keep me company."

"If I did get back to sleep now, I'd be all the more tired for it in the morning."

He opened his mouth, but before he could get the words out, she cut him off. "Don't go apologizing again for getting back late. Better late than—well—the children are mighty glad to have you home."

Shoving away from the table, she grabbed her coffee cup

and carried it to the stove for a refill. "Not that they made much secret of the fact."

Manning jammed a forkful of eggs and grits into his mouth to keep from asking whether she was glad to have him home.

"How did your trip go?" She glided back to the table, her slim, pale fingers clasped around the mug. "Anybody interested in buying our wood or the furniture?"

His mouth full of food, Manning nodded. Once he'd washed it down with a swig of coffee, he gave Caddie a better answer. "Plenty of folks interested in the chairs and tables. We may end up using most of the wood we mill for furniture. That'd save us the cost of hauling it, anyway. Whatever we have left, I figure we can sell cheap to folks in the neighborhood for rebuilding."

"That's good." As she expelled a long, slow sigh, the anxious lines on her brow and around her eyes began to smooth out. "So we're pretty well fixed, moneywise?"

Manning couldn't help but conclude his whole trip had been worth it, just for the look of relief on Caddie's face.

"I can't promise Sabbath Hollow will ever be as prosperous as before—" He stopped himself just before adding *the war*. "But we'll always have a good roof over our heads, clothes on our backs and plenty of food on the table. Money to give Tem and Varina a decent education. That's all we really need, isn't it?"

He was asking her something more, Manning realized with a start. What he truly wanted to know was whether she would always pine for the life she'd once enjoyed. And whether she would always hold him responsible for its loss.

Caddie shook her head. "There's more to life than food, clothes and shelter."

"Such as...?" Slaves to wait on folks hand and foot? Grand tours of Europe? Endless leisure enlivened by genteel vice?

"Never mind." Caddie stroked her brow. To shield her eyes, perhaps? Her voice dropped to a wistful murmur. "I expect the late hour's making me fanciful. After the past three years, a full belly and a snug room for me and mine does sound mighty appealing. Lord knows, life has done its best to keep my expectations modest."

Clearly he needn't fool himself that he had it in his power to make her happy. Why did that thought gnaw at his insides—as if the tasty meal she'd just fed him had been laced with ground glass?

Caddie pushed a paper across the table to him. Though he'd seen it lying beside her coffee cup, he hadn't paid it any mind.

"Right now I'll be thankful if we have money enough to pay the taxes on this place."

"Taxes?" Manning unfolded the paper and glanced over it.

When his eyes fell on one number, he pulled the document closer to his face, turning it to best catch the feeble light of a lone candle. "They can't be serious!"

The anxious look tightened Caddie's face again. "I fear they may be. Perhaps if you talk to the tax collector—"

"Oh, I'll talk to him, all right. This is clean craziness, that's what. How do they expect the South ever to get back on its feet again if they dump a burden like this on it?"

Manning heard his own indignation running away with him, but he couldn't seem to rein it in. He'd seen and heard enough since the end of the war, and particularly during his sojourn in Washington, to know that those in power weren't anxious to rehabilitate the Confederate states.

Besides, he was more than indignant. He was scared. Every asset he had in the world was currently tied up in the business. The orders he'd brought back from Washington would help in the long run, but not to meet a bill this size anytime soon.

"Lon's behind it, of course," Caddie admitted, as though any sin committed by her brother-in-law must be her fault. "You were right about that no-account scoundrel. I shudder to think what would have become of the children and me if I'd been fool enough to let him stay."

Manning had some idea how difficult she found it to speak ill of her kin, no matter how Alonzo Marsh might deserve it. Whether she knew it or not, disparaging Lon in Manning's presence represented a curious sign of trust—a token of acceptance.

The happiness this realization lit in him did battle with his worry about the tax bill, and almost won. If Caddie had learned to trust him, even this little bit, he couldn't let her and the children down.

Unaware of the struggle raging inside him, Caddie confessed something else. "I think I've figured out why Lon's so anxious to get his hands on this place."

Manning raised an eyebrow.

"Treasure—well, silver mostly."

As Caddie told him the whole convoluted story, Manning nodded at suitable intervals and tried to appear as though it was all new information to him. Meanwhile, deep in his mind, painful memories stirred and came to life, like rotting corpses animated by some sinister force.

This wasn't the first he'd heard of the Marsh silver. What's more, he had a pretty good idea where to find it.

Recovering the cache would solve the immediate threat of Sabbath Hollow being seized for unpaid taxes. But to disclose his confidential knowledge of its whereabouts could betray the secret he must protect at all costs.

Now, more than ever.

Chapter Twelve

Manning had come back.

After he finally shuffled off to bed, Caddie sat in the shadowy kitchen, slowly sipping her coffee while she tried to unravel her hopelessly tangled thoughts and feelings.

Manning had come home. Contrary to Lon's confident, sneering prediction.

A tiny grin tugged at the corner of Caddie's lips. She'd give a hundred dollars cash to see the look on her brother-in-law's face when he heard the news.

A fellow like Manning, who stayed put even when there were no fat pickings to be had, could not rightly be called a carpetbagger. Besides, if Lon was in cahoots with the Yankee tax collector, as she suspected, he had no business questioning anybody's motives.

For some reason, the whole idea didn't sit as well with her as it should have. It was one thing for Manning to stick with a struggling business that promised to flourish in time. Quite another to stand his ground while that atrocious tax levy hung over their heads.

Caddie's stomach fluttered, remembering what else Lon had said. Some trash talk about Manning finding out a beautiful woman could still be as cold as creek water.

If only Lon knew! Her coldness was less apt to drive Manning away than her unwelcome ardor. Tonight, for instance…

Any man who'd been anxious to share her bed would have pressed his advantage after she'd kissed him like that. Manning had gone out of his way to ignore her lapse of self-control. Just as a well-bred gentleman might overlook a social gaffe committed by one of his guests. Of course, any visitor who persisted in such offensive behavior ran the risk of being stricken from future guest lists.

Still, carnal desires aside, Caddie couldn't help but wish for a single night of intimacy with her husband. Manning Forbes had proved himself a man of honor, even if he'd been born on the wrong side of the Mason-Dixon line. A consummated marriage would bind him to her and the children far more firmly than their current arrangement could ever hope to.

A fine howdy-do, that! Consummating their wedding vows might strengthen Manning's connection to her family. But any effort she made to lure him into bed would probably send him packing.

When he woke late the next morning, Manning took a few minutes to unpack before heading up to the mill. A strange glow of satisfaction stirred within him as he stowed his modest worldly possessions in their familiar places. It almost felt like the old house was welcoming him back under its eaves the way his family had embraced his return last night.

His family. The notion should have elated him. Instead, it skewered him with guilt.

From the bottom of his rucksack, he pulled out the small wooden box he'd constructed a lifetime ago. Manning passed his hand over its deceptively simple pattern of redbud inlay with a caress of pride. The straight, unsmiling lip of the little casket seemed to glower at him. It demanded he rummage in his pocket for the key, unlock and raise the lid, then sift through the papers inside until he unearthed one from the very bottom.

Since finding Caddie and the children, Manning hadn't reread the letter. Now he did, though he knew every word by heart.

Not that it contained any momentous news. Only the routine account of one young family, written by a soldier's wife to her husband in the field. Millions of similar communications must have circulated on both sides, during the war years.

Ending with the customary salutation "Your faithful wife, Caddie Marsh," it told how tall a boy named Templeton had grown, and how many teeth a baby named Varina had sprouted. Now that he knew the children, Manning gloated over those passages of the letter like a fond father.

Sternly he reminded himself, as Caddie had reminded Varina, he was not their father. Tem and Varina's real father, who'd likely once smiled over this letter, had been killed by the Yankees a few days after he'd received it. Killed by *a* Yankee.

A Yankee named Manning Forbes.

"Manning?" Caddie's voice, accompanied by a brisk tap on the door, set his heart hammering like the pistons of a steam engine under dangerously high pressure.

He wanted to call out to her, but he couldn't forage up enough air from his lungs. His gut kinked and twisted into one untieable knot of panic. If the cooling corpse of Delbert Marsh had sprawled in the middle of his bedroom floor, while he held a smoking rifle, Manning could not have been more agitated.

As the knob turned and the door opened, he thrust Caddie's letter into the box and slammed the lid.

"Oh, you are here, after all." She jumped back at the

sight of him, one hand rising to her breast. "When you didn't answer, I thought perhaps you'd gone off to the mill without my knowing."

"Am I supposed to report my every move to you?" He grabbed the box and slammed it into the top drawer of the bureau.

He didn't mean to be harsh with Caddie, but he couldn't help himself. A rush of anger often came hot on the heels of a bad scare. Once during the war, a couple of drunken fools from his company had stolen up on him during his picket watch. After darn near messing his longjohns, he'd come just as close to shooting the pair of them.

Caddie's face paled and her reply sounded thoroughly chastened. "N-no, of course not. This is your home to come and go as you please."

This is not my home! The damning thought blazed through Manning's mind and nearly came out of his mouth. *This is Del Marsh's home.*

Again Manning turned his anger over the situation against Caddie—and hated himself for it. "Would it be asking too much for a bit of privacy, as well?"

The hurt in her eyes grieved him. But his secret had become a domineering master, stronger even than his bedeviling feelings for Caddie. If he had cared less for her, less for the children, less for the old plantation itself, the secret would not have held him so deeply in its dark thrall.

"I apologize for disturbing your privacy." Caddie's words came out stiff and cold. "I thought I heard you stirring up here, but when you didn't answer my knock… Let me assure you, it won't happen again."

He wanted to apologize for his sharpness, but he couldn't without risking discovery. "What did you want me for?"

"The new county tax collector is sitting out on our front porch. He came by to make sure Dora had given me the bill. I thought you might want to speak to him while he's here, rather than ride off to Westchester.'' The firm, proud set of her lips told him he'd received his last kiss from them.

''I *would* like to speak to him.'' Striding to the door, Manning plucked his coat from its hook.

His misplaced antagonism toward Caddie found a far more deserving target. If the blasted tax collector hadn't come calling, she'd have never blundered into his room like that. Without the tax bill and its threat of ruin, he might never have to risk exposure by retrieving the lost family silver.

Manning descended the stairs behind Caddie with more righteous wrath in his belly for a fellow Yankee than he had ever harbored toward the Rebs on the eve of battle.

Off the top of her head, Caddie couldn't say which of the two Yankees had got her dander up worse. The well-fed, well-barbered tax collector, or her rumpled, irascible husband.

''Mr. Larkin, may I present my husband. Mr. Forbes, this is Mr. Larkin, the new tax collector. He's ridden all the way over from Westchester to make sure we received our assessment.''

Fanning himself with his hat, the man rose from the bare bench where he'd been sitting.

As Jeff Pratt's mother had done with her, Caddie refused to invite the tax collector inside her home. Nor would she offer him any refreshment. With his commission on the tax money he was trying to squeeze out of them, the odious man could afford to drown himself in the finest French brandy.

Larkin held out his hand to Manning. A soft, white, well-padded appendage, compared to Manning's lean, brown, callused one. ''Good to meet you, Forbes. Fine place you've got here.''

"Sabbath Hollow belongs to my wife and her boy, Mr. Larkin." Manning looked as if he'd sooner have shaken hands with a leper. "You might say I'm just a boarder working for my keep."

Did he slant a fleeting glance at her as he said it? Caddie asked herself. Was he trying to beg her pardon in his odd, sidewinding way for being so testy when she'd gone to fetch him?

Well, let him beg. Treating her like she was some kind of spy in her own home…! Imagine how he might take on if he found out she'd searched his room during his absence.

The memory of it provoked a passing qualm of guilt, which Caddie stubbornly ignored. After all, what call did the man have to guard his privacy in so zealous a manner unless he had something to hide? And what could he be keeping in that box he took such pains to conceal?

The tax collector chortled. "Can't say as I'd mind boarding in such a grand house. Or have such a fetching landlady."

Shooting the tax collector wouldn't help their situation any, but at that moment Caddie could imagine few occupations quite as satisfying.

When Manning raised his hand and swatted Mr. Larkin hard on the temple, she couldn't decide whether to kick him or kiss him.

"Sorry about that." He flicked something off his hand— or pretended to flick it; Caddie couldn't be sure. "A nasty old blue-tailed fly was just about to bite you, but I got him."

With a bemused look on his beefy face, the tax collector rubbed a bright welt on his brow. "Ah—thanks."

He didn't say he'd sooner have taken the bite than the swat, but he must have been thinking it.

Caddie sensed her resentment against Manning beginning to erode, and she wasn't sure she wanted it to. Far better to stay annoyed with him than to go around mooning over the man like some calf-eyed girl. Especially when he didn't show the slightest glimmer of returning her feelings—whatever they might be.

"If you gentlemen will excuse me, I know you have plenty to talk about." Hard as she tried to say the word *gentlemen* with unaffected sincerity, a hint of scorn crept in.

Still massaging his head, Mr. Larkin made a little bow in her direction. "Pleasure to meet you, ma'am."

She dropped a stiff curtsy, but did not reply with the polite falsehood that she'd found any pleasure in meeting him.

Withdrawing to the kitchen, Caddie discovered Dora busy cutting vegetables for soup. She could tell the girl's thoughts were a million miles away. Or more likely, half a mile uphill.

"Did you have a nice time at the prayer meeting, dear?"

"Hmm? Oh—yes, ma'am." Dora roused from her reverie. "I mean, a prayer meeting isn't a grand cotillion or anything, but it made a pleasant way to pass the time with other young folks."

Caddie fetched the broom and began to sweep the floor. "Did Jeff Pratt go?"

"Y-yes." Dora emptied a mound of chopped vegetables from the cutting board into a large crock on the back of the stove.

She looked to be struggling to hold something back, but the words burst out in spite of her efforts. "Miz Caddie, do you have any idea how hard it is to flirt with a blind man?"

Work-reddened hands flew to Dora's redder face. "Oh, sugar! I can't believe I said such a thing. Please don't pay me any mind, ma'am."

Setting her broom aside, Caddie put her arm around

Dora's shoulders. "Don't you tell me what I should and shouldn't pay any mind, missy. I can't say as I've ever given much thought to the matter, but I reckon it's not easy for a well-brought-up lady to communicate her interest to a gentleman who can't see her."

No casting glances, followed by a coy smile when one got returned. No putting up hair in a new style to attract a compliment. No letting a fan or a handkerchief fall so a gentleman might retrieve it. How would the poor thing ever attract Jeff's notice?

Dora heaved a little sigh. "I knew you'd understand, Miz Caddie. Life's going on. The old rules and ways of doing things have to change if they aren't working. Don't they? Like you marrying Mr. Forbes so soon after you met him."

"I suppose that's true, dear." Caddie couldn't help feeling Dora credited her with far greater wisdom than she possessed. "Maybe you ought to try putting yourself in Jeff's place. What sorts of things might get your attention if you couldn't see?"

"You mean like wearing scent?"

"That's a fine idea." Caddie returned to her sweeping. She always thought best while her hands kept busy.

"Something distinctive," she added. "Not rose water like every other girl might be wearing. A fragrance that'll let him know you're nearby whenever he smells it. I've got an old bottle of lemon verbena I'd be glad to let you have. That might do the trick. And don't forget your voice. There's a world of difference between the way a lady speaks to a gentleman she wants to encourage, than to one she couldn't care less about."

"I know just what you mean." Dora chuckled.

"You have a pretty laugh, too, dear. Reminds me of sleigh bells. If Jeff Pratt hasn't already noticed it, he's not as clever a fellow as I've given him credit for."

"Thank you, Miz Caddie. I feel so much more hopeful after talking to you."

Suddenly Caddie felt like a fraud. What right had she to give another woman advice on winning a man when she'd shown so little aptitude for it herself? "I'll just go fetch you that bottle of lemon verbena, before I forget."

A happier thought occurred to her. "Perhaps when Manning sorts out this miserable tax business, we can host a dance. You young people need more chances to socialize."

Dora endorsed the idea with an eager nod.

Bustling off to hunt up that old bottle of scent, Caddie found herself wondering what might happen if Manning couldn't *sort out* their tax problem with the odious Mr. Larkin.

The sound of men's voices drifted in through her open bedroom window. One jovial, and more than a little patronizing. The other sharp. From indignation or desperation, Caddie couldn't decide.

"Be sensible, Forbes. Virginia needs tax dollars for rebuilding. As you've probably seen, the state's in bad shape."

"And whose fault might that be?" Manning inquired.

Telling herself not to listen, that it would only rile her, Caddie moved toward window as if she was being pulled.

"Why, their own, of course," replied the tax collector with contemptible good humor. "For starting that terrible war. Which is why they can't expect the rest of the country to foot the bill for their reconstruction."

Somebody ought to shove a hornet's nest down that man's trousers! Caddie's mind seethed like a swarm of those vicious insects.

Manning didn't answer right away. Was he going to agree with his fellow Yankee?

His reply, when it came, was so quiet, Caddie had to lean out the window to hear. "I don't see how driving promising businesses into bankruptcy is going to help revive the South.''

Though part of her wanted to applaud Manning's reasoning, another part wished he'd defend the South with more fire.

Why should he, though? she asked herself. For the better part of four years Confederate troops must have shot at him, killed his friends, taken others prisoner. Perhaps his home in southern Pennsylvania, about which he was so evasive, had been scourged by battle when General Lee marched north in the spring of '63.

For reasons she couldn't fathom, Caddie found herself taking her own advice to Dora. Putting herself in Manning's place. Why had he come and what made him stay, she wondered, if not the desire to get rich quick, as she had first supposed? Nothing about this mysterious Yankee made any sense.

She realized she'd missed part of their conversation when Mr. Larkin suddenly raised his voice to make a telling point.

''The Freedmen's Bureau needs money to operate, too. Our gallant boys in blue didn't fight and die to free those folks just to throw them out of the only kind of work they're fit for.''

A mess of contradictory feelings tugged Caddie this way and that, like a child tormented in a game of blindman's bluff. Her mama had taught her to treat their servants with a firm but gentle hand. Ten years ago, she would have sworn that Mammy Dulcie, Big Amos, Uncle William and the rest were practically family—better cared for than so-called freedmen living in the hungry squalor of Northern cities. She'd been certain they would scorn emancipation.

Until she'd watched her slaves desert her when Grant's army marched into Richmond. Celebrating in the streets like the day of deliverance had arrived.

"I wore a Union uniform for four years." Manning's voice sounded tired. "I wasn't a boy and I sure as hell wasn't gallant. I didn't join up to free the slaves, but I'm glad it came about or that whole war would have been for nothing. I don't know what needs doing to help those folks, but it's a big mistake to grind the Confederate states into the dust in the name of the Freedmen's Bureau. Sow that kind of poison seed and folks will reap a crop of hate around here long after we're gone."

A shiver went through Caddie as she listened. Had women in Bible times experienced this curious mixture of fear and excitement when they heard the Old Testament prophets speak?

Eavesdropping on Manning's conversation with the tax collector, she found herself inclined to echo Varina's initial judgment of the man.

I don't believe he *is* a Yankee.

As Manning watched Mr. Larkin ride off down the lane, he decided he'd throttle the next person who had the nerve to call *him* a carpetbagger. His interview with the tax collector had given him an intimate understanding of all the term implied. And he didn't care to be tarred with that brush.

Another unpleasant thought struck him. What would Caddie say when she found out he hadn't been able to budge the man a penny on their tax levy?

Manning wasn't long finding out.

"Well?" Caddie's voice sounded behind him, though he hadn't heard any warning swish of skirts. "Any luck?"

He hesitated for a moment, not wanting to give her the bad news after they'd started the day on such an unpleasant note. This kind of information wasn't like cheese or whiskey, he decided—it wouldn't improve with age.

"Larkin means to stand firm on his original assessment. Down to the penny. We haven't got long to raise it, either."

"You could have talked him down, if you'd been more agreeable." Why didn't Caddie's voice sound angry?

"Agreeable how?"

He looked out over the property, all green and gold in the sun. The way the lane hooked around that big old chestnut. The tree must have been a good size when Tem and Varina's ancestors claimed this land on a charter from the king of England.

To a man who didn't know the name of his father, let alone his forefathers, this connection between the Marsh family and Sabbath Hollow seemed almost mystical.

Perhaps Caddie sensed his regret over letting them down, for her voice held neither blame nor bitterness. "Agreeable in running down the South. Making us out to be a bunch of proud sinners who need to be humbled. That way Mr. Larkin could feel all righteous about what he's doing."

"How do you know I didn't do just that?"

"I—overheard some of what you told him."

"You didn't need to eavesdrop. I wouldn't have said anything different if you'd joined us."

"I didn't dare stay, or that awful man might have provoked me to violence." Caddie's lips crooked in a wry smile. "Without the excuse of a blue-tailed fly."

In spite of the worries churning inside him, Manning laughed, too, as he remembered the tax collector's dazed look. Considering the jolt of jealous rage that'd blasted through him when Larkin ogled Caddie, it was a wonder he hadn't done the man worse harm.

"I apologize for listening in on your conversation, but I wouldn't change a word of what you said to Mr. Larkin."

Manning told himself not to glance back at her, but his head turned of its own accord.

"I'm sorry I couldn't change his mind...and...I'm sorry

I was so cross with you this morning.'' He scavenged for an excuse that would absolve her without incriminating him. ''Woke up on the wrong side of the bed, I guess.''

The image of waking up in a bed with Caddie blazed in his mind. Hard as he tried to banish it, it wouldn't go away. A bed holding Caddie wouldn't have any wrong sides.

Perhaps his face betrayed a hint of his scandalous thoughts, for she averted her eyes. ''We all do that now and then. No harm in it. I reckon when folks live under the same roof, they can't go tiptoeing around, fearful of giving offense with anything they say or do. Families need to go easy with each other and stand together in hard times.''

Manning nodded slowly. Slowly he extended his hand to her. Somehow he got the feeling she was saying more than he could fathom. He liked the sound of it, anyway.

Just then, the children came tearing around the house.

''Mama, Manning, guess what?'' hollered Tem.

Before they could guess, Varina let the cat out of the bag. ''We made a circus—wanna see?''

Templeton cast his sister a black look. ''We walk on our stilts. Rina can juggle crabapples. And I taught Sergeant some real good tricks.''

Caddie squeezed Manning's hand. ''You two were so quiet this morning, I wondered what mischief you might be getting up to. Do we get to see this great circus, or just hear about it?''

''You can watch,'' Varina assured her mother. ''Dora, too.''

''Around back by the pump,'' added Tem. ''Give us a few minutes to get ready, then come.''

With that, they raced away again.

For a moment Manning forget everything but how much he loved those children. ''You've done a fine job raising those two.''

Caddie shook her head. "You wouldn't say so if you'd seen how they moped while you were gone."

She still hadn't let go of his hand. "Would you do me the honor of escorting me to the circus, Mr. Forbes?"

Every particle of sunshine in the whole day seemed to concentrate on the spot where he stood. "The honor would be mine, ma'am."

That shimmering warmth followed him around to the flat, shaded spot where Tem and Varina put on their show. Manning laughed more in the next quarter hour than he had in the previous fifteen years combined.

Yet hard as he tried to bend his full attention on the children, his eyes kept straying to the pump behind them. What pretext could he invent for taking it apart and poking around the well beneath, without provoking Caddie's suspicion more than he had already?

Worse yet, what if he'd misinterpreted the last ramblings of a dying man—and the lost Marsh silver *wasn't* hidden under that water pump?

Chapter Thirteen

"What's this?" Caddie stared at the big metal chest crusted with dirt. Sergeant sniffed around it suspiciously.

Manning's expectant look and Tem's barely contained jubilation told her what it must be, but she didn't even want to hope until she was completely certain.

"It better be worth digging up the well." She peered past her husband and son at their messy excavation.

For some reason it made her recall the day Manning had shown up at Sabbath Hollow and how she'd watched him wash at the pump.

"Open it up," ordered Varina.

"Can't you see it's locked, silly?" Tem fairly vibrated with excitement.

Caddie shook her head. "I don't have a key."

"I do," said Manning.

Her already speeding heart beat faster still. How had Manning gotten his hands on a key to this box…unless…?

Grinning like a fool, he pulled a crowbar from behind his back. "This big ugly key will open pretty near any lock."

Caddie fought down the urge to swat him as some of the

tension seeped out of her. "Go ahead. I want to find out if..."

Wild superstition kept her from elaborating on that *if*.

"Yes, ma'am." He dug the wedge-shaped end of the crowbar under the lid, then in a burst of power that set Caddie's pulse fluttering in her throat, Manning wrenched it open.

A ridiculous stab of disappointment hit her when she saw only brown bundles of various sizes.

Manning plucked out one fat cylinder and untied it. A long roll of leather unwound across the grass.

It jingled.

"Oh, my," Caddie breathed as she sank to her knees and began pulling piece after piece of silver flatware from pouches that ran the length of the specially crafted holder. "I can't believe it. You really have found the Marsh silver."

"*Forks?*" Varina infused that word with perfect disgust. "All this fuss over a mess of forks? I thought you found something good, Tem."

"Shows what you know, Rina Marsh. These here are *silver* forks and they're worth a whole heap a money. So there!"

"Yes, they are, darling." Caddie unwrapped an elaborately engraved silver tray. Maybe she'd serve Lon and the tax collector a big old roasted crow on it. "This'll take care of our money worries for a while to come, I should think."

Pay the taxes. Begin refurnishing the house. Maybe buy a filly of good blood to start rebuilding their stock? Too soon for that. A milk cow and a few shoats would be more practical.

She looked from Manning to Templeton and back again. "I don't understand how you found it—in the well of all places."

"It wasn't down in the water, Mama," Tem explained patiently. "There was a shelf built just a little way down."

Manning shook his head as he looked over the contents of the dirty old box with obvious satisfaction. "The boy knew where to find it. I suppose his pa or his grandpa must have spoken about it when he was around, forgetting that little pitchers have big ears and long memories."

"Why didn't you tell me about this sooner, Son?" The child looked proud enough to bust. Also a little scared, Caddie sensed, unless her motherly intuition was misleading her.

Templeton shrugged and gave the answer boys had likely been giving their mothers since back in Bible times. "Don't know."

If only they'd found this hidden windfall the first night they'd arrived from Richmond... Caddie balked at the thought. She wouldn't have had to marry Manning Forbes. How much poorer her life and the children's lives would be now.

"The important thing is, we have it now when we really need it." She pulled Tem down beside her and wrapped her arm around his shoulders to let him know he mustn't feel bad.

Manning kept opening bundles and laying their precious contents before Caddie, like an emissary from olden days bringing tribute to a queen. "I don't think the boy recognized the significance of what he'd heard until I told him about the Marsh silver. I had a hunch he might know something—even if he didn't realize he knew it."

"You're our hero, precious." Caddie hugged her son again. "Years from now, you'll tell your grandchildren how you found a hidden treasure and saved Sabbath Hollow. Why, look at this!"

She unwrapped a glass cylinder sealed with wax that held some rolled-up documents. "Unless I miss my guess, this is the original royal charter for the very first Marsh who claimed Sabbath Hollow, back when Virginia was a young colony.''

She handed it to Templeton, who looked properly impressed. ''We'll make a nice frame for it and hang it up in the house.''

Glancing up, she saw her daughter investigating the spot Tem and Manning had dug up. ''Varina, scoot away from that hole right this minute! Nobody needs you to cap off an exciting day by falling down the well.''

Before she got those words out, Manning had seized Varina around the middle and pulled her out of danger. The child squirmed and giggled in his arms.

A soft tide of contentment stole over Caddie as she returned the silver and other valuables to their wrappings. As she looked back, her life before the war seemed like a golden dream—one she hadn't suitably cherished at the time. The years since Fort Sumter had been a cruel nightmare that still haunted her. The simple, peaceful existence she enjoyed now felt real and lasting.

She looked around at Manning and the children. ''I believe we should celebrate and share our good fortune by hosting a barbecue and dance.''

''That sounds like a fine idea.'' Manning's eyes met hers and a long, intense look passed between them.

Was he picturing what she was picturing? Gliding and twirling in his arms to the smooth lilt of a fiddle on a sultry summer night?

Caddie's mouth went dry as she thought of it, and her sweet milk of contentment soured a little. Her present life did lack something, after all. Hard as she tried not to hanker after it, she couldn't seem to stop herself.

''What about you, Tem? Varina?'' She tried to divert her wayward thoughts by focusing on the children. ''Would you like us to get up a barbecue?''

The boy's earlier excitement seemed to have burned itself out, for he only gave a grudging nod in reply.

Several hours later, Manning dropped onto one of the kitchen chairs, his hair stiff with sweat and the cloth of his shirt sticking to his damp skin.

"I got the hole filled in," he puffed. "And the pump seems to be working all right again."

Caddie held up a big glass jar. "Would you like a drink of lemonade? I just brought this up from the cellar."

"Please." Manning flexed his tired muscles. Maybe a drink would give him the energy to go bathe in the creek.

"I still can't believe it." Caddie shook her head as she strained the pale yellow liquid through cheesecloth into a tall glass. "The Marsh silver. Providence sure does work in mysterious ways."

"Uh-huh." Manning knew that for a fact.

How often had he pondered the divine or diabolical plan that had brought him and Delbert Marsh together, scrambling their lives like eggs in a frying pan? Finding the family valuables had been a carefully contrived plan of his own that seemed to be working.

Caddie handed him the glass and he drank the cool, tart lemonade in great thirsty gulps.

"I wonder what's ailing Templeton?" she mused. "He seemed so excited at first, but by the time he went to bed he'd gotten real quiet and thoughtful."

His last swallow of lemonade went down the wrong way. Manning choked and coughed, trying to catch his breath. Maybe his clever plan wasn't unfolding so smoothly, after all.

"The boy's probably just played out," he managed to gasp at last. "We had quite a chore digging the hole and hoisting that heavy box up."

Caddie didn't look quite convinced.

"Besides, you know Tem." Manning held out his glass for a refill. "It's not in his nature to be excitable. Maybe he's pondering what would have happened if we hadn't found his grandpa's stash. Or wishing he'd found it sooner, like you said. So his ma wouldn't have had to marry a Yankee."

"I'm sure it's not that!" Caddie's hand trembled and the lemonade sloshed over the table. "You know how fond the children are of you."

The mild acid of Caddie's lemonade seemed to eat away at Manning's innards. Loving Tem and Varina gave his life meaning in a way it never had before. But for them to love him corroded his soul with guilt. Like a treasure tainted by murder and theft.

He searched for a topic that would distract Caddie from her worry about Tem, and himself from thoughts he couldn't bear to dwell on. "We need to talk about your brother-in-law."

Caddie cast him a questioning look, perhaps wondering about the abrupt change of subject. "Lon?" Her nose wrinkled. "He'll be fit to be tied when he hears we found the silver."

"Oh, yeah." A chance draft sent a chill rippling over Manning's sweat-soaked body. "Can't blame him much, either. By rights, half of it does belong to him. I think we should do the fitting thing and give Lon his share."

"Have you lost your mind, Manning Forbes?" Caddie looked ready to baptize him with the rest of that lemonade. "After everything that man's done? Trying to claim squatter's rights on Sabbath Hollow. Turning the neighbors against us. Setting that Yankee tax collector on us."

"You don't know that for a fact."

"No, but I don't doubt it, either. If you could have heard the way he went on about the children and me needing a friend. Saying you'd never come back from Washington."

"Well, he was wrong, wasn't he? And you managed to make the neighbors see reason—all the ones who count, at least. Isn't it time to stop this feud, before it gets out of hand?"

He could tell he was winning her over. And she didn't want to be won.

"Do you reckon Lon would give the children and me so much as a silver teaspoon, if he'd been the one to find it?" she asked, like a desperate gambler playing her last trump card.

Manning thought for a moment, then shook his head. "I don't suppose he would. Which is all the more reason for us to do what's proper. You don't want Tem and Varina growing up to act the way Lon would, do you?"

Her lips pressed together so tightly they all but disappeared, and her eyes flashed with fury. "I reckon not," she conceded, almost against her will.

"Don't worry, we'll have plenty to pay the taxes and keep us going until the business starts to turn a profit. Maybe once Lon knows the silver's been found and he's got a share, he'll quit making trouble for us."

"There's where you're dead wrong, *Mr. Right and Fitting.*" Caddie poured herself a glass of lemonade. "Half of anything will never be enough for Lon."

For once in her life, Caddie wished she hadn't been right.

At Manning's suggestion, they'd met with Lon outside the Methodist parsonage—the parson, Dr. Mercer and Bobbie Stevens acting as their witnesses.

When Manning pulled the tarpaulin off the battered old box, Lon looked as though he'd been struck by lightning. "Where the hell did you find this, Carpetbagger?"

Manning's fists balled tight, but he answered in a voice of controlled reason. "The where part hardly matters. What's important is that the valuables your father hid have been found, on our property. We figure you're entitled to half."

The parson beamed. "If only the family states of our poor country had treated one another so fairly."

"Fair?" Lon spat on the ground.

It was almost worth a half share of the findings, Caddie decided, to see the smirk wiped off her brother-in-law's face.

"And just who's to decide what constitutes a fair division of *my* family's valuables?" Lon glared his challenge. "A Yankee like the ones who looted the Stevens place?"

Much as she hated to admit it, Caddie knew Lon had a point. Without an expert appraiser on hand, how could they hope to reach an agreement over any division? If they let Lon do the choosing, they'd be lucky to end up with a quarter share. Any split she and Manning suggested, no matter how generous, would have Lon claiming he'd been grossly cheated.

Something about the look on Manning's face told her he'd anticipated Lon's objection. "You go ahead and divide what's here into two lots you consider equal."

Lon's glacial eyes lit up. Caddie opened her mouth to protest Manning's noble but foolish integrity.

"Then," added Manning, "Caddie and I will choose which of the two halves we want."

For an instant Lon appeared ready to object. Then the full implication of Manning's proposal hit him, and he gnawed the end of his cigar in speechless fury.

The parson murmured something about "the wisdom of Solomon," while Bobbie Stevens cracked a grin so broad, Caddie worried his face would split in two. Doc Mercer, who'd looked dubious about the whole proceeding from the start, seemed to regard Manning with newfound respect.

"If you'd rather, we can divide and you can choose

first." Though he had every right to gloat, Manning made
the offer in earnest.

Any trace of resentment Caddie'd felt toward him for
doing the right thing melted like hailstones after a summer
storm. The man might have high principles, but he wasn't
a fool. A new ingredient slipped into the mix of contradictory, combustible emotions Manning Forbes stirred in her.
If she didn't look out, they might cook up into that sweet,
poisonous cake called *love*.

By suppertime a deal had been struck that appeared to
satisfy everyone but Lon. As Caddie and Manning rode
home with their share of the Marsh valuables, a light rain
began to spit.

"Shame we have to sell these things that have been in
the family so long." Manning sighed. If they'd been his
own family heirlooms, Caddie doubted he could have
sounded more regretful.

"If it'll let us hang on to Sabbath Hollow, I don't mind
parting with them." Caddie tried not to think about her
family's special possessions and what might have become
of them during Sherman's scourge of the Carolinas.
"There's a little cameo that belonged to my mother-in-law.
I'd like to hang on to it for Varina, if we can."

Manning nodded. "I wondered why you chose that half.
We shouldn't waste any time taking this stuff to Washington to sell. It'd probably fetch a better price in New York,
but that's a long trip to make with the children."

"Go wherever you need to." Caddie tried to keep her
tone matter-of-fact, as though this was not a decision she'd
struggled over. "I'll stay here to keep an eye on the business. The city's no place for children in the summer.
They'll be better off staying put."

Had he heard her? Did he understand the risk she was
taking? The hard-won, still-fragile trust she offered in

atonement for all the suspicion and antagonism she'd directed at him in the past.

Finally he looked over at her. "You sure about this?"

Caddie could tell by the gravity of his tone and the searching blue gaze he aimed at her that Manning understood, perhaps more than she did herself.

Why, then, did he not look happier about it?

By rights, Templeton Marsh should have been a happy boy. Any lad in his position might have dreamed of finding hidden treasure to save his home and restore the family fortunes. Well, he'd been credited with doing just that. His mother's eyes held a special glow of pride when she looked at him now.

His stepfather had gone to New York and returned with money to pay the taxes, promising business contacts, and presents for the family. Tem's gift had been a book, *The Silver Skates,* about a Dutch boy who'd also saved his family from ruin. Reading about Hans Brinker's courage and honesty made Tem feel like a fraud.

"Say, Tem, want to go catch toads out back of the stable?" Varina tucked her new doll into the cradle Manning had built.

"Maybe later." Tem leaned against the porch rail and stared off down the lane. Sergeant sprawled at his feet, panting and swishing his tail in a lazy rhythm.

It wasn't honorable to take credit for something you hadn't done, and even at the age of eight Templeton had a finely honed sense of honor. His grandpa had often lectured him on the subject when he'd been just a little shaver back in Richmond. Only since Manning Forbes had come into his life had Tem begun to understand the day-to-day living of an honorable life.

"Want to go pick blackberries?" Varina marched over

and leaned against the railing in a perfect imitation of her brother.

Sergeant's ears pricked up, as if he sensed the opportunity for some fun.

"In a while, maybe." Long ago Tem had learned that saying no to his little sister just got her riled up. And if there was one thing he hated, it was folks getting riled up.

He had an unpleasant suspicion honor demanded doing the right thing even when it riled folks. The way Manning had stood up to his uncle Lon, and the way he'd risked riling Mama by insisting they share all that silver his grandpa had hidden.

"You been no fun since you found them old forks." Varina flounced over to the cradle and pulled out her doll. "Miz Maymie and me are going for a walk and you can't come—so there."

The dog raised his face to Tem, an expectant look in those faithful dark eyes.

"Go on if you want to, boy. Go with Rina and keep her out of trouble." After a brief show of reluctance, Sergeant barked and loped off after Varina and Miz Maymie.

As Tem watched his sister stalk away with the dog at her heels, he almost hollered after them that toad catching or berry picking sounded like good fun. It was no use. While his conscience ached like a sore tooth, it took the fun out of everything.

Behind him Tem heard the front door open and close. Soft, sure footsteps approached. Mama.

"Are you feeling poorly, Son?" She laid a cool, graceful hand on his forehead. "You haven't been yourself lately. Is the heat bothering you?"

"No, ma'am." It might have been easier to pretend some minor ailment, but that would have been like telling a fib, and Tem didn't want to overburden his conscience just now.

His mother sighed. Tem stole a guilty glance to find her wearing the *old look*. The one where puzzlement and worry mixed with the love. Tem liked the other look far better. The one so full of pride and wonder it glowed.

Too bad he didn't deserve it.

"Then what's the matter, precious? At first I thought you were just moping for Manning to get back. Now I'm wondering if you need a good dose of sulphur and molasses?"

Tem made a face.

"What else am I supposed to think? You're off your food. You don't want to play with your sister or the dog. Are you provoked because we had to sell off the things you found?"

Tem shook his head. It seemed as though the more he studied on his problem, the bigger it grew. Like a bubble full of air, it just grew and grew until it popped.

"Mama, promise not to be awful mad if I tell you something."

His mother wrapped her arm around his shoulders and tilted her head until it rested against his. "That's a pretty hard promise to make before I know what you're going to say. What I can promise is that I'll respect you for telling me the truth, and I'll weigh that in your favor."

"I...didn't find that silver and such."

A little noise broke from his mother that might have been a wet laugh or a happy cry. "Is that all you're upset about? Well, of course you didn't dig the heavy old box up by yourself. But you told Manning where to look and that's what—"

"No, ma'am!" Tem shook his head hard. "I *didn't* tell him where to find it. Manning knew—he *knew!* Oh, he asked me all sorts of questions about Grandpa and back in Richmond, and did Grandpa ever talk about Sabbath Hollow."

"Y-yes, but—"

"See, Mama? I don't deserve you to make a fuss over me for finding those things. Manning does. He talked about different places—the stables, the woodshed, the pump. He kept coming back to the pump until I said, 'Maybe,' then we started to dig."

"I see." Mama sounded queer—like she was talking in her sleep. Rina did that sometimes, so Tem knew.

"I'm sorry I let you make a fuss over me instead of Manning. Sometimes I think you don't like him much, Mama, and I sure wish you would." Aw shucks, he was going to start bawling like a big old baby. Templeton squeezed his eyes together real tight until the tears leaked down into his nose.

"Listen to me, Templeton Randolph Marsh. You've got no call to be sorry. I'm prouder of you for telling me this than if you dug up fifty treasure chests with your bare hands. Understand?"

Tem opened one eye and looked into Mama's. The pride was there, all right. But so was something else. Something wild that frightened him. "Yes, ma'am, I understand."

"Good." The way her slender fingers dug into his shoulders scared Tem so bad he almost wet his drawers. "Now you run along and play with your sister. And no more moping."

"Yes, ma'am." Who'd be fool enough to mope with Judgment Day at hand? Somehow Tem knew a storm was brewing that might be on that order.

And he had unleashed it.

He tore down off the porch and around the house, his bony chest heaving beneath his shirt. There he stopped and listened.

Mama was talking to herself. Words that didn't make sense, about how she should've known, questions about why he'd do this.

The front door slammed shut, and when Tem mastered

his panic enough to peek around the corner of the house, his mother was gone. Inside, feet thundered up the stairs. Surely that couldn't be his composed, light-stepping mother.

Tem's stomach felt as if he'd swallowed a handful of tadpoles, as Rina had once dared him. Part of him—almost all of him, as a matter of fact—wanted to tear off after his sister and stay clear of the house until this ruckus passed.

But another part—a tiny one and new to his nature— insisted he take responsibility for whatever he'd set in motion. Set things right, if only he could figure out how.

He nearly jumped a foot when a familiar hand reached up from behind and tousled his hair.

"What ya doing, Tem? Playing hide and seek with Varina? You'll have to find a better hiding place than this. Sorry, Son, I didn't mean to startle you."

"You're home early, Manning."

"Benefit of owning your own business, boy. You can come home early on a fine summer day. Think you and Varina might like to go splash around in the creek with me?"

"Ah...sure, let's go."

Manning laughed. "Give me a minute to lose my socks and work boots and find a towel. You round up Varina."

"I—I wouldn't go in the house if I was you. Mama's not in a real good humor."

"Tem—Templeton, what's going on?" Against his advice, Manning strode into the house, and almost immediately his voice blared through the open window of his bedroom.

Tem's mother shrieked her answer, words that sounded like, "Well, why are you doing this to me?"

Tem clamped his hands over his ears to protect himself from the anger in Manning's voice and the anguish in his mother's. The harsh words that rang in his thoughts were at least as bad as anything they could say in real life.

He had to stop them—even just for a little while. Give them something else to think about besides their quarrel. He could think of only one distraction serious enough to qualify.

Chapter Fourteen

Tem's blurted confession tore the blinders off Caddie's eyes once and for all.

Why had she been too weak and stupid to do it for herself long before this? Manning Forbes and Delbert Marsh had to be the same man.

But *why?* If Del wanted to pass himself off as a Yankee, why come back to Virginia to do it? Was it like Bobbie had suggested—wanting more than anything to be on the winning side? By the time he'd disappeared in the spring of '64, the fate of the Confederacy had been written on the wall, in blood, for anyone who had the courage to see it.

Surely, it must be more than that. Caddie paced the front porch, muttering to herself in a fever of speculation. Maybe Del had taken a head wound and woken up in some Yankee hospital without a full recollection of who he was? He might have returned to Sabbath Hollow, the one thing he did remember, looking for answers.

A third possibility occurred to Caddie—one that left her bilious. Had Del come back in the guise of a Yankee, to tempt her into betraying his memory? To prove that fidelity wasn't as easy as she might have thought?

She had to find out. She had to know.

If Manning…or Del…or whoever he was wouldn't tell her, Caddie had a pretty good idea where she'd find some answers. Wrenching the door open, she charged up the stairs, almost tripping over her skirts in her haste. She tore down the hall and skidded to a halt in front of her husband's bedroom.

For a minute or two, some unseen force kept her from crossing the threshold, almost like a magical ward. Her craving to know the truth proved an even stronger counterspell.

She yanked open the dresser drawer into which she'd last seen Manning thrust that wooden box. It was still there. But when she tried to open the lid, it wouldn't budge. Caddie made a brief search for the key but couldn't find it. Very well—there was more than one way to skin a cat.

Pulling out one of her hairpins, she jabbed it into the lock and commenced to wiggle it around. She didn't have a clue what she was doing, but years ago she'd seen her brother, Gideon, unfasten a lock this way.

Click!

That faint but portentous sound set Caddie's pulse rushing faster than a drumroll.

Then she heard another sound that set her whole body aquiver. The heavy, rapid clatter of a man racing up the stairs.

When Manning reached the doorway of his bedroom, he found just what he'd feared.

Caddie sat on the edge of his bed with the wooden box on her lap. Somehow she'd managed to pick the lock, which had never been intended to deter serious prying.

It didn't look as though she'd read any of the papers inside, but that did nothing to quiet the ferocious alarm that reared and raged within him.

"What the hell are you doing in here?" He swooped in and grabbed the box from her.

He was less furious with Caddie than with himself. Why couldn't he just burn the damn letter, or tear it into a hundred pieces and scatter them to the four winds? It wasn't like he was apt to forget his promise without that tangible reminder. The whole business made no sense, and things that made no sense scared Manning—especially when it came to his own behavior.

Nothing fueled anger like a good charge of fear.

"If you don't quit spying on me, woman, so help me I'll—" What would he do? What *could* he do?

Not a damned thing. No matter how grave a threat she posed to his one chance at redemption, he'd let the devil take him before he'd harm one flame-kissed hair on her beautiful, dear, dangerous head.

"Just get out and leave me be!"

Caddie rose to her feet, her eyes searching his face as if it was a far more cryptic lock she intended to pick. Her whole body trembled, surely in the grip of emotions as intense and contrary as his own.

Her lips parted. Lips he could never see or think of without remembering the kiss she'd given him. And without feeling his whole body catch fire, like a heretic at the stake.

Of all the words that might discharge from those lips, the last Manning ever expected was, "Del?"

As Caddie reached for his face, Manning found himself frozen to the spot. "Del Marsh, that *is* you in there, isn't it? Why are you doing this to me?"

That was what she'd suspected? As understanding crashed upon Manning, Caddie's charge seemed both completely inevitable and completely impossible.

For one mad instant, he considered saying yes.

After all, he'd assumed most of Delbert Marsh's earthly responsibilities. Would it be so much of a stretch to assume his identity? Never again would he bear that hateful title, *carpetbagger*. Never again would Caddie discourage the children from calling him Papa. Never again would he have to hold back the floodgates of his desire for this woman.

"No!" It was the hardest word he'd ever had to say.

Manning staggered back from Caddie, lest her gentle touch pummel his battle-weary scruples. "I'm *not* your husband. I mean I am, but not your real husband. That's craziness!"

"It's not craziness. It's the only answer that makes sense. The first time I laid eyes on you again, I knew it had to be you. But I let myself be persuaded otherwise."

He should have known this might occur to her. Till the day he died, and maybe even after, while he burned in hell, Manning would remember that soul-chilling instant when he'd rolled a mortally wounded rebel officer onto his back and seen a face too much like the one that stared out of his tiny shaving mirror every morning.

"I swear to you, Caddie, I am *not* Del Marsh. What do I have to do to prove it?"

Thank goodness he hadn't yielded to the temptation to pretend he was Del. That would have meant a lifetime of lies compounding his other sins.

Caddie's hard stare bored into him, drilling for the truth. "If you aren't Del, then who *are* you, Manning Forbes? And what have you got in that box you don't want me to see?"

He'd sooner she'd ordered him to strip naked and march through Mercer's Corner. For a mad instant, he considered showing her Del's letter and concocting some story about getting it from Del before he died. But Manning knew his guilt would blaze from his face and scream from the tone of his voice. Then Caddie would know…and hate him. His fingers tightened convulsively around the box.

Then it came to him.

Could he offer another secret, a smaller shame to divert her attention from the big one? Knowing Caddie's proud nature and unblemished pedigree, even this might cause her to rethink their paper marriage, now that Sabbath Hollow was no longer in peril.

It was a risk he had to take.

"Very well." He lifted the lid and sifted through the papers inside, making certain to leave Caddie's own letter undisturbed at the bottom.

He handed her a stiff, yellowed document. "This should provide the answers to both your questions."

Caddie willed her hand not to tremble as she reached for the paper. But how could she hold it steady when the rest of her body quivered like it had the palsy?

Finally she was about to discover what Manning had been hiding. Perhaps what had been standing between them like a thick, transparent wall of ice. Would the information in this document break that invisible barrier? Or would it destroy the fragile, precious understanding between them?

For a mad instant, she wanted to shove the paper back at him without looking at it. If she did, perhaps Manning might look at her the way he'd looked when she trusted him to take the Marsh silver away for sale. But trust had to run both ways to be worth anything. If Manning had trusted her, he would have shared his secret with her before she forced him to.

She snatched the piece of paper from him and wilted back onto the bed as her quaking knees gave way. After carefully unfolding it, she began to read.

From what she could make out, it was a baptismal certificate issued by a church in southern Pennsylvania. For the adopted infant son of a couple named Prudence and Jeremiah Forbes, natural child of an unnamed mother, deceased. The date on the document tallied with her own estimate of Manning's age, about a year younger than Del would have been.

So Manning Forbes was a Yankee, after all. Then Del must really be dead. She would have no magical second chance to mend what had gone wrong between them. To forgive and to beg forgiveness.

"*This* is what you've been hiding?" Compared to her imaginings, it seemed pretty tame. "The fact that you were born on the wrong side of the blanket, as my late mother would so delicately have put it?"

Manning nodded, and Caddie had no doubt he was telling the truth. The man's face had paled to the color of putty.

"Maybe it was different here in the South when you grew up." He stared resolutely at the floor as he spoke in a tone as bitter as raw turnips. "Where I come from, that kind of thing's a stain you carry with you your whole life."

An enormous lump rose in Caddie's gullet. Where she came from, bastardy was like a dead horse in the middle of your great-aunt's parlor—folks would choke to death on the stink before they'd speak of it. Up until her marriage to Del had started to sour, the worst moment of her life had been discovering one of the house slaves was her natural half-sister.

She'd never met a white person of illegitimate birth.

"I reckon you have a point."

No wonder Manning had come South after the war—for a chance to escape his tainted birth and enjoy a position of relative power.

"Would you have accepted my offer of marriage if you'd known about this from the start?" He glanced up, pinning her with his gaze.

She could lie, of course, but he'd know it in a minute. She'd come within a hairbreadth of rejecting his proposal, anyhow. If she'd known about his parentage, or the lack of it, she would have refused him for sure.

Before she could speak or shake her head, Manning divined her answer. "I thought not."

He sounded like a man who had spent his life trying to push a heavy rock up a hill, only to have it roll back over him and all the way down again.

"Those Forbes people, were they good to you?"

Caddie wasn't sure what made her ask. Perhaps she still needed convincing. Some intangible proof that tied this man to this document and this identity. Once and for all.

"They meant to be, I think." Manning stared at the pattern of inlay on the top of his wooden box. "At least my pa did. Looking back, I don't suppose they should have taken me. They'd had a son who died, see? Pru took it hard—pined for him. I didn't find that out until after she passed on. Pa must've figured another child would help her get over it. Maybe it was too soon or maybe it wouldn't have mattered."

That wistfulness she'd sensed in Manning from the first moment they'd met suddenly took on form and shape. Somehow Caddie felt more guilty about prompting this confession than she had about looking through his papers.

"Pru might have looked on loving another child as disloyal to the memory of her own boy." Manning shrugged. "When I was small I figured it was because I didn't behave well enough. Later, when I found out about my real ma, I wondered if it was the way of my birth that kept Pru from caring for me."

The hurt in his voice was so raw and rough, it rasped on Caddie's motherly heart. When she tried to tell Manning he needn't say anything more, her throat was too constricted to speak.

For a moment he fell silent, as though he had read her

intention. Then he passed his hand over the lid of the box in a kind of awkward caress.

"Things were a lot better with my pa. The best times I recollect as a boy were working beside him in the wood shop or once in a while going fishing. He was careful not to make too much of me around Pru, though. We both knew she wouldn't like that. Pa passed on the year I turned fourteen and Pru died a month or so after the war started."

Suddenly Caddie realized how wealthy her childhood had been. Not just in money and the things it could buy, but in the company of her brothers and sisters, the love of parents so constant she could take it quite for granted. Even Mammy Dulcie and Uncle William had loved her. Now that she'd begun to guess how much they must have longed to be free all those years, Caddie marveled at their bountiful affection.

Manning sighed. "That's all there is to tell, really. Pa and Pru saw to it I ate well and had decent clothes and a pretty fair education. Pa gave me a start on learning a trade. I owe them a lot and I never really got the chance to pay them back."

As she struggled to frame some kind of reply, Caddie heard footsteps pounding up the stairs, accompanied by loud barking.

"Mama!" Varina hollered at the top of her capable young voice. "Come quick!"

She hardly needed to add the latter, since Manning and Caddie came running almost before she got the words out.

Manning scooped the child up in his arms. As Caddie shushed the dog, she remembered all too vividly the comfort and protection *she'd* found in Manning's embrace. Could he have held her with any more compassion or tenderness if he'd been a lawful heir of the old Southern aristocracy? On the contrary, a lifetime spent on the fringes of polite society had better equipped him to offer a sympathetic hand to anyone who needed it.

"What's the matter, precious?" Caddie checked Varina for blood or obvious bruises. "Are you hurt?"

"Smoke!" Varina gasped. "Up on the ridge."

"The mill!" Manning thrust the little girl into Caddie's arms, then barreled down the stairs, his feet striking every third or fourth step. The dog shot after him.

A queer, bottomless feeling lodged in Caddie's stomach. What if they were to lose in minutes what Manning had spent months working so hard to build? Would he vanish from their lives just as quickly? Or would her shameless prying drive him away?

Setting Varina on her feet, Caddie took the child's hand and started down the stairs. "Come on, dear. Let's see what we can do to help. You were a real smart little mite to come find us."

Drawn by the commotion, Dora came running from the kitchen.

"It looks like there may be a fire up at the mill." Caddie nudged her daughter toward Dora. "You two go call for Templeton, then you all come back to the house. Don't stray too close to the ridge, now."

She headed for the door.

"Where are you going, Mama?"

"To ride around and call the neighbors for help. We'll have that little spark out in no time—you'll see." Caddie could tell by their faces neither the young woman nor the little girl were fooled by her false optimism.

She'd never saddled a horse by herself, but thoughts of Manning battling the fire on his own spurred her. If only she hadn't relied all her life on strong, able black hands to do such tasks for her, she wouldn't be losing precious minutes now. Fortunately, the gray gelding was a patient animal, or the whole plantation might have burned before Caddie was ready to ride.

At last she set off cross-country, praying Manning's horse could jump a fence if necessary. She tried to ignore the plume of dark smoke drifting skyward from the top of the ridge. Her alarm eased a little after she called at Gordon Manor and the Stevens place to find that neither Bobbie nor Alice had returned home yet. Caddie settled for borrowing several tin pails and riding off to the mill with them.

When she arrived, the mill yard was boiling with activity that put her in mind of an anthill kicked open. Alice Gordon and another girl scurried back and forth from the wood shop ferrying containers of varnish and oil to Bobbie Stevens's wagon, while Jeff Pratt held the skittish horse still.

Flames crackled and a pall of smoke hung in the air, haunting Caddie with images of that harrowing night Richmond had burned. At least the fire had not yet spread from the nearby trees to the piled lumber or the buildings. It would only take one shift of the fickle wind to change that.

"More buckets!" Bobbie Stevens lurched toward Caddie and relieved her of her burden. "Bless your quick thinking, ma'am."

She peered around through the haze of smoke, but saw no sign of Manning. "How can I help?"

"Go fetch Doc Mercer. We don't need him yet, but we may before this is over."

Part of Caddie longed to put as much distance as possible between her and the fire that stirred so many terrifying memories. Yet something inside her recoiled from the prospect of leaving when she might finally help Manning. A token repayment for all the help he'd given her since coming to Sabbath Hollow.

She slid from the gelding's back, fanning the smoke away from her face. "Doc Mercer isn't likely to come on my say-so. Alice, can you ride?"

The girl nodded.

Caddie handed her the horse's reins. "Then go into town and fetch the doctor. After that, could you stop at Sabbath Hollow and make sure Dora and the children are all right?"

Alice glanced at Bobbie, who nodded.

As the girl rode off, Bobbie handed Caddie back the last of her pails. "Fetch water from the millpond and wet down anything that looks likely to burn." He glanced up at the sky. "And pray those clouds do something more than hang there looking black."

It took over an hour for the storm clouds to enforce their threat. Once they made up their minds, however, the rain quickly gathered momentum.

With her aching arms as limp as a couple of wet rags, Caddie blessed every drop of water from heaven. Even when they sent sodden locks of hair straggling over her forehead, and icy droplets slithered down her back.

The business was safe. For now at least.

"Looks like we can stand down, folks," someone called.

Caddie and the others staggered from the millpond back to the yard. Two horses, one of them Manning's, stood hitched to a post near the wood shop. Dr. Mercer's resonant tones carried from inside. He must have commandeered the place for a makeshift surgery, she decided, mildly surprised that the doctor had heeded their summons.

After confirming with Alice Gordon that all was well with the children, Caddie once again looked around for Manning. She hadn't laid eyes on him since he'd dashed out of the house. A fresh chill snaked down her spine, and this time the rain was not to blame.

She caught the eye of Joe McGrath—at least that's who she thought it was beneath the soot. "Have you seen Mr. Forbes?"

The boy bobbed his head and pointed toward the woods. "Saw him head that way with an ax awhile ago, ma'am."

"An ax? Are you sure?"

"Yes, ma'am. Reckoned he was fixing to cut a firebreak. Keep it from coming back this way if the wind shifted." Joe squinted at something over Caddie's shoulder. "Reckon that might be him coming now, ma'am."

Caddie spun around.

It was him, all right. His shoulders bowed with exhaustion. A layer of soot on his face so dark the whites of his eyes seemed to glow in contrast. Hair bristling like broom corn. Not since her return from Richmond to find the plantation house still standing had Caddie beheld a more welcome sight.

Forgetting the harsh words they'd exchanged such a short time ago and the lack of enthusiasm with which he'd greeted her last embrace, she launched herself at him.

"Manning, thank God you're all right!"

Circling his neck with her arms, she drew his face down to hers. At the last instant, mindful of the young folks who might be watching, she kissed him on the cheek instead of on the mouth. A faint bristle of whiskers rasped her lips and she tasted smoke, seasoned with sweat.

She couldn't begin to make sense of the outlandish patchwork of feelings this man provoked in her, so much of it hopelessly tangled with her unresolved feelings for Del. Only one thing she knew for certain. Every time she faced the threat of losing him from her life, it frightened and grieved her as the loss of her first husband never had.

Manning accepted her embrace passively. The poor man was probably too tired to raise his arms.

"Let's go home, wash up and get something to eat." She reached for his hand.

A sharp cry broke from his lips.

"Manning?" She turned his hand palm-up. "Dear Lord!"

The sight of raw, burned flesh made her gorge rise. She examined his other hand and found it almost as bad.

"Doctor! Somebody get Doc Mercer. My husband's hurt."

What if the doctor refused to treat him? Doc Mercer hadn't made any secret of his contempt for her new husband and his outrage over their hasty marriage. She hadn't done much to win him over, sassing him that day at Gordon Manor. If it would persuade him to use his medical skills on Manning now, she'd beg Doc Mercer's pardon on her knees.

"What have we got here?" The doctor emerged from the wood shop and strode toward them.

"My husband's burned his hands while fighting the fire."

"Let's have a look then." The doctor's tone sounded brusque, but he examined Manning's scorched palms with an uncommonly gentle touch.

Manning kept his mouth tightly clamped and his strangely vacant gaze averted from his injuries. Caddie's own palms tingled with a faint echo of the pain he must be suffering.

"Could be worse," pronounced the doctor. "I can clean and bandage them. Apply some salve. They're going to hurt like hell for a while, though. More than if the burn had been deeper. Let's get this man back to Sabbath Hollow, where I'll have better light to work and a dry roof over my head."

Caddie nodded, and after a brief exchange with Bobbie, she and Manning squeezed onto his wagon with Jeff, Alice and the others for a ride home, while Joe McGrath rode Manning's horse.

As they drove off, the weathered shingles of the buildings faded into the gray downpour. In the distance, charred tree trunks spiked the air like the jagged black tines of the devil's own pitchfork. Reminding them how close they'd come to losing their precarious foothold on the future.

To Manning, it felt as though that short wagon ride back to Sabbath Hollow would never end. The rest of his body might have turned to stone for all the sensation he felt in it. Only his hands were alive, pulsing with pain beyond anything he'd ever known. It took every scrap of will to keep from crying out.

In a futile effort to distract himself, he thought about Caddie throwing her arms around his neck and kissing him. For a magical instant he'd forgotten he had hands...or feet, or most anything but a heart. Then she'd clutched his hand, firing the pain to a whole new level of intensity.

Perhaps he should have expected that. From the moment he'd met Caddie, she had lofted him to heaven one minute, then hurled him to hell the next. Not that she meant to most of the time, he conceded, his sense of fairness rising to the fore. She no more guessed his feelings for her than she'd known his hand was burned when she grasped it. That was just the way Manning planned to keep it.

He was vaguely aware of the wagon pulling up outside the plantation house and Caddie ushering him into the kitchen. After checking with Miss Gordon that the children were safely tucked in bed, Caddie sent the girl to catch a ride home with the others.

Collapsing onto a chair, Manning sprawled forward with his arms stretched out on the table before him. He heard the doctor murmur something to Caddie about warm water and a clean cloth. The next thing he knew fresh barbs of pain raked his right palm.

Roaring the foulest curse he could think of, Manning tried to wrench his hand back. The leathery old physician held on with a strength of grip that surprised him.

"Go ahead and yell, Yankee," said the doctor. "Lord

above knows you've got good cause. I'm sorry I have to do this, but there's no help for it.''

"Don't want to wake up the children," Manning muttered through clenched teeth. Then a blanket settled over his shoulders and he heard Caddie's voice just behind him. "Do you have anything you can give him for the pain, Dr. Mercer?"

"Laudanum's too dear these days," the doctor grunted, "but I have a little flask of whiskey in my bag that you're welcome to. Wish I'd thought of it sooner. It's home brew and mighty strong, so don't go giving him too much."

Manning could hardly remember the last time he'd tasted whiskey. It was long before coming to Sabbath Hollow, and now seemed like a whole other lifetime.

When he smelled the reek of raw spirits, he pursed his lips, eager for anything that might numb him. The first swallow burned all the way down, as though it had been distilled from hot coals.

He gasped and choked, then begged, "More."

The second drink went down a little easier than the first. The third easier still. By the time Dr. Mercer had cleaned and bandaged his hands, Manning had taken several more swigs. His hands still pained, but he felt as though the sensation was reaching him from a long distance away.

He even thanked the man for putting him through hell.

"Don't mention it, Forbes." Dr. Mercer spoke with a kind of gruff camaraderie. "I've often thought I'd like to be paid to torture a Yankee. Get some rest, you hear?"

Manning lolled back in his chair as a lazy warmth kindled in his belly. He heard Caddie's anxious tone as she asked the doctor what she could do.

"Anything that might take his mind off it. Even with the whiskey, I doubt he'll get much sleep tonight. Keep the wounds good and clean. Change the bandages as often as he'll let you. Call me if you see any sign of infection.

Fortunate nobody else was hurt. Any notion how that fire got started?''

"I have more than a notion." The cold rage in Caddie's voice sent an answering chill down Manning's back. "And I expect you do, too, Doctor. I've got plenty of witnesses who heard my brother-in-law going on about how sawmills and fire don't mix. Flicking his cigar ashes around."

"Be careful about pointing fingers, child," advised the doctor. "Lon may talk big, but he'd never do worse than talk."

"Talk all the neighbors into turning against us," Caddie fumed. "Talk the tax collector into coming after us. Maybe Lon just talked somebody into setting a little fire near the mill."

Perhaps it was just his whiskey-addled brain, but that didn't make sense to Manning. Lon had been given his share of the family silver—why should he continue to cause trouble for them?

Manning puzzled over it as Caddie and the doctor moved out of earshot and a door opened and closed in the distance.

"Is that whiskey doing you any good?" Caddie asked when she returned to the kitchen. She sounded hesitant— almost timid.

Manning raised his heavy eyelids and peered at her. The steady downpour on their drive from the mill had washed the soot from her face. She looked cold, wet, tired, bedraggled and so beautiful he could hardly stand it.

He tried to remember why he was supposed to fight the desire she kindled in him. The reason wafted just beyond the reach of his suddenly sluggish mind, dancing like a windblown scrap of paper. A letter, the writing of which he could no longer decipher…

When Caddie's fine aristocratic brows drew together in a look of concern, he realized she was waiting for an answer to her question. What had the question been? Oh yes—about the whiskey and whether it had dulled his pain.

"Some." His tongue felt thick and awkward, as if it, too, had been blunted by the whiskey. "My hands still hurt, but I don't care so much."

"In that case I reckon you'd better get out of those wet clothes and into a warm bed."

Manning lifted his bandaged hands. "There's only one way I'll be able to shuck these clothes."

Yes sir, Doc Mercer's potent moonshine had managed to dull his pain, his memory, his reflexes. Everything but his desire. That it had sharpened like a knife on a whetstone.

He felt a slow, befuddled smile spread across his face. "That's if you take 'em off me."

Chapter Fifteen

Take his clothes off? The notion nearly toppled Caddie onto her backside.

She'd never so much as unfastened one of Del's collar buttons. Not even when… Her tinder-dry mouth suddenly watered and a mellow heat shimmered between her legs.

Hadn't she been hoping for a chance to consummate this marriage, if only Manning would cooperate? His drowsy, teasing grin and the improbable gleam of admiration in his eyes told her he'd be more than cooperative tonight.

Now that this golden opportunity had presented itself, a host of doubts tempered Caddie's eagerness. What did she know about seducing a man, after all? What if he woke tomorrow morning angry with her for taking advantage of his drunken state?

She sucked in a deep breath and squared her shoulders. "Let's worry about getting you upstairs to your bed before we bother about clothes. With that much home brew in your belly, you won't likely be too steady on your feet. Can you stand up?"

Manning tried. He got halfway to his feet before collapsing back onto the chair like Varina's new stuffed doll.

"Guess I'm going to need a little help with that, too."
He sounded cheerfully resigned to the prospect.

Perhaps he wasn't in any shape to make use of her to
night, anyway. Caddie tried to ignore a pang of disappoin
ment.

Kneeling beside Manning's chair, she wedged her shou
der under his arm and slid her own arm around his wais
He felt lean and solid to her touch. Though the rain ha
scoured away the worst reek of smoke and sweat, a pro
vocative trace of it still lingered.

"All right then." She didn't trust herself to turn her fac
and look at him with such a dangerously short distanc
between his lips and hers. "On the count of three
One...two..."

"Thu-ree!" Again Manning faltered halfway up, but b
that time, Caddie had planted her feet under her and wa
able to steady him until he could rise the rest of the way

"Do you feel dizzy?" she asked, savoring the pleasar
weight of him listing against her.

"A bit."

Well, he wasn't the only one. His nearness set her hea
spinning as surely as a swig of moonshine. "Reckon yo
can walk?"

"I'll try."

His long arm hooked around her neck and his hand dar
gled down over her bosom. Not that it could get up to
whole lot of mischief, burned and bandaged as it was. Stil
imagining how his strong bronzed hand might feel on he
soft pale breast set a delicious hum of desire through Cad
die's flesh.

Gracious! If she didn't do something to distract herse
from such carnal thoughts, she might let Manning fall t
the floor, with herself on top of him.

"Come on, then." They staggered off into the darkene

house toward the stairs. Their slow, weaving progress gave Caddie too much time to savor her contact with Manning.

She cleared her throat and forced out the words. "We got interrupted before I could apologize."

A cold rain of shame fell on the smoldering embers of her attraction. What kind of hypocrite preached to her children about the importance of good manners, only to commit the most grievous invasion of privacy?

"I'm sorry I went into your room and pried into matters you'd rather keep to yourself." Apologies didn't come easy to her, but it galled her pride a little less, begging Manning's pardon when she didn't have to look into his eyes.

"Should've told you myself," he murmured. "Right from the start...only..."

Only. That one word held a lifetime of wistfulness, spoken in that soft deep rumble she'd grown to like so well. With his lips so close to her ear, the sound of his voice had all the intimacy of a touch. Or a kiss.

"Only?" Husky with emotion, her own voice emerged in almost as deep a timbre as his. She could no longer resist the temptation to turn her face toward him.

His whiskeyed breath caressed her face. "You had more than enough reasons to turn me down." In the softest whisper, as if a thought had escaped directly from his mind, he added, "And I sure did want to marry you."

He wanted her? Not just as one of the inconvenient trappings of a business arrangement, but as a wife? As a woman? The thought made Caddie's knees tremble.

Without a single pair of reliable legs beneath them, they collapsed onto the stairs. Neither of them seemed to notice.

Her lips found Manning as his came searching for her. Unlike the night he'd returned from Washington, this time neither was taken by surprise. Unless by the intensity of their kiss. Why had she never noticed his full, sensuous lower lip? Now Caddie doubted she'd ever see it again without wanting to kiss him.

Their kiss was raw and potent, like the taste of sour mash on his breath, and every bit as intoxicating. She opened her mouth to him. Their tongues tangled, both ripe for conquest and surrender. Eager. Ravenous.

Caddie's whole world wobbled on its axis. Even after five years of marriage and two children, she'd never imagined kissing a man could feel like this, or that it could ignite such a blaze of sensation in the rest of her body.

She pried her lips away from Manning's long enough to release a gasping whisper. "We can't...ooh..."

Deprived of her lips, Manning nuzzled her neck just below her ear. The sweet torment made Caddie want to crawl out of her skin. Or at the very least, out of her clothes.

She tried again. "We can't spend the night...here on the stairs."

Manning kissed his way up her throat to her chin. "Right now, I wouldn't care if I was lying on a bed of nails."

"It's the whiskey."

He dipped his head to rest on her bosom. "I don't think so."

Caddie's voice stuck in her throat. She rubbed her cheek against his hair, which was still damp and smelling of smoke. She struggled to bring her breath, her voice and her raging emotions back under control. One of them had to be practical, and Manning was clearly in no shape for it.

"Will you be a good fellow and come up to bed?"

He heaved a sigh of perfect contentment. "I like it here just fine."

"What if I..." Could she say it? "...promise to stay and keep you company once we get there?"

He swiped his jaw across the bust of her dress, over the stiff peaks of her breasts, which strained against the top of er corset. "Now *that* puts a whole different complexion n things."

Hooking his elbow over the banister, he gained his feet, auling Caddie upright with him. They continued their urching ascent, though much more rapidly than before. Iad Manning been dawdling to prolong their closeness? Caddie wondered.

Or had she?

Near the top of the stairs he teetered for a moment, and he feared he'd crash all the way down, breaking his neck. t the last second, he caught his balance and charged the nal few steps to the second floor.

"Shush, now," he whispered to her, as though he wasn't he one making most of the noise. "We don't want to wake he young'uns."

He chuckled, and Caddie couldn't help but smile at the ound. There was something strangely touching about hearng a person so quiet and controlled carrying on a little illy. Maybe she ought to try it herself sometime.

"I like that word—*young'uns.*"

She liked the warm note in his voice when he said it.

"Come on now, it's just a few steps more." She tugged im down the hall toward his room, before his racket oused the dog, who'd make it his business to rouse the vhole house.

As they crossed the threshold of Manning's room, a flash f lightning illuminated every nook and cranny. The little vooden box sat on top of the bureau, where he'd tossed it few hours ago. His baptismal certificate lay on the floor vhere she'd dropped it.

When she'd left this room, Caddie had feared her half aarriage with Manning might be over. Now, instead, she ound herself with an undeserved opportunity to make it rhole. But did she dare to take that chance and risk another ailure?

Thunder rumbled in the distance and the bed frame squeaked in protest as Manning collapsed onto it, his leg dangling over the side.

Maybe by the time she got his boots off, he'd be sound asleep. Then she could settle for covering him with a blanket and stealing away.

Off came one. Then the other, after some pulling. His socks were wet, so Caddie took those off, too, running her hands over Manning's long narrow feet to warm them. Her fingertips brushed rough calluses on the ball of each foot. From marching, most likely.

Yes, he'd been a Yankee soldier, Caddie conceded, her bitterness waning. But that didn't matter like it once had. It didn't matter that he'd come south with most of his possessions in a rucksack—the soldier's equivalent of a carpetbag. It didn't even matter that he'd been born out of wedlock. Nothing mattered but the man himself, who had grown dearer to her with each passing day. If only she cared about him less, the thought of sharing his bed might not unsettle her so.

She began to wonder if he might have fallen asleep, but Manning flexed his toes. "Have I got cold feet?" His voice took on a teasing note. "Or have you?"

Fortunately the lightning didn't flash just then to betray Caddie's embarrassment. If the weather had been fine, the soft glow of twilight would have bathed this corner room. Tonight, the storm had left it wrapped in shadows.

Thank goodness.

No matter what she'd promised Manning, Caddie simply could not have stayed if he'd been able to see her more clearly. What a fright she must look with her hair a damp tangled mess and smudges of soot on her face. In the last months she'd put on a little weight, but she was still too skinny. Not round and lush like Lydene.

Caddie tried to shield both her doubts and her desire

behind a show of brisk practicality. ''I'm surprised the two of us aren't freezing in these wet clothes.''

As she fumbled in the shadows to unfasten Manning's suspenders, her fingertips brushed across the lap of his trousers. Caddie's hand flinched away, but she did manage to swallow the squeak that rose in her throat. She hadn't been married once already without learning to tell when a man was ready for a woman.

Hearing a soft rumble, she wondered for an instant if it might be far distant thunder. Then she realized the sound had come from Manning.

''Mmm. That felt awful nice. Suppose you'd mind doing it again?''

A fierce, prickly blush started down in Caddie's toes and swept up to the roots of her hair. She wished she'd taken a swig or two of Doc Mercer's whiskey to calm her nerves. Why, she hadn't been this bashful and flustered as a green virgin on her wedding night!

Of course, there hadn't been time. It'd all been over before she knew what was happening. And Del hadn't expected her to take any active part. Tonight would be different. Her old role as the reluctant instrument of her husband's relief would not do.

She unfastened Manning's suspenders with her left hand while her right hand strayed lower, passing over the firm ridge of flesh that strained beneath his trousers. When a low groan shuddered out of him, she knew better than to ask if his hands hurt.

The glow of heat between her own thighs intensified.

Light-headed from the whiskey, and without the use of his hands, Manning was at her mercy. A sense of power swelled within her—provocative, dangerous and liberating.

With a blatant caress that made him writhe beneath her, Caddie slid both her hands up to the collar of his shirt and began unbuttoning it. Now her fingers moved with deft, sure purpose. When she reached the lowest buttons, at the waistband of his trousers, she unfastened them, then slid her hand down to tug the rest of his shirt free.

Acting on a daring impulse, she let her fingers wander lower and glide over the hot, smooth crown of his manhood. Her reward was his gasp of astonishment, which subsided into a purr of pleasure.

"If this turns out to be some drunken dream, I pray to heaven I don't wake up anytime soon."

The ragged edge of Manning's voice drifted over her like the most arousing caress, stripping away another stifling layer of restraint. Then, as if powered by his will instead of hers, her left hand rose to the bosom of her blouse and tugged it open. Caddie's pulse sped to the wild tempo of the rain as it lashed against the window.

Suddenly impatient with her own layers of clothing, she interrupted her sweet torment of Manning to peel off everything but her shimmy and drawers. Then she pulled the pins from her hair and shook her head until it cascaded over her shoulders.

As the lightning blazed again, Caddie saw an answering flicker in Manning's eyes. She also caught a glimpse of his bare chest through the open front of his shirt. A thatch of dark hair laced across those firm, bowed muscles lured her to touch. His skin was hot and smooth, his chest hair crisp, yet silky.

She stroked and petted him, deliciously shocked by the thrill of exploring a man's body. And when her hands had sated themselves, she grew unbearably brazen, whispering her lips over him, resting her cheek above his heart, savoring the thunderous throb of his pulse, which *she* had excited.

He pressed his chin into her hair, making soft crooning noises that set her aquiver.

"I fear I'm going to die of delight before you get done with me, woman."

"Funny, you don't sound scared."

When Caddie lifted her face to answer, Manning strained forward and claimed a kiss. It wasn't as fierce and wild as the one they'd unleashed at the foot of the stairs, when their long-checked attraction had broken its bonds. This time was slow, deep and sensual.

In a past that now seemed too far removed to have been *her* childhood, Caddie's family had always summered at the luxurious sulphur springs resorts in the Blue Ridge Mountains. She hadn't thought of that in years.

Now she immersed herself in Manning's kiss as she'd once relaxed in the hot water with soft warm mud oozing between her toes and tiny bubbles of gas tingling on her skin. Even the faint smell of smoke that clung to them both revived memories of the pungent odor surrounding the springs.

By the time Manning released her lips, she felt as flushed and weightless as she once had at the end of a long, hot soak. Not to mention other sensations, entirely new in her experience.

He blazed a trail of kisses, starting at her chin and moving down her throat. To prevent him from wrenching his neck, Caddie had to stretch herself up to meet his lips. Her insides quivered like jelly when she realized his ultimate goal.

Manning caught the top of her shimmy between his teeth and pulled it down, setting one breast at liberty. His whisker-stubbled cheek rasped against the smooth, rounded flesh of her bosom, until his questing lips located the exquisitely sensitive crest and closed over it.

As her head began to spin in a dusky haze of pleasure, Caddie realized she'd forgotten how to breathe. Manning caressed her nipple with his hot whiskeyed tongue until her veins seemed to pulse with tawny moonshine. She whimpered her delight and her need.

When her lover paused for breath, Caddie fumbled out of her shimmy to allow him easy access to her other breast, which ached for his attention.

"Get me out of this damned shirt!" Manning's voice had lost its earlier teasing drawl, becoming tight and urgent.

"Careful now, you'll hurt your hands," Caddie cautioned, easing one sleeve off over his bandages, then the other.

"You're not going to stop there, are you?"

Even with the darkness deepening, Caddie fancied she could see a flash of quicksilver in Manning's eyes as he challenged her.

"Not if you don't want me to." Knowing there was little chance of that, she dispatched the last of his clothing, and hers, to the floor.

She hesitated for a heartbeat before climbing back onto the bed. She'd already failed once as a wife, without truly understanding how or why. What if she did everything she could to please Manning and it still wasn't enough?

Winding its way out of the shadows, his voice soothed her fears and rekindled her anticipation. "You aren't going to get all shy on me now, are you? Not after you've got parts of me burning worse than my hands?"

He probably wouldn't remember anything in the morning, Caddie told herself. Something in that thought saddened her, even as it seared away her last shreds of restraint. She wanted to make this a night *she* would remember, even if a sober Manning decided to keep her at arm's length again.

"I reckon I might know how to quench that fire of yours." She slid her naked body up the length of his, relishing the smooth, delicious friction.

"Mmm." Manning writhed beneath her. "You sure know how to stoke it up, sweet lady."

"I don't want to be sweet tonight." Her tongue made a circuit of his lips, then slipped between as part of a hot hard kiss. "And I sure don't want to be a lady."

They kissed some more. She touched him all over. First with her hands. Then, as his eager reaction made her braver, with her lips and tongue.

She felt the explosive heat building within him, which fired a back burn in her. At last she slid over him, taking him inside her.

A faint sense of regret tugged at Caddie, for she had never associated this marriage act with pleasure. She pushed the thought from her mind. She would partake of Manning's pleasure, satisfied that she had done everything possible to make it good for him.

But what was happening to her?

Manning's hard length inside her coaxed Caddie's body to the same wondrous state she'd experienced when he kissed her, and when he favored her breasts with his mouth.

Only…so much more…intense.

A fierce yearning radiated from the place where his body became one with hers. He had not invaded her sanctum; she had invited and welcomed him to become part of her, never guessing it would feel like this.

Manning flexed his hips, pulling slightly away, then plunging in again. Ripples of bliss washed through Caddie, crashing harder and faster as Manning bucked beneath her, his breath gusting in her ear like a storm wind.

Keening for something she could not imagine, she pressed her face into the hollow of his broad shoulder. He filled her with one final deep thrust, then he shuddered under her as though he might break into a million pieces. A hoarse cry broke from his lips, pained as a confession extracted under torture.

Did her ears deceive her, or had he uttered the word *love?*

With the force of a hurricane, ecstasy swept Caddie clean out of her thrashing body. Some while later, it washed her up, spent and sated, on the warm shore of Manning Forbes.

From the slow, rhythmic rise and fall of his chest, she could tell he'd fallen asleep. Caddie couldn't make up her mind whether to be glad or sorry.

Of course she wanted him to sleep while he could, escaping the pain of his burns. But a selfish streak in her wished she could snuggle against him and talk. Learn everything she could about him. Share parts of herself she'd never shared with anyone else. Plan their future together as a real family, with Tem and Varina...and perhaps other children, bred in the kind of passion they'd discovered tonight.

With a sigh of contentment unlike any she'd felt before, Caddie surrendered herself to sleep.

She could hardly wait to wake up to a new day and a new happy future.

Chapter Sixteen

Manning woke the next morning to a temple-splitting headache and fierce stinging in his palms. Both were mere annoyances compared to the crushing burden of guilt on his conscience.

He tried to keep from looking at Caddie, splendidly naked in the soft first light of day. Sometime during the night she had rolled off him. But her head still rested in the hollow of his shoulder, as though divine providence had fashioned that part of his body for just such a purpose.

The gentle swell of her breasts pressed against his side, beneath his lowest rib. It reminded him of the old Bible story of Genesis. He understood, now, that God's final and most perfect creation had been woman.

But there was more to the story. Beautiful Eve had tempted Adam into sin. In that golden dawn so dark with regrets, Manning could guess how. She'd simply offered him a taste of paradise.

Much as he would have liked to soothe his guilt by blaming last night on Caddie or on the whiskey, Manning knew better. This divine, desirable woman was in his bed for one reason only: because he had wanted her there. Had wanted her there, truth to tell, from the first night he'd slept under Delbert Marsh's roof.

Now here he was, three months later, sleeping under Delbert Marsh's roof, perhaps in Delbert Marsh's own bed. With the man's wife curled up naked beside him, the musk of their lovemaking filling his nostrils and making him want her all over again.

He'd longed for her every night for three months, yet at that moment he longed for her more fiercely than ever. Because she had given him a foretaste of heaven.

Now he glimpsed the fires of hell.

Somewhere, Manning had read about the witch trials of early colonial days. Most of the accused witches had been hanged, but one had been pressed to death—a slab of wood laid over her, on which large rocks were set one by one until their weight crushed the life out of her.

This morning Manning felt as if he was being pressed to death. It didn't help matters that he had quarried every one of the stones himself and piled them on.

A lifetime of sober, selfless penance might have absolved him of killing Delbert Marsh in the first place. Nothing he could do would acquit him of stealing the man's home, his family and his wife. If he kept on the way he was going, Manning feared the day would come when he'd congratulate himself for what he'd done. Be willing to do it again if Marsh suddenly returned from the dead to reclaim the life of which Manning had robbed him.

The longer he continued to lie there beside Caddie, stealing glances at her heavenly body and reliving what he could remember of their shadowy, storm-tossed lovemaking, the swifter would come the day of his ultimate damnation.

As gently as he could manage, given the state of his head and his hands, he eased himself away from her. The whisper of her rich mahogany hair against his skin was almost too sweet an enticement to resist. He hated himself for surrendering to his weakness last night. Hated himself for wanting her more than salvation itself. Before he had dragged himself from the bed and begun to fumble for his clothes, he almost hated her for being so damnably desirable.

As if wakened by the intensity of his feelings, Caddie stirred and opened her eyes. Perhaps realizing she was naked, or recalling the abandon with which she'd given herself to him in the night, she blushed the pearly rose hue of a new dawn. Then she gazed up at him with those bewitching eyes, the color of a green Eden swathed in the silver-gray mist of creation.

"Heading off to work so early?" Caddie asked, her smile an invitation. "You won't be able to do a whole lot at the mill with your hands in the shape they are."

If he hadn't wanted to yield to temptation so badly, Manning might have been able to keep the sharpness from his voice. "I can have a look around. See what damage has been done. Try to figure out what caused the fire."

If she minded his curt tone, Caddie chose to ignore it. "I reckon we both *know* who started that fire, and so does everyone else hereabouts. Why don't you come back to bed, and I'll see what I can do to make you forget your hands hurt."

Manning felt as if he was engaged in a tug-of-war. Him on one side with the rope biting into the seared palms of his hands. Caddie and a strong team of horses pulling on the other.

He tried to dig in his heels. "I don't think that would be a good idea."

Caddie's luscious lips crinkled up at one corner and sweet, seductive mischief beckoned in her eyes. "Is that so? Well, you look a little willing to me."

"Damn!" He didn't need to look down to know what she was talking about. His face blazing hotter than his hands, Manning raked his trousers from the floor to cover his traitorous body.

For good measure he turned away from Caddie, blushing more furiously still when he saw the admiring glance she cast over his bare backside. How could he resist his own baser nature when she seemed intent on taking its part? Last night had taught him that fighting his runaway desire was a losing battle. If he was to have any chance in this skirmish for his soul, he had to break up the alliance against him.

"Let me tell you something. A man's pretty near always willing for that sort of thing. The world would be in a damn mess if we went around acting on it whenever we felt the urge."

"I thought maybe last night was something more than that." The wistful tone of her voice and the plea in her eyes tore into his gut like a load of buckshot fired at close range.

Manning almost surrendered. But General Secret and his subaltern, Guilt, ordered a suicide charge.

"Don't fool yourself." He struggled in vain to dress himself. "Last night happened because I was drunk and because you felt sorry for me. Or maybe some kind of obligation."

That much was true at least.

His agitation made his bandaged hands more awkward still. Manning felt himself growing more exasperated by the second at his helplessness.

"If either of us has any sense or pride, it's not something we'll look to repeat."

His suicide charge had wounded her badly. The hurt he'd caused couldn't have been more plain if her heart had spurted blood. *Had* last night meant more to her than pity or duty?

Manning knew he didn't dare let himself believe it, or his private civil war would be lost for sure.

* * *

If either of them had any pride? A nauseating chill of shame settled over Caddie.

For many years she had cherished her pride. Defended it at all costs. In turn, it had come to her defense—when she had discovered Del's betrayal and after the fall of Richmond.

Lately she'd begun to question whether excessive pride was such an asset, after all. She'd begged Manning's pardon more in the three months of their marriage than she'd done Del's in all her years as his wife. And she'd forgiven Manning more often and more readily than she'd ever forgiven Del.

Last night she'd thrown pride, and pride's twin sister, propriety, clean out the window, crawling into the man's bed with no more invitation than his drunken ramblings and her own wishful thinking. She'd taken advantage of his susceptible state to satisfy her carnal lust and bind him tighter to her family. She'd carried on with him in ways that made her cringe to remember in the unsparing light of day.

If ever it could be said that a woman had taken a man against his will, then that's what she had done.

But did he need to humiliate her quite so thoroughly to drive home his point? Caddie's battered pride dusted itself off, shot her an indignant glare and rode to her rescue once again.

With deliberate hauteur she rose from Manning's bed and began to dress. "If that's how you feel, Mr. Forbes, I suggest you stay clear of strong drink after this."

She ignored the glances he stole her way, taking her time to wriggle into her drawers and cover her bare breasts with her shimmy. The trousers Manning held so awkwardly before him couldn't disguise his body's reaction, and how helpless he was to curb it. Caddie took a measure of vindictive enjoyment in tormenting him.

"I don't see why you need to go acting like some old maid schoolmistress, anyhow," she taunted. Against all sense, her hands ached to ruffle his hair just once more, to touch the firm muscles of his chest, to caress the tight, rounded flesh of his bare backside. "We're legally wed, in case you've forgotten, and have been for a good spell now. I'm sure there's not a soul in the world who'd take it amiss that we shared a bed for the night."

"Maybe I am just a Yankee prude." Now that Caddie was decently covered, Manning allowed himself to look at her openly. "But I believe a man and a woman oughtn't do that kind of thing unless they love each other a great deal—even if they have a piece of paper that says it's legal."

Was that an invitation to confess how she felt about him? Caddie concentrated on gathering her scattered hairpins from the floor. Even if she could sort out her hopelessly tangled emotions and decide that what she felt for him *was* love, would she dare make herself vulnerable by admitting it?

Fortunately she had to hold the pins between her lips while she twisted her hair into a tight knot on the top of her head. Otherwise some rash admission might have slipped out—a pitiful plea for him to keep on bedding her.

By the time she was able to talk again, she'd managed to marshal her defenses. "No need to run on about it. You've made your feelings on the subject abundantly clear. I promise that henceforth your virtue will be safe with me."

He nodded, trying to appear dignified in spite of his undress. "I'm glad we understand one another."

Caddie swept him a look cold enough to freeze running water. She started to flounce out of the room, never to darken it again, supposing dust gathered an inch thick on all the furniture and the windows grew too dirty to see through.

"Ah…Caddie?"

"Yes, sir?" She spun and faced him, taking spiteful pleasure in being fully dressed while he was so thoroughly exposed.

"You removed my clothes," he growled. "I think the least you could do is help me put them back on again."

Caddie heaved an impatient sigh, as if he'd asked her to perform some odious chore. "Very well. As long as you aren't afraid I'll take unwelcome liberties with your person?"

He shot her a wry look. "Just help me dress, please."

It sounded so easy.

Much as Caddie wanted to get a little of her own back at the expense of Manning's modesty and independence, she could not enjoy an undertaking that roused so many strong feelings in her. The most intense being regret.

She'd spoiled everything with her haste to consummate their marriage for all the wrong reasons. Protest though he might, she *knew,* in the way women throughout history had known, when a man was drawn to her. If only she'd just bided her time and let that tightly clenched bud blossom on its own, Manning might have welcomed her into his bed under more congenial circumstances.

With this mortifying finale to their lovemaking, Caddie doubted he would ever make another overture. Vexed as she was with him, she knew deep in her heart she wanted him to. After last night, she would burn for him until she was gray and wrinkled, and folks would be scandalized to think of a refined old lady harboring such feelings.

Desperate to distract herself from those thoughts, and from the unseemly urges the sight of his bare body provoked in her, Caddie searched for something—anything—

to talk about. Dangerous silence cried out to be filled with words that must remain unspoken.

"Now that our finances are on a more stable footing, I'd like to host that barbecue we talked about. Give the young folks in the neighborhood a chance to socialize." Standing behind him, averting her eyes from his shapely backside, Caddie pulled Manning's drawers up his legs and over his hips. "With your permission, of course."

She spoke with the excessive politeness Southerners reserved for their dearest enemies.

"This is your house." Was it her imagination, or did Manning's voice sound a little higher in pitch than usual? "You're free to do as you like with it."

Except come into my room at night. He didn't say it, but as Caddie circled around and began to button the waistband of his drawers, the unspoken prohibition hung in the air between them.

"In that case I'll invite folks for a week from Saturday." It would take a superhuman effort to ready Sabbath Hollow for company. Just the kind of diversion Caddie needed to keep her from mooning over this man.

She struggled to keep her fingers steady as she fastened his shirt buttons. At the same time she tried to ignore the sheen of sweat that had broken out on Manning's brow. He might not love her, and some streak of Yankee puritanism might make him keep her at arm's length. But while he might not admit it, even to himself, he wanted her just the same.

Surveying the fire damage, Manning wiped the sweat from his forehead with the back of his bandaged hand.

A blanket of hot, sultry air had settled over the area in the aftermath of the storm. That didn't heat him up as much as a passing thought of Caddie.

Part of him wished he'd been worse drunk, blurring his

recollection of their mating, so it wouldn't taunt and tempt him at every unguarded moment. A streak of unrepentant sin in his nature made him wallow in every vivid memory.

One thing he knew for sure, he'd have to get Doc Mercer to modify these damned bandages so he could feed and dress himself without Caddie's assistance.

"Bobbie," he called, "can I get you to drive me into town?"

"Reckon so, boss." The young man ambled over, eyeing the drenched, blackened piece of woodland. "Good thing that rain came when it did."

Manning nodded. "Queer, isn't it? If that fire was set on purpose, why not wait for a dry day? And why start it off in the woods? One match in the right place would have sent the shop up like a torch."

Bobbie shrugged. "Maybe it was just meant for a scare."

"Maybe." Manning couldn't decide whether to bless or curse whatever agency had started the fire and driven Caddie into his arms.

As they drove into Mercer's Corner, the two men talked more about possible causes of the fire and measures they might take to minimize the threat in future.

They were just drawing up to Doc Mercer's surgery when Bobbie nodded toward a well-dressed couple parading down the road. "Well, speak of the devil. That Lon is nothing if not brazen."

"Don't pay him any mind." Manning climbed down from the wagon as awkwardly as he'd been doing everything today.

The temporary loss of his hands gave him a heightened sympathy for the soldiers, North and South, who'd lost limbs for good. Did anybody truly *win* a war?

"That fellow could be a dangerous enemy," he added. "I've got more of those than I need already."

Caddie, for instance. Had he made an enemy of her with his behavior this morning?

"I'll try to hold my peace." Bobbie pretended to ignore Lon and Lydene as they came closer. "That's all I can promise."

Manning took a few steps toward the doctor's door.

"Hold on there, Carpetbagger!"

His faint hope of avoiding a confrontation with Del Marsh's brother expired. Reminding himself to keep a lid on his temper, Manning turned to face Lon.

By the looks of them, part of the proceeds from the Marsh silver had gone to prosper some fashionable tailor and dressmaker. Lon's wife in particular was decked out like a showpiece in a flounced summer gown sprigged with roses.

"Morning, folks." Manning nodded. To Mrs. Marsh, he added, "I beg your pardon for not tipping my hat, ma'am. My hands aren't quite up to the task today."

Lydene regarded him with a bold stare and a sly little smile that might have been inviting. Or had his night with Caddie left him reading lewd intentions into everything?

Lon looked ready to spit on him. "Isn't that just like a Yankee? Making all mannerly to a fellow's face, then slandering him behind his back."

What was it about this man that got under his skin so bad? Manning wondered as he mentally counted to ten. "Whoever claims I've slandered you has either been misinformed or is looking to stir up trouble. In case of the latter, I don't intend to give them the satisfaction of succeeding. I suggest you don't, either."

Hearing Bobbie Stevens mutter, "…fine one to talk about slander," Manning shot the young fellow a glance, begging him to leave well enough alone.

"Don't you go telling me what I should and shouldn't do, Carpetbagger." Lon's lip curled in an ugly sneer.

"Maybe Yankees don't care about things like keeping a good name. Maybe y'all don't have good names to keep."

His temper flared at that, though Manning reminded himself that Lon couldn't possibly know about his illegitimate birth. "What am I supposed to have done to sully your *honor?*"

"First you made a damned fool of me over the family silver, now you're telling folks I set that fire up at your mill." The man looked truly outraged. "I ought to call you out right now."

Having contented himself with casting dark looks at the Marshes, Bobbie Stevens could restrain himself no longer. "That's real gallant, Lon. Challenge a man to a duel when he can't hold a sword or a pistol."

"Bobbie, please..."

Clearly the young man wasn't about to back down. "Mr. Forbes hasn't said a peep to anybody about you trying to burn down his mill, but I have. Reckon you ought to call *me* out? If I'm wrong I'll gladly apologize, but what was I supposed to think after the way you threatened Miz Caddie—saying fire and sawmills mix too well?"

Lon's face blanched. "Just stating a fact was all," he sputtered. "I didn't mean anything by it."

Maybe part of the reason he disliked Lon Marsh was because the man had a much more legitimate claim to be Caddie's and the children's protector, Manning admitted to himself. How could he fault Lon for wanting to usurp Delbert Marsh's place when he had done that very thing?

"You see how easily rumors like that can get started?" Manning had held out one olive branch to Lon already, only to have it thrown back in his face. Would it kill him to try again? "If you give me the benefit of the doubt, I'll do the same."

Malice warred with common sense for control of Lon; every skirmish played across his face. At last he drew himself up tall and fixed on his most engaging smile. "We might have gotten off on the wrong foot at that, Forbes. I reckon neither of us has much to gain by feuding."

The minute Lon Marsh saw anything to gain, they'd be declared enemies again—Manning wasn't about to fool himself. Still, this was someplace to start.

"I'm glad you see it that way, Marsh. Say, Caddie's planning a barbecue a week from Saturday. We'd be happy to have you folks come if you care to. Might put some of these fool rumors to rest."

"Well now, a barbecue at Sabbath Hollow." Lon nodded slowly. "Be just like old times. Give Lydene a chance to show off her pretty new dress."

A little of the tightness seeped out of Manning's shoulders. "We'll look forward to seeing you there. Now if you'll excuse me, I need to consult with the good doctor about my hands."

Lon tipped his hat. "We won't detain you further. I'd offer to shake hands on our new understanding, but that can wait till you're healed up a little better. At the barbecue, perhaps?"

Ignoring Bobbie Stevens's doubtful expression, Manning replied, "I'll look forward to it."

As the couple strolled off, Lydene glanced back at Manning with a smile that might have been flirtatious. Or more likely he was just imagining it, and the woman was simply grateful to him for providing an opportunity to flaunt her new finery.

Heading into Doc Mercer's surgery, Manning congratulated himself on calming hostilities with Lon Marsh. If only he could strike a truce with Caddie that easily.

Chapter Seventeen

"You've invited *whom* to the barbecue?" On her knees scrubbing the parlor floor, Caddie glared up at Manning. Was he deliberately trying to provoke her?

"I don't intend to repeat myself." Manning flexed his fingers, now freed from the bandages that encased his palms. "I'm sure you heard me the first time."

In deference to her civilized upbringing, Caddie refrained from hurling her soapy scrub brush at his head. "Did Doc Mercer ladle more moonshine into you, or have you just plain taken leave of your senses?"

"What's so wrong with inviting Lon and Lydene to join us?" Manning demanded. "Maybe if folks on both sides had been willing to mend fences, we could have avoided that damned war."

"Lon doesn't want to mend fences." She scoured a spot on the floor, imagining her brother-in-law's face in the wood grain. "He wants to burn 'em down. Did you ask him to bring a bucket of coal oil and a box of matches to warm up the party, while you were at it?"

"Lon didn't set that fire and you know it." Manning paced the floor where it had dried. "If he had, the mill and the shop would be nothing but a pile of cinders now."

Could this be the same man who'd set *her* aflame in bed last night? Now the only thing he kindled was her temper—Caddie wished. "Maybe you'd think differently if you'd heard Lon as good as threaten to burn the place to the ground."

Why were they arguing about Lon, anyway? It was Lon's *wife* Caddie didn't want darkening the doorstep of Sabbath Hollow. No amount of torture would persuade her to tell Manning why. Still smarting over the way he'd rebuffed her this morning, she didn't need a reminder of her shortcomings as a wife.

"The man said sawmills catch fire easily." Manning started to plow his fingers through his hair, then seemed to think better of it. "I could have told you the same thing. It's more than that, though, isn't it, Caddie?"

Of course it was more than that. It was about Del and Lydene. It was about last night...and this morning.

Manning had his own ideas. "Lon had the gall to be living in your house when you got back here from Richmond. Are you going to hold that against him forever?"

"Some things can't be forgiven!" The words gushed out like poison from the festering wounds in her pride, and she wasn't talking about Lon and Sabbath Hollow.

Caddie hadn't noticed her voice and Manning's growing louder and sharper with each exchange until Varina appeared at the parlor door bellowing, "How come y'all get to holler in the house and I get told to shush?"

Her voice didn't sound much louder than theirs had become.

"That'll be enough impertinence from you, young lady." Caddie snapped.

"She has a point, though." Manning stooped to address Varina eye to eye. "Sometimes grown-up discussions get a little heated and folks don't realize how loud they're talking." He grabbed the end of one red braid and tickled her nose with it. "If you hear me hollering in the house any-more, go ahead and shush me."

The warmth in his voice made Caddie's throat tighten. She would have given every piece of the Marsh silver if he'd spoken like that to her this morning. Manning Forbes might not love her enough to make her his wife in more than name, but he loved her children as much as any father could.

Why couldn't she be happy and satisfied with that, rather than jealous of her own young'uns?

"Once your behavior is entirely correct, Varina Marsh, *then* you can go ahead and criticize others. Now, run along and play with your brother like a good girl."

"I don't know where he got off to." Varina shrugged. "We heard you hollering, then Tem and Sergeant runned off. I think he was crying—old baby!"

Manning turned to Caddie, a look of shame and concern blazoned on his face. "I'll go look for him."

"In a minute. Varina, you go see if Dora needs a hand bringing in the wash."

"Chores." Varina rolled her eyes. Then, seeing her mother's warning look, she trudged off toward the kitchen.

As her forceful little footsteps faded in the distance, Manning remained crouched by the door, his head bowed and his shoulders slumped. "Go ahead and say what you're thinking."

He sounded so...defeated. Caddie didn't dare say what she was thinking. "I don't know what you're talking about."

"Of course you do." He sighed, and in spite of everything, she ached to put her arms around him.

"You're dying to say, 'Now see what you've done.' Go ahead and spit it out."

The lye soap began to sting Caddie's hands. The stuff was as caustic as anger.

"I have no intention of saying anything of the sort." She gentled her voice, as he had done to reassure Varina. "It takes two to make a fight. You're no more to blame than I am. Probably less. I know you meant well inviting Lon and...all. It's just..." She couldn't tell him.

Manning drew his own conclusions. "I know." He struggled to his feet, as if a heavy pack was strapped to his back. "This is *your* house. I should have let you do the inviting."

It sounded so petty. Better he should think her petty than guess the truth and feel sorry for her.

Caddie could abide anything but that.

"What do you want me to do?" Manning asked. "Tell Lon the invitation's withdrawn? Cancel the barbecue?"

On no account would she let the threat of Lydene's presence force her to cancel this gathering. Until that moment Caddie hadn't realized how much she was looking forward to it. This would be a welcome chance to pretend, for a few sweet hours, that they were back in the easy, prosperous days before the war.

But how could she get Manning to retract his invitation without making him look like a henpecked fool, reinforcing the notion that he was little better than a lodger at Sabbath Hollow, working for his keep?

"What's done is done." Caddie rose from her knees, wiping her smarting hands on her apron. "We might as well put the best face we can on it. Who knows? Maybe if Lon shows up here and eats our vittles, he'll have to behave himself after this where we're concerned. Otherwise the neighbors will think worse of him than they do already."

Manning might not understand why, but he seemed to sense how hard a decision this had been for her. He smiled at her, and something like fondness glowed in his eyes. "Thank you, Caddie. I hope you're right. From now on I promise I'll ask your leave before I invite anyone into your house.''

''*Our* house.''

For some reason, Manning's smile faltered. ''I'd better go find Tem.'' He headed off.

Caddie went over and opened the windows to let the lye fumes escape. In some strange way, she felt as though a window had been opened in her heart just now, letting in a warm, clover-scented breeze. They'd had *words,* more heated than any she'd ever exchanged with Del, and yet she felt good about the compromise they'd reached, instead of seething with bitterness.

Maybe if she could forget the night they'd spent together and stop herself yearning for him, she and Manning might manage a halfway decent marriage, after all.

She was a better woman than he deserved, but that went without saying.

In his search for Templeton, some instinct beckoned Manning toward the creek. Whenever he felt low or troubled, the sound of water never failed to soothe and revitalize him. Last night, it had been the sensual music of the rain drumming on the roof and windows of Sabbath Hollow, as much as Doc Mercer's whiskey, that had made his desire for Caddie flood its banks and burst the dam he'd built to contain it.

He'd pushed her away this morning, to ease his guilt. Which might also have been the reason he'd invited Lon to the barbecue, if he was honest with himself. Both had provoked Caddie's anger, but beneath that, he'd sensed her hurt, and it tore at him.

As Caddie had said, some things couldn't be forgiven. Killing her first husband would surely be at the top of that list.

Manning shied away from that painful thought the way

he'd have avoided trying to lift a heavy object with his burned hands.

"Tem," he called. "Templeton Marsh, it'll soon be time for supper, Son."

The boy gave no sound or movement to betray his whereabouts, but the dog had no scruples about calling attention to both of them. It came bounding through the underbrush toward Manning, barking a greeting, tail beating back and forth against the leaves. Once confident of having caught his attention, Sergeant wheeled about and made for Tem with the unerring precision of a well-aimed bullet.

As Manning had suspected, the boy sat on the creek bank, skinny arms wrapped around equally skinny legs. As the dog romped around him, saluting Manning's arrival with more loud barks, Tem continued to stare out at the water, ignoring them both.

"Good boy, Sarge." Patting the dog as best he could with his bandaged hand, Manning sank down beside the boy on grass still a little damp from last night's rain.

He addressed his next words to Tem. "Stick close to Sergeant, here, and you'll never have to worry about getting lost. Maybe in the fall, you and me can go hunting. Something tells me this fellow could track and flush game like nobody's business."

Tem didn't reply or give any sign he'd even heard. His silence implied that the dog was no asset when his master just wanted to hide and be alone.

"This is a nice spot." Manning looked around, slowly nodding his head in approval. "When I was your age, I used to have a place something like this where I'd go."

It wasn't easy for him to talk about, but he sensed the boy needed to hear it. "You know…when I was troubled about something. Listening to the water always made me feel better. Sometimes I'd talk to the water, too. Tell it what was bothering me. Maybe it couldn't really hear me or do anything to help, but just putting my bad feelings into words and getting them outside of me… Probably sounds foolish to you, doesn't it?''

By gradual, hesitant degrees, Tem's face turned toward him. Manning could see that Varina had been right. The boy'd been crying.

It pained Manning's heart. In a different way, and somehow deeper than any hurt on his own account. Those were his and he could bear them. But he ached to relieve Tem's hurts, knowing full well he couldn't.

He held the child's anguished gaze, saying nothing, asking nothing. Like the flowing water, just being there to receive whatever Tem was ready to disclose.

"How come you and my ma got married if you don't like each other?''

If a cannonball had come whistling out of the heavens and blown apart the stretch of creek bank where he sat, Manning's composure could not have been so thoroughly shaken. A hundred possible answers to Tem's question exploded in his thoughts. None of them he dared utter.

Perhaps if Tem had been ten years older, Manning could have said he liked Caddie far too much for his good, or hers, and the young man might have understood. No way on earth could he look into the dear, anxious face of a boy he'd come to love like a son, and tell him the truth. That he'd put a bullet into Tem's real pa, then had sworn a vow to look after Del Marsh's family.

Manning sighed. "Templeton, you're a big boy, so I'm not going to give you a baby's answer. I know at your age, lots of things seem simple. A man loves a lady, so he marries her. When you get older, you'll understand it can be way more complicated than that. Your ma's a fine lady and I've got all the…respect in the world for her.''

His mouth had a tough time forming those words, as if

it wanted to say something else altogether. Manning wasn't sure what, nor did he dare to think about it too closely.

"Is there some other gal you like better?" the boy demanded.

"No!" Manning almost wished there was. Why had his fool heart taken a notion to the one woman he'd the least right to? "No, Tem. It's just…well, you don't want your ma forgetting your pa, do you? Some folks aren't lucky enough to find love once in this life, let alone twice. But that doesn't mean they should do without the help of a husband or wife for the rest of their lives. Especially if they have children to raise."

Tem looked grave and thoughtful—even more than he usually did. "My ma and pa didn't fight like you and her do."

Of course they hadn't. Caddie and Delbert Marsh would have had a whole world in common. Del wouldn't have grated on her aristocratic sensibilities like sandpaper on fine-grained hardwood. When Del roused her considerable passion, he'd have been entitled to satisfy Caddie and himself.

Manning opened his mouth to apologize for what Tem had overheard.

The boy's sensitive brow furrowed deeper, as if digging for long-buried memories, then sifting to make sense of them. "They didn't fight, but I don't think they loved each other the way you said, either."

"I see." He didn't. Manning struggled to digest Tem's words.

"It's *my* fault you and my ma get cross with each other." The statement exploded out of Tem like something rotten left in a corked jug to ferment. "If it wasn't for me, maybe you'd get to like each other."

Even before the child finished speaking, Manning had started shaking his head. "No, Tem. No. You've got to believe me. One of the few things your ma and I agree on is how much we care about you and Varina, and what fine young'uns you are.''

For reasons Manning could not guess, his intended reassurance backfired. Tem buried his head in the nest of his arms and knees and commenced to sob his tender young heart out.

Words heaved out with his tears. "I...told Mama...I didn't find that treasure. That's when...she went in your room."

The dog whimpered and tried to lick his master's face.

Manning winced. He never should have made the boy an unwitting confederate in his deception. No wonder Caddie had been driven to snooping through his papers. "It's all right, Son. Your ma and I worked all that out...sort of..."

"'Cause you had to run off on account of the fire."

True enough. Manning wasn't sure where their confrontation might have led if the fire hadn't interrupted. It had given him and Caddie a chance to back away from their highly charged feelings and each to look at the situation from the other's point of view. In spite of his burns and the fear of losing what he'd worked so hard to build, Manning couldn't say he was sorry the fire had started when it did.

Maybe that's why he felt more forgiving toward Lon than Caddie did.

"I started that fire."

The words could only have come from Templeton, but Manning still found himself peering around for another source. Surely the boy couldn't mean it?

"I didn't aim for it to get so big." Tem sniffled. "I only wanted to make some smoke so you and Mama would quit fighting and come see."

"Oh, Tem." Manning's insides quivered like cold jelly

to think what might have happened. "Thank God you weren't hurt!"

Shoving the dog out of the way, he gathered the child in his arms. How could he live with himself knowing his actions had driven the boy into danger?

Tem burrowed into Manning's embrace, soaking his shirt with tears. Finally, when the child had cried himself out, he asked in a quiet, hesitant voice, "Aren't you mad at me?"

"Sure am." As much as he could with his bandaged hands, Manning ruffled the boy's hair. He tried to keep any sharpness out of his voice, while still impressing on the boy what a serious matter this was. "You could have been hurt, Tem. Maybe killed. We could have lost the mill. I want you to promise me you won't set any more fires."

Tem's head thumped vigorously against his chest. "No, sir. I sure won't."

"Then I guess we can let it go at that. I know how hard it must have been for you to tell your ma the things you did, and to tell me about the fire. It's brave to do things we're scared of when we know they're right. I'm real proud of you for that much, Tem."

If he had half this little fellow's courage, he'd tell Caddie the truth about Del's death. Manning tried to justify himself by asking if that *would* be the right thing for her and the children. Perhaps if Del hadn't been a model husband, as Tem implied, Manning could redeem himself by doing his best to make her happy.

Even if it afforded him the kind of pleasure he ill deserved.

"Tem set the fire? Are you sure?" A chill went through Caddie, though the July evening air on the porch was oppressively hot. "When I think what could have happened…"

She half rose from her seat on the porch to go check on her son and satisfy herself that he was safe. Manning's next words froze her and made her collapse back onto the bench.

"Seems the boy was trying to distract you and me from the hollering match we were having."

"Oh dear." She could hardly face the thought that she had put her child in danger. "I reckon I owe Lon an apology. And you for the things I said this afternoon."

Of course, her unfounded suspicion of Lon had only been a pretext to vent her impotent rage at the thought of having Lydene as a guest in her home.

Caddie picked up the material she'd been sewing into a fancy summer dress for Varina, stabbing her needle into the dotted muslin. She'd had no right to blame Manning for that. How could he know about Del and Lydene when Caddie would have sooner slit her throat than tell him of her humiliation?

"This isn't your fault, Caddie. It's mine."

She glanced up from her sewing to find him staring off into the distance. His elbows rested on his knees and his shoulders rounded to accommodate the invisible load he carried.

How she wanted to slip her arm around those broad, burdened shoulders and ease whatever troubled him. Swallowing a sigh, Caddie forced her attention back to her sewing. Manning had made it clear he didn't want that kind of bond with her. She owed him so much already, she couldn't bring herself to beg for more.

Though part of her wanted to so bad she could almost taste it on her tongue, like the fumes of moonshine whiskey.

Neither of them said anything more for a while as a chorus of frogs tuned up for their nightly concert down in the hollow. Caddie kept her eyes firmly on her sewing, though her ears strained for the soft rumble of Manning's voice, and her nose greedily inhaled the tang of wood sap and sawdust that hung about him. She remembered how he looked without a stitch of clothes on and how delicious his bare skin felt against hers.

"Caddie?"

The unexpected caress of her name on his tongue made her tremble. She clutched Varina's dress tighter and lowered the cloth to her knees. "Yes?"

"I've tried to keep things businesslike between you and me." Manning scratched his brow and shook his head, clearly pondering a riddle that admitted of no easy solution. "Because of how we started out together and the differences between us. Marriage is hard to do right by at the best of times. I thought it might be better not to try at all than to try, and fail."

He glanced over at her, his expression earnest and somehow wistful. "Does that make any sense?"

Too much. "I believe it does." Her voice caught in her throat. Only a strong push of will succeeded in dislodging it. "Has something made you change your mind?"

"Maybe not change, exactly." He looked half-afraid of admitting more. "But question."

Question was a start. Caddie's heart broke into a skip-to-my-loo. She wanted to reach out and run her fingers through his hair. Pull him close and kiss him until his eyes crossed. But she'd carried on too brazenly before. Played with fire and gotten singed for her trouble.

So she sat there on the porch on a summer evening, like a demure Southern belle entertaining her first suitor. Trying to give the proper encouraging signals without appearing too forward.

She pretended to examine her sewing again, then glanced back up through her lashes. "Did you have something more you wanted to say?"

"No!" He blinked, as if waking from a spell her eyes

had cast on him. "I mean…yes. Tem seemed pretty upset. Not just about the fire, though that was part of it. He asked me why you and I got married if we didn't—"

As he spoke Caddie nodded. "He told me he thought I didn't like you much, and that he wished I would."

If only Tem could understand. She hadn't wanted to like Manning Forbes. Certainly hadn't wanted to feel whatever emotion plagued her at the moment. But her heart hadn't given her any choice in the matter.

"Then maybe…" Manning reached over and laid one bandaged hand on top of hers "…we ought to see if it's possible to get along a little better. For Tem and Varina's sake. Act as if we married for some reason other than just salvaging Sabbath Hollow."

Caddie tried to swallow a big lump that suddenly materialized in her throat. The provocative touch of Manning's fingers, the deep, soothing melody of his voice and the soft twilight glow in his eyes all filled her with a fragile, frightening sensation of hope.

She reminded herself he was forcing himself to do this on account of the children, and perhaps compassion for a woman so desperate for a man's regard.

"For now," whispered her heart. He might not start out to care for her, but if she tried hard, she might win him just the same. Curb her pride, try to see his side of things, be quicker to apologize if she wronged him and to forgive if he wronged her.

And if that *still* wasn't enough? Could she stand to live with a man she hungered after, but who didn't want her?

"I—I'll try." Those words might have been fifty-pound cannonballs for the effort they cost her to push forward.

Manning smiled. The kind of smile she'd only seen him offer the children, until now. A smile that lit his whole face with the warm, rosy-golden hues of sunset.

"Good. So will I."

She was pretty sure he was going to kiss her. The expectation of it hung around them in the sultry, fragrant summer air.

"Caddie?"

"Yes?"

"You and Del—did you have a good marriage? Did he make you happy?"

From out of nowhere, a raw January wind tore through Caddie. What had her son been telling Manning? What had a sensitive child like Tem guessed about the state of his parents' marriage?

Some lingering vestige of Southern clannishness wouldn't let Caddie disparage the husband who'd given his life for the Confederacy. Early on, her mama had taught her that well-bred folks never spoke ill of the dearly departed.

"Del was a fine Southern gentleman." For the most part. "We loved each other and had a happy marriage. Why do you ask?"

"I just…wondered." The smile bled out of Manning's face and the tide of an approaching kiss ebbed. "You never talk about him."

"I think about him plenty." Caddie battled to keep the disappointment from showing in her eyes. Once again she'd spoiled something that could have been very special.

If she'd told Manning the truth—about the slights, the silences, the growing discontent, the final betrayal—she knew he would sympathize. That's the kind of man he was. But she didn't want his pity; she wanted more. Somehow, this dear baffling Yankee had made her feel she deserved more.

Even if he couldn't be the one to give it to her.

Chapter Eighteen

Caddie had loved Del Marsh. Probably still did. Maybe always would.

I think about him plenty. Her words haunted Manning as he helped prepare for the barbecue.

He should have known better than to pin his hopes on his own wishful thinking, and the recollection of a little boy whose memories had been colored gray and black by the war.

If the Marshes' marriage hadn't been happy, Manning would have jumped at the chance to make it up to Caddie. Now he didn't know what to do.

Mulling over her passionate response to him the night of the fire, he wondered if she might have been lonely for a man in her bed. Any man who could substitute for Del Marsh in the dark.

That didn't explain the honey-trap look she'd dangled in front of him the next morning. Before he'd dashed it off her face with his guilt-ridden gruffness.

They hadn't fought any since his talk with Tem. Manning almost wished they would. If he couldn't provoke Caddie's passion in bed, at least it was something to see her magnificent eyes flash and cross verbal sabers with her.

Instead they acted like cordial strangers separated by a trench full of eggshells.

"Hey, boss!" Bobbie Stevens's cheerful hail nudged Manning out of his puzzled, regretful musings. "Where do you want the boys to set all this stuff?"

Manning turned to see Bobbie perched on the driver's seat of the big draft wagon they'd bought for hauling their wares to the rail depot in Westchester. The wagon bed had been loaded with chairs...and a surprise for Caddie. Manning could hardly admit to himself how much he hoped she'd like it.

"Let's set some of the chairs out here on the porch." Manning made a sweeping gesture indicating the front of the house. "The rest we can put around the edge of the parlor for folks who want to be near the dancing."

"You heard the boss, boys." Bobbie alighted from the wagon, using a special rung Manning had installed for the purpose. "Who knows but I might have a go round the dance floor if they play something good and slow."

With a broad grin stretched across his face, Bobbie bent down and tapped one of his wooden legs, a hollow sound that never failed to twist Manning's gut in knots. "These make a fine excuse to hold on to a young lady a little tighter than might be polite otherwise."

"I guess that's one way to look at it."

"The only way, boss." The young man held himself with a certain jaunty belligerence, as if daring self-pity to take him on. "Unless you want to throw away the rest of your life. I know plenty of boys didn't make it after amputations. I reckon they'd have been glad to trade me places, so I'd better do all I can with a life I'm damn lucky to have."

To Joe McGrath and the other young fellow, Bobbie called out, "Careful with those chairs, mind! We want to sell them once they've done their duty here, and nobody's going to buy them if they're all scratched and dented.''

Something prompted Manning to speak. The words had scarcely left his mouth before he wished he could recall them. ''Do you ever think about the man who shot your legs up?''

''Hate him, you mean?'' Bobbie sniffed the air, redolent of smoldering oak and hickory. ''Suppose I might if I let myself ponder on it any. I don't, though, 'cause then I might have to ponder on the fellows I shot. If you'll excuse me, I'd better go keep a close eye on the boys so they don't bang up those chairs.''

''Go ahead.'' With all his heart, Manning wished he could adopt Bobbie Stevens's practical philosophy.

He would like to have taken his mind off their conversation by helping carry more chairs in. His hands weren't up to it, though. So he settled for directing the boys where to put them, and later holding open doors when they toted in their other delivery. When they'd finished unloading everything, he sent them off to the kitchen for a drink of lemonade to cool off.

''Hope you're going to have a little something stronger than lemonade on hand at the barbecue.'' Bobbie winked.

''Maybe a *little* something,'' Manning allowed. Not that he'd be drinking any of it, then using that as an excuse to make a fool of himself over Caddie.

He followed Bobbie and the boys back to the kitchen. The sound of Caddie's voice lured him outside, where she and Miss Gordon were supervising the barbecue pit in consultation with Jeff Pratt.

''Does that smoke smell right to you, Jeff?'' Caddie looked dubious.

Jeff inhaled. ''Maybe a little more hickory, Miz Caddie. I was always partial to plenty of hickory smoke in my barbecue.''

"I agree entirely," said Miss Gordon. She stood beside Jeff, his hand tucked in the crook of her elbow.

Safe in the knowledge that Jeff couldn't see her, Caddie was watching the pair with a sweet, brooding look. No doubt remembering her courtship with Del Marsh.

"What do you think, Mr. Forbes?" asked Jeff. The young man had developed an almost spooky ability to identify folks by their scent or the rhythm of their walk.

"Smells fine to me, but I can't claim to be any great expert on the subject. I'll defer to you and Miss Gordon. Caddie, could I get you to come inside for a minute? There's something I'd like *your* advice on."

"Certainly, my dear."

She'd begun calling him that around the children. Perhaps the habit was starting to stick. Manning wished he didn't like the sound of it quite so much.

As she swept through the door he held open for her, she asked, "What's the problem?"

"Not a problem, really." He inhaled the faint aroma of spices that hung around her from all the baking she and Miss Gordon had done. "I wanted to make sure you approve of the way we've set up."

Caddie stopped abruptly. Following close on her heels, Manning bumped into her. When he tried to draw away with an apology for his clumsiness, Caddie caught him by the suspenders and held him close.

"It's all right," she whispered, "if you were just trying to get me inside so Jeff and Dora could have a few minutes alone. I was looking for a reason to excuse myself."

"I'm glad to oblige you." Finding they were near the dining room, Manning spun Caddie toward the door. "But there's a little more to it than that."

For what seemed to Manning like a very long time, Caddie didn't move, speak or react in any way to the sight of a large table occupying the center of the room.

Did she not like it? Before the fire, Manning had spent many hours carving the table legs in a simple but decorative style. Maybe it wasn't as elegant as whatever table used to be here, but folks could eat off it just the same.

He tried to keep the disappointment from his voice. "I wasn't sure if you'd want it in the middle or pushed over against the wall."

"The middle's fine." The tight, wavery sound of Caddie's voice told Manning she was fighting tears.

"If you don't like it, I can sell it and make you another one." It wouldn't be a surprise, but at least Caddie would have what she wanted.

She turned on him so quickly, Manning didn't have a chance to retreat a single step. He hovered over her as she looked up into his eyes and spoke.

"Don't you dare think of selling it! It's the most beautiful table I've ever seen." A soft film of tears filled her striking eyes. Together with the urgency in her voice, it told him this practical, unromantic gift meant more to her than he could have imagined.

Apart from all the other impediments that held him back, Manning told himself it was ridiculous to kiss a woman on account of a…table. The unexpectedness of the moment and Caddie's nearness overwhelmed his scruples more thoroughly than Doc Mercer's whiskey.

He closed the tiny distance between them, which seemed to shimmer like air above the hot mouth of a cannon. Then he kissed Caddie in broad daylight, cold sober, with half a dozen people watching them, for all he knew. Manning wasn't sure he could have stopped himself on threat of death.

Their lips met and molded together in unspoken harmony. To Manning she tasted as smooth and sweet as a saucer of strawberries and cream, with a delightful wild tang. For one reckless moment, he wanted to toss her onto that brand-new table and gorge on a banquet of Caddie.

The sound of a poorly smothered giggle jolted him back to his senses. He pulled away from Caddie just enough to see Tem and Varina watching them. Varina's plump little hand was too small to stifle her enormous grin and her eyes danced with gleeful mischief. Templeton's cheeks glowed like hot coals, but his eyes shone with a rare, shy felicity Manning could not bear to cloud by recanting what he'd just done.

And Caddie?

At the same instant, they looked from the children to each other. What Manning saw in her face—something promising and expectant—made him want to kiss her again, even with an audience present. It also made him want to turn tail and run worse than a raw recruit getting his first taste of enemy fire.

"I'd b-better go fetch some more chairs," he sputtered.

Then, for the sake of the children and possibly Caddie, he forced himself to smile as he raised his hand and caressed her cheek with the back of his fingers. "Save me a dance tonight."

She hadn't been this nervous before her first cotillion. As Caddie put on the prettiest dress she'd worn in the past five years, she fought to quiet the anxious little hummingbird that tickled her insides. But every time she thought about Manning's kiss, she fancied the tiny creature's wings picking up their frantic flutter again.

She told herself not to read anything into it, any more than she should pin her fragile hopes on the diffident brush of his fingers against her cheek or the request to save him a dance. Manning had played it all for the children's benefit—Tem's, mostly. While Caddie loved him for it, an ember of resentment smoldered just the same.

Loved him? Her rational faculties went on alarm. Surely she meant attraction. Or fondness. Or gratitude. Or some hopelessly mixed-up combination of those sentiments.

Love, Caddie's heart insisted, exhilarated and terrified to put that intimidating name on her feelings.

Perhaps Manning could love her, too, if only he'd let himself. True, that wasn't why they'd married, but did it mean they must resist the feeling if it grew between them?

"Mama!" Varina pounded up the stairs. "Manning said to tell you company's coming!"

"I'll be right down."

Caddie twirled around to enjoy the rustle of petticoats under her creamy, pale yellow ball gown. In the tiny mirror above her washstand she gave herself a critical look, then fussed with the clusters of auburn ringlets on each side of her head that whispered over her bare shoulders.

Had all the blushing she'd done in the past few months been good for her complexion? she wondered as she peered into the looking glass. The woman she saw there appeared much closer to twenty than thirty.

She hadn't needed a mirror, after all, Caddie decided as she descended the staircase. The appreciative glow in Manning's eyes assured her that she looked quite presentable.

His appearance, on the other hand, unsettled her. In more formal attire, carefully shaved and with his hair slicked down, he resembled Del even more than usual. Hard as she tried to ignore it, Caddie found herself moving and speaking more stiffly than she intended.

Not half as stiffly as Mrs. Pratt, however. That lady sailed through the entry a few minutes later with scarcely a word to Caddie, countering Manning's outstretched hand with a glare of withering disdain. Jeff followed with his sister Ann and her young son. Ann looked less peaked than when Caddie had paid her a call at Willowvale.

In a skittish whisper, she thanked Caddie and Manning

for the invitation. "Remember the parties we used to have? All that seems like a dream now."

From the parlor, Caddie overheard Jeff laying down the law to his formidable mother. "If you can't behave with a little civility, I'll get someone to fetch you home."

Varina pounced on Ann's son. "Say, what's your name? Want to come and play with Tem and me? We got a dog, but he's tied up so's he don't get at the barbecue."

The boy blinked in wonder, as if the existence of females his own size was a revelation. "What's barbecue?"

"Some kind of vittles they cook on a fire—smell."

Both children inhaled deeply, then ran off giggling.

Manning caught Caddie's eye. "Maybe when fall comes we can hire somebody to teach the children?"

The Stevens clan appeared just then, leaving Caddie with no opportunity to answer. She hoped her smile would tell Manning how much the idea pleased her.

It froze on her face when she spied Lon and Lydene driving up in a fancy new buggy.

"If you'd be so good as to greet the rest of our guests, my dear, I really must go check on the barbecue." Bad enough she had to suffer Lydene under her roof; Caddie wasn't about to welcome *that woman* to Sabbath Hollow. "I see Jeff brought along his fiddle. I'll ask him to strike up a tune in case folks want to dance."

Manning nodded. "Don't forget about the dance you owe me."

Sweet anticipation rippled through Caddie. "I'll be looking forward to it." She cast her husband a challenging glance to warn him he'd better not disappoint her.

She had barely taken a step toward the parlor when she heard the first notes of "The Last Rose of Summer."

Spotting Doc Mercer standing outside the room, she pulled him inside. "You know how bashful folks can be about getting started dancing. Let's set them a good example.''

"That's pretty bold, missy,'' the doctor teased, "but I don't suppose a gentleman ought to turn down his hostess.''

Perhaps because they'd had neither the opportunity nor the desire to dance in quite a spell, the rest of the guests were quick to follow Caddie's and Doc Mercer's lead. By the time Jeff struck up a new tune and Caddie pushed the doctor toward Mrs. Pratt, several other couples had taken the floor, including Bobbie and Ann.

As she watched Dora serving lemonade, her wistful gaze straying frequently to the fiddler, a soft ache of regret stole over Caddie. If only they still had a piano, she might have been able to fumble through a simple piece or two so Jeff and Dora could have a dance.

"Nothing wrong, I hope?'' Warm with concern, Manning's voice wrapped around her.

"Not hardly.'' Caddie glanced back to find him caressing her bare shoulders with his gaze. Her voice almost faltered. "Nothing important, anyhow.''

"Why don't you let me be the judge of that?'' He held out his arm to her. "You can tell me all about it while we dance.''

Caddie gave a pointed look at Jeff and another at Dora as she took Manning's arm. "I wouldn't care to be overheard.''

His head dipped toward her, and for an intoxicating instant, Caddie thought he meant to kiss the base of her neck. Instead, he whispered in her ear. "In that case, you talk softly and I'll lean good and close to hear you.''

They were far from the most graceful dancers on the floor, but Caddie didn't care. As long as she had an excuse to feel the tender strength of Manning's arms around her and the whisper of his breath against her hair.

"So what's this unimportant problem that had you looking so thoughtful?'' Manning murmured as he held her even closer.

Caddie liked the sound of his voice in her ear almost as much as she liked the taste of his kisses and the press of his body against hers.

''Do you know how hard it is for a lady to flirt with a gentleman who's blind?'' she asked.

For a long time Manning had seemed blind to her as a woman. Fortunately, his vision had improved of late.

''Ah…'' He looked toward Dora Gordon. ''Are you sure you'll be doing either of them a favor promoting that match? Young Jeff has plenty of responsibilities already, to his womenfolk and Ann's boy, when he has a hard enough row to hoe just looking out for himself.''

''I know,'' Caddie confessed. ''But she's dead gone on him and I think he could care for her if he'd let himself. I reckon folks ought to grab the chance for a little happiness when it comes.''

''You're a real sensible woman, Mrs. Forbes.''

He'd never called her by that name before. Caddie's spirits rode a rush of pleasure so high and fast it frightened her.

He steered her in Jeff's direction. When the young man lifted his bow, Manning called out, ''I haven't got anything like your skill, Jeff, but I'll spell you long enough to have a drink and maybe take a turn around the floor yourself.''

''I'm fine, boss.''

''Nonsense.'' Caddie plucked a tray of lemonade glasses out of Dora's hands and elbowed her toward Jeff. ''You and Miss Gordon have both been working too hard. We want you to enjoy the party as much as everybody else. Now, you will be a gentleman and ask her to dance, won't you?''

When Manning put his hands on the fiddle and bow, Jeff surrendered them. He seemed to sense Dora's presence, for he turned toward her. "Will you take pity on me, Miz Dora? I reckon I can count on you not to let me bump into too many other folks on the dance floor."

Dora glared at Caddie and Manning, perhaps not realizing her exasperated look was tempered with gratitude. "I'd be honored to dance with you, Mr. Pratt."

With a tentative touch, Manning played the opening bars of "Believe Me if All Those Endearing Young Charms." Jeff and Dora took to the floor with equal hesitation, but with each note and each step, both the musician and the dancers grew more confident.

Other couples crowded onto the floor, including Lydene with old Mr. Stevens. Her stylish new dress in a silvery-green shade made all the other ladies look shabby and twice-turned. Caddie tried to quell a pang of envy, but failed.

Lon was keeping Mrs. Pratt and Mrs. Gordon amused with reminiscences about the good old days at Sabbath Hollow, talking at a volume that threatened to drown out Manning's fiddle playing. At least Lon and Lydene were staying out of her way, for which Caddie was thankful.

Confident that her guests seemed to be enjoying themselves, she bustled off to check on the barbecue. Awhile later, when heaping trays of pork and chicken had joined bowls of boiled greens, pans of corn bread and other hearty fare on her new dining table, Caddie returned to the parlor to call everyone to supper. The words froze on her lips as she stood in the doorway staring at the dancers.

During the time she'd been gone, Manning had relinquished the fiddle to Jeff again. Now he glided around the room, easy as you please, with Lydene clinging to him the way Spanish moss clung to big cypress trees in the Low Country. Suddenly she glanced Caddie's way, her sassy dark eyes glittering with insolent triumph.

A scary sensation rose in Caddie, hot and cold at the

same time, like the queer warmth of frostbite or the clammy chill of a breeze on sweat-slick skin. It made her want to rage and scream, yet it tightened her throat until she could barely breathe, let alone speak.

Was the sensation that overwhelmed her jealousy? Caddie couldn't think what else to call it.

As she watched Lydene whisper something in Manning's ear, then let out a high-pitched giggle, Caddie quivered with barely suppressed violence. The sickening sense of betrayal and humiliation she'd experienced the night she'd caught Lydene in bed with Del had been a mere fancy compared to this. How could she have been such a fool as to grant Manning Forbes this terrible power to hurt her?

He must be hearing things.

As Lon Marsh's minx of a wife sashayed off at the end of their dance, Manning stuck his pinkie finger in his left ear and wiggled it around hard.

He thought she'd cooed some nonsense about meeting him upstairs later for a little party of their own. Unless she was trying to torment him, which Manning didn't discount, he couldn't imagine why Lydene Marsh might make such a scandalous suggestion.

Maybe he'd been thinking too much about Caddie. How badly he wanted her, yet how wrong it would be to surrender to his desire. Somehow that might have gotten mixed up with whatever shallow pleasantry Caddie's sister-in-law had uttered.

The sound of hands clapping for attention hit Manning like a hard slap on the cheek.

"Ladies and gentlemen," Caddie called from the parlor door. "Come and eat before the barbecue gets cold."

Her voice sounded strange—hollow, as if echoing through an empty room, instead of a crowded one. And her face had paled to an ivory shade that looked striking in contrast to her vivid hair. Manning didn't like it, though.

Had the barbecue brought back too many bittersweet memories for her? Had it made her yearn for life at Sabbath Hollow as it used to be? For the husband she'd once loved, whom Manning was luring her to forget?

He fought his way through the press of guests streaming toward the dining room, trying to get close enough to Caddie that he could ask her what was wrong. He wasn't sure he could bear to hear it.

Either circumstances were against him, or Caddie was deliberately making an effort to avoid him. Hard as he tried, he could never seem to make any headway in reaching her. He was beginning to feel like a fish swimming upstream to spawn.

A flounce of green drew his gaze to the wide arched entry of the dining room. Lydene flashed him a smile brimming with sultry mischief. A smile that told him he hadn't been hearing things, after all. When she glanced upward, there could be no mistaking her meaning.

Manning barely resisted the urge to yank out a handful of his hair. The last thing he needed right now was Lon Marsh's wife poking around upstairs. He began to battle his way out of the dining room.

Doc Mercer loomed before him. "Appreciate your hospitality, sir." By the smell of his breath, Manning guessed the good doctor had laced his lemonade with something a trifle stronger.

"Glad you're enjoying yourself." Manning tried to step around him.

"Many's the fine time I've had at Sabbath Hollow over the years." The doctor's face took on a faraway look, for which the whiskey he'd consumed was only partially to blame.

"I hope you'll have many more in the years to come."

Picturing Lydene on the prowl upstairs, Manning pushed the doctor toward Dora's mother. "You and Mrs. Gordon will have plenty of good old times to talk over, I'm sure."

As he threaded his way through a press of guests, he knocked Bobbie Stevens off balance and almost barreled into Jeff Pratt. "Sorry, folks! Swear I haven't had a drop stronger than lemonade."

In case anybody might be watching, he resisted the urge to dash up the stairs two at a time. Just the same, his breath was coming fast when he reached the upstairs landing. Though he knew with nauseating certainty where Lydene Marsh must be, Manning cast a passing look into the nursery and Caddie's room. There was no trace of the woman.

He found more than a *trace* of Lydene in his own room.

Dark curls hanging loose around her shoulders, she lounged back in his bed, the picture of wanton allure.

Manning stood at the door. "Mrs. Marsh, if you're feeling tired or unwell, I suggest you ask your husband to take you home."

"Silly man." She laughed as if he'd just told the funniest joke she'd ever heard. "I'm not one bit tired—except of that poky old barbecue. I'll bet you and me can have plenty more fun right here by ourselves."

Manning reached back to rub the tightly bunched muscles in his neck. "I doubt your husband or my wife would take kindly to that idea, and I can't say as I'd blame them. Now, why don't you just act like a lady and come on downstairs?"

"I like it here just fine." Her little raspberry mouth pulled into a pout some men might have found bewitching.

Manning wanted to shake some sense into her. "I've asked nicely, now I'm telling you. Get off my bed. Get out of my room. And get the hell out of my house!"

Lydene started to sit up, and for an instant Manning thought she was going to do as he'd asked. Instead, she began to unbutton the front of her dress, until a tempting expanse of plump breast strained over the top of her corset.

"If you want me out of here so bad, why don't you come and get me?"

Manning swallowed hard. A fellow would need to be made of marble for the sight of a woman in such a provocative pose not to stir him the least little bit. He didn't want Lydene Marsh, though. Not the way he wanted Caddie—with his whole heart and most of his soul as well as his body.

Just then he heard voices coming up the stairs—the loudest of them Lon's. Suddenly Manning understood what had brought Lydene to his bed, and it wasn't any kind of fancy for him.

He knew he needed to beat a retreat. If the Marshes had conspired to spring this trap on him, he should put as much distance as possible between himself and Lydene. He had no intention of leaving her alone in the same room as his box of papers, though.

As for trying to manhandle Lydene off his bed... "I'll leave that chore to your husband, Mrs. Marsh. I believe I hear him coming."

Swearing that he'd burn Del's letter before another day dawned, and cursing himself for not doing it sooner, Manning stepped toward the bureau to grab the box and be off. He nearly choked when he felt a small but forceful hand snag the waistband of his trousers from behind.

"I'm...not...used to being turned down by men, Mr. Carpetbagger." The woman had considerable strength for her size.

Caught off balance, Manning staggered back toward the bed. His arms flailed out, grasping for something to break his fall. Only when he heard the high-pitched shriek of ripping cloth did he realize that he'd latched on to some part of Lydene's gown.

She cried out in a very believable pretense of distress— or perhaps she was genuinely upset about the dress.

The rest unfolded as neatly as a stage play. The aggrieved husband rushed in on cue, conveniently accompanied by two witnesses in the persons of Mrs. Pratt and Mrs. Gordon. They all made proper noises of horror.

Manning didn't bother trying to explain. What was the use?

At last Mrs. Pratt withdrew, huffing, "I'll see to it that Caddie knows what kind of shenanigans are going on under her roof."

Manning caught Lon in a smirk of triumph that told him he'd better start packing up his carpetbag.

Chapter Nineteen

Caddie knew.

"Of all the no-account behavior!"

"I good as told her something like this would happen!"

"What did she expect, marrying *one of them?*"

Deep in the pit of her stomach, she knew. If the look Lydene had shot her while dancing with Manning hadn't been enough, the vindictive glee in Mrs. Pratt's and Mrs. Gordon's voices, masquerading as neighborly concern, slapped Caddie in the face.

She didn't need to hear the women recount every disgusting, humiliating detail. But she let them run on, holding her peace with a show of cool dignity when all she wanted to do was scratch Lydene's eyes out, shriek at her husband like an ill-bred scold, then fall on her bed and cry till her eyes ran out of tears.

Lon and Lydene appeared behind Mrs. Gordon and Mrs. Pratt, Lon's coat covering the ruin of his wife's dress in a pointed pose of gallantry. If she'd been carrying on with another man, why didn't he seem the least bit angry at *her?*

Caddie knew very well why.

The crowd of guests parted and fell silent as Manning made his way toward her. His hang-dog look brought Cad-

die nearer to losing control than the women's nattering or
the gloating gleam in Lon's eyes. For it told her he was
dead guilty on all counts, yet at the same time coaxing her
to feel sorry for him when that was the last thing she
wanted to do.

Perhaps not the last. The very last thing she wanted was
to give Lon and Lydene the satisfaction of mortifying her
in public.

Stonewalled by Caddie's implacable silence, Mrs. Pratt
and Mrs. Gordon finally sputtered out. In the hollow hush
that followed, the sound of Manning clearing his throat
thundered like a full battery of artillery.

"Caddie...I can explain, if you'll let me."

"There's nothing to explain, my dear." She glared at
Lon and Lydene, not daring to glance at her husband's
stricken face, for it might smash her brittle composure. "I
knew from the moment my brother-in-law accepted your
generous invitation, he'd only be coming to make trouble.
I'm disappointed such a sly fellow couldn't dream up something more original than this tiresome farce."

The shock on Lon's face was almost worth what it cost
Caddie to hide her anguish. At least when she'd discovered
Del's unfaithfulness, the whole neighborhood hadn't been
witness to it.

He puffed up like a rooster at a cockfight. "How dare
you accuse me...?"

A swell of muttering in support of Caddie and Manning
drowned him out.

"I know what I saw!" insisted Mrs. Pratt.

"Mother!" Jeff pulled her away from Caddie, none too
gently. "You have shamed our family, making these kinds
of vile accusations against Mr. Forbes. We are going home.
Mr. and Mrs. Forbes, I apologize for my mother's disgrace-
ful behavior."

Awestruck by her son's outburst, Mrs. Pratt let herself be led away, as meek as a lamb.

As Dora bore down on her, Mrs. Gordon recanted. "It might not have been as bad as it seemed. My eyesight isn't what it used to be."

"Now see here..." Lon tried to protest, but outraged scowls from the other guests drove him and Lydene into ignoble retreat.

There could be no salvaging the party after such a spectacle. Caddie didn't even try.

Leaving Manning to bid their guests goodbye, she went looking for the children, to satisfy herself they hadn't overheard anything that might upset them. She found them out back feeding pork bones to the dog.

"How come Rafe had to go home so soon?" Varina demanded. "Just when I'd almost coaxed him to dance."

"He's a nice little fellow," Templeton agreed. "His pa got killed in the war, too. In the navy. He said he might get a new one, though, if his ma marries Mr. Stevens. Varina and me wished him luck on it. Why'd everybody leave all of a sudden, Mama?"

"Maybe on account of it's as far past their bedtime as it is past yours." Caddie shooed them into the house and put them to bed as the last of the wagons trundled off up the lane.

When Manning finally ventured back into the house, she was carrying a stack of dirty dishes out to the kitchen.

He began to clear some glassware from the dining table. "Why don't you go on to bed—I'll see to this."

Everything in Caddie's upbringing urged her to go on upstairs without another word, nurse her tattered self-respect in private and sweep this whole unpleasant matter under the rug. But she deserved better from Manning Forbes, and she was going to demand her due, even if it let him see how much he'd hurt her.

"You could wash dishes till the day you die, and you still wouldn't come close to making amends for what you put me through tonight."

Manning almost dropped the glasses he'd gathered up. His mind and heart were still reeling from the way Caddie had taken his part against Lon's accusations. After all the secrets he'd kept from her, the half-truths he'd told her, he didn't deserve the faith she'd shown in him. Not to mention the way he'd thrown the precious gift of her lovemaking right back in her face.

He had wandered out to take leave of their guests in a daze. If Caddie could stand by him after what had just happened, was it possible he could tell her the truth about his past, daring to hope she might understand? Perhaps even forgive him?

Her words hit him like jagged bits of shrapnel. He should have known she'd only defended him as a means of defying her brother-in-law.

"It happened like you said, Caddie. Lon and Lydene set the whole thing up. I didn't—"

"Who invited them here in the first place?" Caddie slammed the dishes down on the table. "And how did Lydene get you up in the bedroom with her? Toss you over her shoulder and carry you? Or maybe she put a pistol to your head?"

Not a pistol—but a threat. A threat he himself had furnished with his lunatic refusal to destroy Del's letter or hide it where no one would ever find it.

"Did you hear something?" Manning set down the glasses and started for the entry hall. He didn't want Tem to overhear them fighting again. Who knew what danger the boy might court trying to distract them?

Caddie was not about to be distracted by anything. "Don't think you're getting away that easy, Manning Forbes. I know you had your reasons for marrying me, and love didn't likely come in the top ten, but we took vows and I mean to hold you to them.''

Didn't his vow to a living woman count at least as much as his vow to a dead man? Was it too late for him to mend what he'd marred again and again?

Before he could say anything, Caddie issued her terms. ''If you wish to remain under my roof, I'll need your solemn undertaking that you'll never have anything more to do with *that creature*.''

Was that all? Maybe he could promise not to eat live slugs while he was at it.

''Oh, Caddie…'' The noise he thought he'd heard completely forgotten, Manning crossed the room in two long strides and took her in his arms.

''Don't you 'Oh, Caddie' me, you Yankee hypocrite!'' She made a token swat at his chest, then turned away from him. But she didn't struggle to free herself from his embrace. ''Preaching about it being wrong for legally married folks to sleep together if they don't love each other, then carrying on with another man's wife!''

She wouldn't care about this so much if she didn't care about *him.* The hope of it might have brought Manning to his knees, if he hadn't been holding on to Caddie. It made him wrap her even tighter in his arms.

Pressing his cheek against her hair, he whispered, ''You don't think for a minute I could prefer her to you?''

The fight seemed to leach out of her. ''What else am I supposed to think? I know Lon set a trap for you, but that doesn't excuse how fast you went for the bait.''

''There's a whole lot more to it than that, Caddie. And I promise I'll tell you all about it in good time.''

He would, too. Once he sensed there was a possibility she could forgive him, he'd tell her everything. For now, he must convince her to give him one last chance to make her happy. Or die trying.

"I promise you, I'll never willingly go within a mile of Lon's wife ever again. I swear it wasn't any hankering for her that took me up those stairs awhile ago. You're the only woman I want, and I've been a damned fool to pretend any different."

He bent his head, brushing his cheek down her ear and the slender line of her neck, along the elegant contour of her bare shoulder. There it came to rest.

"Can you blame a man who's never known love for not recognizing it when it coldcocks him right between the eyes?"

Beneath his bandages, his palms grew clammy. Though he tried to still them, his knees trembled. He'd been plenty scared on the eve of several battles, but never like this. Caddie's answer mattered more to him than anything in this world or the next.

If Del Marsh had suddenly risen from the grave and come between them, Manning feared he might kill the man again. Damn the consequences. And doubly damn his soul.

Did she dare give her heart to a man who could make the iron ramrod of her pride melt into a pitiful puddle? The notion frightened Caddie worse than the fiery sack of Richmond.

Looking back, she realized her marriage to Del had been a lot like the war. They'd waged their battles of will with no outward show of violence, not even angry words. There had been victories and defeats just the same. Occasional truces, renewed hostilities and escalating bitterness.

In the end, they'd both lost.

There had to be a better way. Could she and Manning both find victory in mutual surrender?

She couldn't find the words to ask him—wasn't sure she had the courage to speak them, anyhow.

Instead, she settled for nuzzling his crisp dense crop of hair with her neck. When he turned his face and pressed his lips to the base of her throat, she could not hold back a keening, quivering sigh that betrayed her longing for him. Her mouth hungered for his kisses with the kind of hollow ache that had lodged in her stomach during the bleak days after the Confederacy fell.

But she would not kiss him or beg him to kiss her. That one stubborn nub of pride restrained Caddie. If Manning cared for her the way he made it sound, was it too much to hope he'd finally scale or smash whatever barrier held him back from her?

The waiting became sweet torment as Manning hovered behind her, laying siege to her exposed neck and shoulders with his lips and the tips of his fingers. Caddie shut her eyes, the better to concentrate on the wonder of his touch. Fiber by fiber, he eased the tight knots that anger and hurt had tied in her flesh, telling her in a language deeper and truer than words how precious she had become to him.

And she had no choice but to believe.

With every runaway lurch of her heart and every stormy gust of her breath, her craving to touch *him* grew. Memories of their first time together broke free of the wards she'd placed on them—riding roughshod over judgment and propriety.

Why a man of such fierce restraint should provoke such wildness in her puzzled and frightened Caddie. But confusion and fear only whetted a sharper edge on her recklessness.

Just when she was sure she could stand it no longer—certain she must scream or swoon, or turn and plant a scorching kiss on Manning—he spun her toward him. Their lips collided, and Caddie could almost picture a shower of sparks exploding around them.

No woman who'd been kissed the way Manning kissed her now could entertain any serious doubts about his desire or her desirability. The mellow taste of hickory and the sweet tang of lemonade mingled on his breath without the faintest taint of moonshine. If he cut loose now, there could be only one excuse.

Passion.

At last Manning gathered his composure, like a pack of hunting dogs in full bay straining on their leashes, and pulled away from her.

Caddie clung to the lapels of his coat. "If…you're about to lecture on morals…" She gasped for air. "Or warn me that we shouldn't go any further…so help me, I'll pick up those dishes and throw them at you!"

A smile lit Manning's face, even brighter and warmer than the special ones he reserved for the children. He laughed like Caddie had never heard him laugh before—as if he wasn't holding anything back.

"Oh, Caddie-girl." He took her face in his bandaged hands with a gentleness that bordered on reverence, but the fire in his eyes said he wanted her in a way that was anything but sacred.

Or maybe it was sacred, after all.

His voice hushed to the soft murmur of distant waves breaking against some lonely stretch of Low Country shore. "I know I already asked you to marry me, but we both meant something different back then. Now I need to know, are you willing to let me be a husband to you?"

Caddie drew a deep breath to fuel her reply, then found her throat too constricted to speak.

Perhaps Manning misread her hesitation. "I know I can't take Del's place, and I don't want to."

She pressed her finger against his lips to hush such talk. The last thing she wanted him to do was take Del's place, but now wasn't the time to go into all that. Sometime, though, when she felt a little more secure in his love for her and hers for him. Right now they were a pair of wobbly foals, just finding their feet after a difficult and dangerous birth.

In her desire to reassure him, she found her voice again. "You don't need to take *anybody's* place. You've made your own place in my heart and my children's."

His gaze wavered before hers. Had she misspoken?

The significance of what he'd called himself dawned on Caddie—*a man who's never known love.* Remembering what he'd told her about his childhood, so much about the baffling man became clearer. Why he worked so hard to win her affection, then shrank from accepting it. Like some mistreated animal who snarled when you went to pet it, because it had learned to expect blows from an approaching hand instead of caresses.

She hadn't made it any easier for him. Once bitten, twice shy, she'd been too quick to pull back.

Well, not tonight.

Her finger still lingered on Manning's lips. Now Caddie ran it over them. "In so many ways you've been a fine husband to me. Maybe it's greedy to want more, but I do. And I want it tonight—right now." Her lips twisted up in a fleeting half smile. "Before you think better of the idea."

Kissing the pad of her finger, Manning glanced at the table. "The dishes?"

Tempted as she was to say they'd keep until morning, Caddie didn't want them drawing flies, either. "We can scrape them off and set them to soak—that shouldn't take long."

It didn't, either.

Caddie chuckled to herself at the zest with which they tackled the chore. The speed of their movements betrayed their eagerness for one another. When she caught Manning watching her with wistful hunger in his eyes, her knees would go weak. Meeting in a doorway, they would brush against each other in passing, making Caddie's bosom tingle.

By the time they had all the dishes soaking, the pair of them practically tripped over one another racing up the stairs.

"My room tonight," Caddie whispered as she tugged Manning over the threshold.

She didn't want any unpleasant memories of the morning after their last encounter to taint her enjoyment of this one. Nor could she stand the thought that a ghost of Lydene's strong perfume might still haunt Manning's bed.

He couldn't blame it on moonshine this time.

Manning's heart hammered hard and fast against his ribs—almost as much from the dread of what he was about to do as from his potent desire for Caddie.

Everything in his conscience screamed that this was wrong. He remembered the old Bible story from the Book of Samuel, how God had cursed King David after the king sent Uriah to die in battle, so he could have the dead man's wife. For the first time, Manning pitied David.

Caddie seemed to sense the struggle within him. "You don't have to do this if you don't want to. I won't kick you out of the house or anything."

It would hurt her, though. She tried not to show it, but Manning could tell just the same.

"I want to." Surely she would hear the raw need trembling in his voice, and believe him.

Her hunger to be cherished and desired must come before everything. Even before his warped urge to punish himself.

Manning shut the door behind him. He pictured himself shutting out his doubts, his dread and anything else that might cast a shadow over the loving he was about to give this woman.

Late-summer twilight deepened and a warm breeze wafted in the partly open window.

"In that case—" Caddie stepped toward him and began to untie his cravat "—could I get you to unfasten my dress? Some of the hooks are fearful hard to reach."

Manning shrugged out of his coat. "I guess I could manage that, seeing as you had to undress us both last time."

Presenting her back to him, Caddie lit a candle on top of her bureau. "May as well be able to see what you're doing."

She meant to keep her tone light and casual, Manning was pretty sure, but a beseeching note crept into it in spite of her. For some reason, this mattered to her.

It mattered to him, too. Manning's fingers fumbled with the tiny hooks down the back of her dress. This wasn't a case of all cats being gray in the dark. Caddie didn't want just any warm male body as a substitute for the husband she'd lost.

She wanted *him* and he must not fail her.

Turn about, they undressed one another. Only the quickening rasps of their breath frayed the edge of their intent silence. When the last of Caddie's undergarments had parted company from her glorious body, Manning could keep silent no longer.

"I can't believe it." He shook his head, amazed.

"Believe what?" Caddie glanced down at herself, a spasm of embarrassment contorting her features.

Manning reached out and stroked a long red-brown curl that dangled over her shoulder. "That you could be any more beautiful than I remembered."

She couldn't dismiss his words as flattery when his body bore such compelling witness to their truth.

Manning leaned past her to twitch back the bedclothes, then he took Caddie in his arms and eased her down onto the sheets. As a warm July night enfolded the Virginia countryside, Manning satisfied Caddie, by touch and kiss and whispered word, that she was everything he'd ever dreamed of in a woman. And so much more than he had ever hoped to find.

He fashioned himself into an instrument for her pleasure, all his senses alert to the faintest sound or movement that might suggest what she wanted next.

He couldn't deny that part of what she wanted was to caress him, explore his body and give him pleasure, too. Something in him tried to resist the seductive power of her touch, withholding a scrap of reason to sit in judgment on the rest of him. In the end, he could resist her no more than oil-soaked tinder could resist the kiss of the flame.

The first time they'd made love, on that drunken stormy night, he'd felt enough to pierce the thick fog of his pain and stupor, winging him away to bliss. Tonight the intensity of sensation tread a razor-fine edge past which pleasure must become pain—perhaps even death.

Leisurely at first, their kissing and fondling grew more and more fevered until they blundered together, straining for release. As Caddie whimpered and panted in his arms, her body clutched Manning in a series of delicious spasms that pulverized his consciousness into a handful of glittering dust and scattered it to the four winds.

When he woke to a pearly dawn, Manning held Caddie and stroked her hair. He didn't give her a chance to look into his eyes, though, in case she should find some lingering regret there and mistake its cause.

"Whereabouts are you going to sleep tonight?" she teased him.

After a long simmering kiss, he replied, "Wherever you want me to."

They both chuckled, knowing where that would be.

After breakfast, they washed up the dishes from the party. Then the whole family went to church in Mercer's Corner, where their neighbors politely pretended as if nothing untoward had passed at the barbecue.

For lunch they ate a cold collation of food left over from the party. At Tem and Varina's urging, all four of them, and the dog, went fishing. Though they didn't catch so much as a tadpole, the whole family had a fine time.

Finally, late in the afternoon, Manning stole away to his bedroom, determined once and for all to destroy Caddie's last letter to Delbert Marsh.

When he could not find it in the wooden box on his bureau, at the bottom of his rucksack or in the breast pocket of any of his coats or shirts, he understood at last why he had kept it all this time.

Because deep down, some part of him had wanted to be caught and punished for what he'd done.

Now he would be.

Chapter Twenty

Something was eating that man alive from the inside out. He thought he had her fooled, the way he managed to fool the children, but Caddie wasn't deceived. If there had been such a disease as consumption of the soul, that's exactly what she would have diagnosed. As the golden days and warm fragrant nights of summer passed, Caddie pondered the possible cause of Manning's condition and searched with growing desperation for a cure.

Many men fretted over their business affairs, but Caddie knew that couldn't be Manning's trouble. She kept the books, after all. Ever since the sale of the family silver had paid off their back taxes and provided a small cushion of capital, orders had begun to pour in. Manning and Bobbie were talking over plans to build a second shop, closer to the main road and fully enclosed so they could continue to make furniture even after the creek froze and the mill sat idle during the winter months.

If anything, the load that seemed to weigh her husband down lightened when he was engrossed in his work.

From her seat on the porch, shelling peas, Caddie heard the whoops and squeals of the children playing with Jeff Pratt's little nephew. Tem and Varina provided a powerful but temporary antidote to whatever ailed Manning. When he became absorbed in one of their games, or in reading to them here on the porch before bedtime, Caddie would watch and brood over the three of them, tantalized by visions of the truly happy life they could have. If only...

The front door opened and Dora appeared with the broom. She began to sweep the porch, humming a tune under her breath and moving with swaying, dancelike steps. Her sweet, dreamy smile put Caddie in mind of a velvety pansy, dark and demure.

"Once you're finished here, why don't you leave early today, dear? Ann told me you'd offered to walk little Rafe up to the mill to meet Jeff."

Dora broke from her private musings with a guilty blush. "I believe I'll take you up on that, Miz Caddie. Thank you."

"Does that mean you and Jeff are courting?"

"Something like that." Dora sighed. "Ann and Bobbie have asked us to stand up with them when they get married. Jeff has this prideful notion that a blind husband would be a great burden to me."

Caddie shook her head. "Men! Their minds just don't work the same as ours. I hope you're succeeding in talking some sense into him."

"I reckon I'm making headway." Dora tried to look demure.

"Good for you." Caddie chuckled. "Now scoot off and see if you can make a little more."

When Dora had gone, still humming the fiddle tune to which she and Jeff had danced at the barbecue, Caddie wandered inside to start supper.

If work wasn't the problem with Manning, she decided as she fried a mess of chicken, and neither were the children, could it be her? Old doubts about herself as a woman and a wife insisted she must be to blame. But when she remembered how Manning worshipped her in the privacy of her bedroom, a stubborn confidence took root, assuring her that was not the trouble, either.

Part of her wanted to keep up a cheerful facade and ignore whatever was wrong, hoping and trusting it would go away in time. Experience warned her that life's challenges needed to be faced and overcome. Tonight she would cradle him to her bosom and ask him to tell her what was wrong. Beg him if necessary.

And if he didn't unburden himself tonight, she'd ask again tomorrow and the next night and the next, assuring him that she would love him no matter what.

Perhaps she could find the courage to trade him one painful secret for another, by telling him about Del and Lydene.

When Manning saw Lon Marsh, he knew his own personal Judgment Day had arrived at last.

His crew had all left for the day and he'd been just about to head home for supper.

"What do you want, Marsh?" he challenged, as if he didn't know.

Leave it to Lon to wait awhile before confronting him. Playing him like an increasingly exhausted trout on the end of a fly rod. Letting uncertainty and worry snag him like a sharp hook. Paying out just enough line to tease him with false hope. Now Lon had come to reel in his catch.

With slow, mocking movements, Lon drew from his breast pocket...a cigar.

As Manning released his bated breath, Lon made a leisurely ritual of trimming and lighting his smoke. "It's not so much what I *want,* Yankee. You and I both know what that is."

Again he reached into his pocket. "It's more about what I've *got.*" This time he withdrew a piece of paper.

Manning didn't have to ask what it was. "How'd you get hold of that?"

"Does it matter?" Lon grinned. "Let's just say my wife doesn't often miss a trick. I take it as a grave personal insult you spurned Lydene's favors when she offered them. She told me you must have something in that box on your bureau that you didn't want folks to see. I came back in later and had a peek. Danged if Lydene wasn't right."

Lon turned the paper in his hand, looking at it from several different angles. "What beats the hell out of me is why you kept it around all this time? Were you brazen, or forgetful, or just plain stupid?"

Manning didn't reply. He'd finally figured out the answer to that question himself, and he didn't owe Lon Marsh the truth of it.

His silence seemed to vex the man worse than a scornful retort.

Del's letter clutched in his fist, Lon stabbed the air with his forefinger. "The only reason folks around here have accepted you is because they think you're my brother masquerading as a Yankee." He gave a harsh snort of laughter. "As if Del'd be smart enough to dream up a scheme like that.

"We both know better, though, don't we, Carpetbagger? The only way you could have come by this letter is if you took it off my brother's dead body. Right after you killed him."

Not right after. Several long hours—the worst of Manning's life—had passed between firing that shot and receiving the letter. And he hadn't taken it. Del had given it to him. None of that altered Lon's charge, or the verdict.

"Guilty!" cried Lon. "It's written all over your face."

Manning shrugged. "What are you going to do about it? No court's going to convict one soldier of killing another in battle."

That rocked Lon back on his heels, but only for a second. "I don't need no judge and jury to make you swing, Yankee. What do you reckon Caddie'll say when she finds out it was you made her a widow? Or those young'uns you make so much of. How are they going to look at you when they hear tell you're the Yankee who shot their pa? What about all these folks who work for you and take on like you're the Second Coming of Stonewall Jackson? I reckon they'll change their tune when they find out you aren't my brother, after all, but a real live Yankee who cut him down in his prime."

Backed into a corner with nothing left to lose, Manning found his self-respect again. He pulled himself up tall. "In that case, what are you doing here? Why aren't you down in the parlor of Sabbath Hollow telling all this to Caddie?"

Lon took a long draw on his cigar, expelling the smoke in a leisurely breath. He smiled at Manning like a schoolmaster whose star pupil had just ciphered a complicated equation.

"You know the answer to that as well as I do. I've got something you want—this letter and my silence. And you've got something I want." He jerked his head in the direction of Sabbath Hollow. "This plantation. Nothing's going to bring my brother back, so I might as well salvage what I can for myself."

"And your brother's widow and children can go to hell?" snapped Manning.

"Or Oregon." Lon shrugged. "Makes no difference to me. If you can convince Caddie to deed Sabbath Hollow to me, you can take her and the young'uns wherever you want to start over."

"You mean it?"

He'd thought the hour of reckoning was upon him. Instead Lon was offering to let him off with all that really mattered to him. Now that Caddie'd had time to realize

Sabbath Hollow would never be more than a shabby shadow of its former glory, she might be prepared to go elsewhere. Someplace not haunted by ghosts from the past. Someplace a boy like Tem could make his own way in the world, rather than being weighed down by family tradition and the expectations of his elders.

Manning had the skills to make a decent living for them wherever they went. It would be even easier in the booming economy of the North than here with the upkeep of that grand house like a millstone around their necks.

And yet...

"What if I can't talk Caddie into it?"

With a flourish, Lon tucked the letter back into his coat pocket. "You'd better try to be real persuasive, Carpetbagger. I'm givin' you twenty-four hours to be off my property."

He pivoted on the toe of one well-polished riding boot and sauntered back to where he'd tethered his horse. Mounting with careless grace, Alonzo Marsh rode away without once looking back.

Manning watched him go, wondering what he'd have done if he'd been carrying his Union issue rifle just then. At least if he shot Lon Marsh, he'd have a reason.

For what seemed like a long time after Lon rode off, Manning stood in the mill clearing while his heart wrestled his conscience for control of his future. Finally, when each had beaten the other bloody, he stumbled back to Sabbath Hollow.

To talk with Caddie.

They must talk.

Whether she had to threaten, wheedle, badger or plead, Caddie refused to let another night go by without finding out what was eating at her husband.

She watched him at supper with the children, pretending

to enjoy her fried chicken and beaten biscuits, exclaiming over the children's account of their day, while his eyes betrayed the anguish inside of him.

"Rafe helped us learn Sergeant a new trick today," announced Varina.

"Did he, indeed? And what trick might that be? Not picking pockets, I hope."

"Uh-uh."

"Well, that's a relief. I don't suppose you taught him to howl 'The Star Spangled Banner'? A body could make good money in the music halls with a stunt like that."

"No-oo!" Varina wrinkled up her nose. "That's silly."

"I guess it is." Manning winked at Tem, who shook with laughter. "It's no use hoping you'd taught the Sergeant a real exciting trick like jumping through a barrel hoop. That'd be far too hard."

"We did it! We did—honest."

"Well, that's truly amazing. Any chance you'd put on a show for your ma and me after supper?"

"Yessiree! Come on, Tem. We got to practice."

After the children darted off, Caddie cleared their plates in silence. Returning to the table, she stopped behind Manning's chair and slipped her arms around his neck. "*That* was quite a performance. Tem and Varina will never guess there's anything bothering you, but you can't fool me."

His shoulders bowed. "Then it couldn't have been much of a performance, after all."

She nuzzled his hair with her cheek and tightened her hold on him. "I can't let this go on any longer. One way or another, I am going to find out what's been tearing at you. Now. Tonight. I didn't survive everything I have by taking no for an answer."

A sigh gusted out of him—the saddest, weariest sound Caddie had ever heard. "Give me this one more hour before the children go to bed. That's all I ask."

He sounded like a condemned prisoner requesting a last meal. Caddie almost recanted her demand for answers. If the trouble was that bad, maybe she'd be better off *not* knowing about it. But she couldn't let Manning continue to shoulder the burden alone.

She tightened her embrace, pressing her face into his hair, willing her love and support into him. "Whatever's wrong, maybe we can find a way to fix it."

For the longest time he didn't reply, just sat there. Then he disengaged one of her hands from around his neck and raised it to his lips.

"You said it yourself, Caddie—some things can't be forgiven." The hoarseness of his voice rasped across her heart. "And some things can't be fixed."

Could the man be dying of some incurable disease? she wondered as Manning put on a brave face to watch Sergeant's tricks and help her put Tem and Varina to bed. If he was, she hadn't seen or felt any sign of it on his lean, firm-muscled body during the nights they'd spent together. Were their nights together numbered, too?

Closing the children's door behind them, Caddie reached for Manning's hand. "I know I said I wanted some answers tonight, but now that I think on it, perhaps it can wait till morning. Things always look better after a good sleep."

Did the husky note of desire in her voice tell him she wasn't thinking about sleep?

Perhaps.

Manning shook his head, but reluctantly, as though his body wasn't anxious to cooperate. "One more night with you would only make it harder to do what I have to do, Caddie-girl."

He headed for the stairs, towing her behind him. "Let's go sit on the porch. I don't want the children overhearing us."

"All right."

A whippoorwill called from the hollow as they seated themselves. For some reason the odd whistling cry struck Caddie as plaintive. As if the little woodland bird was bidding its mate farewell or calling in vain for one it had lost.

"Can I get you anything?" she asked when several protracted minutes passed without a word from Manning. "There's a drop or two of moonshine left over from the barbecue."

"No, thanks. I want my head clear to say what I have to. If I drink I'm liable to make a damn fool of myself on top of everything else."

"Suit yourself."

"Where the hell do I start?" Manning kneaded his knotted brow with his fingers.

Caddie's patience snapped. "Anywhere! Just tell me and be done with it."

He turned and looked at her, chastened, accepting the rebuke as his due. "I'm not trying to drag this out, Caddie, honest. I just want to lead into it so it doesn't come as too bad a shock."

"I believe I could abide a shock better than this waiting and imagining all sorts of terrible things."

Manning nodded. "Very well. I guess you and I were set on a course toward one another early in May of '64."

Caddie's heart seemed to swell and rise until it blocked her throat. She couldn't speak—struggled to breathe.

"We were inspecting one of our pickets on the right flank when half a dozen rebel cavalry blundered into us," Manning began.

She might not have been sitting there struggling to take in his words. Manning would never have known the difference. In his mind he was back at that spring day over two years ago. On the right flank of that tangle of forest near Chancellorsville.

"The whole bloody mess was over in a few minutes. I

ended up with a couple of nicks and a busted ankle. The rest were all dead, except for a cavalry officer I'd shot.''

Caddie felt as though someone had shot *her* and every drop of blood was draining from her body.

"Off to the left I heard the battle commencing. I knew I wouldn't be any use to my company, the shape my leg was in. I didn't dare try to move the wounded man—I could tell he wasn't going to make it. If I'd had the stomach, I might have finished him off, but he didn't seem to be in too much pain, just weak and fading..." Manning's voice trailed off.

I'm sitting here beside the Yankee who shot my husband. I've let him live in my house all these months. Taken him into my bed. This can't be happening. It must be a nightmare.

Letting loose a shaky sigh, like a distant locomotive shuddering into motion, Manning began to speak again. "Either he didn't know it was me who shot him, or it just didn't make any difference to him. He talked about his home and his family, mentioned the pump out behind the stable over and over. I couldn't figure why at the time.''

The pump. The silver. Tem had told her Manning knew. None of his explanations or proof of his identity had explained how that was possible. Once she'd been satisfied he wasn't Del, she'd looked no further. Now her stomach had joined her heart up in her throat. Caddie strained to swallow a mouthful of bile.

"I'd shot plenty of the enemy during my soldiering days. But he was the only one I had to watch die. And when I looked in his face, I saw my own. Before he died, he gave me your last letter. He made me promise to find you and his children after the war and look after you. That's what I've tried to do.''

He didn't love her—never had. The certain knowledge

sickened Caddie worse than anything she'd heard about Del's death.

Manning Forbes had married her out of guilt, then bedded her out of pity laced with lust. She felt so dirty she wanted to rub herself raw with the harshest lye soap she could lay hands on.

"I'm sorry, Caddie." Manning reached for her. "I didn't mean for you to find out like this."

"Don't touch me!"

She leaped from the seat like a scalded cat and backed away from him as though his confession had made him a stranger again. A dangerous stranger armed with all sorts of intimate knowledge about her.

"How could I have been such a blind fool?" It all made a kind of macabre sense now. All the questions, the suspicions, the baffling inconsistencies. Caddie looked back on the idyllic life she thought she'd been leading and saw one huge lie.

He'd played a warped black joke on her and she'd been too gullible a love-starved fool to see it. Even as she gazed at him hunched over on the porch seat, his face buried in his hands, some weak, pathetic little ninny inside her wanted to lie naked beneath him and quiver at his touch.

His power over her infuriated Caddie as much as any other wrong he'd done her.

"Get out of my house, you lying carpetbagger, and don't ever come back. I rue the day I first laid eyes on you!"

Manning rose from the seat. "I was afraid that's what you'd say. I'm sorry you had to hear it like this, Caddie. I'm sorry I wasn't honest with you from the beginning. I'm sorry—"

"Don't!" Caddie clamped her hands over her ears. Next he'd probably tell her how sorry he was about letting her lure him into her bed. "Just go!"

He nodded, and Caddie saw his lips form the words, "Yes, ma'am."

She removed her hands from her ears and wrapped them tightly around herself to keep from reaching for him. Then she turned away, so the sight of him wouldn't stir unwelcome feelings in her. Feelings like passion...or compassion.

"I'm going to send you money for the children, and I want you to use it. Not for my sake, but for theirs and for...your husband's. He wanted you looked after."

He had a fine way of showing it. Caddie swallowed the bitter retort. Was there a woman in all the former Confederate states who chose worse husbands than she did?

Manning persisted. "I'm going to keep in touch with Bobbie Stevens. If you or the children ever need anything, I want you to let him know so he can get a message to me."

"Fine. I'll do that." Promise him whatever he asked to get him out of there before her resolve weakened.

Caddie listened as he walked to the front door, opened it and went inside. Presently, through his open bedroom window above, she heard the sounds of him packing his few worldly possessions.

She held herself still. Frozen like brittle ice, she didn't dare move lest she shatter.

Behind her the door opened and shut again, and Manning's footsteps moved away. Then they paused.

"I had no right to love you, but I couldn't help myself. Goodbye, Caddie."

The frigid force of pride and stubbornness held her together long enough for Manning to retreat out of earshot. Then the ice statue that was Caddie melted onto the porch floorboards in a thaw of bitter tears.

Chapter Twenty-One

Considering he'd just passed the worst night of his life, Manning felt at peace with himself for the first time in months—maybe years.

As he had on that long-ago night in April, Manning sat on the rise overlooking Sabbath Hollow, keeping watch on the sleeping house. He'd get Bobbie to hire someone to guard the place at night for a while. He'd also let Lon Marsh know, in no uncertain terms, that he'd be quick and ruthless to avenge any harm that came to Caddie or the children.

Caddie and the children.

He'd carry them forever in his heart, a constant ache that would remind him he had lived and loved. If it weren't for the fact that his lies had hurt Caddie and his leaving would hurt the children, he would not regret anything he'd done on his own account. He'd trade the whole rest of his life, before and since, for this one bittersweet summer when he'd been a husband and father. Loving and beloved.

The sun had risen awhile ago. Time for him to be on his way. Maybe now and then in the years to come, he'd return to this spot and listen for the dog's bark, Tem and Varina's laughter, the sound of Caddie's voice calling them in to supper.

Manning hefted the rucksack over his shoulder and turned away from the one place that had been a home to him.

"Where're you going?" Tem's query slammed into Manning like an artillery shell, blowing his stoic composure to smithereens.

He turned. The truth might hurt them both, but he was done with lies, no matter how well intentioned. "I'm not sure, Son."

"When're you coming back?" Tem yawned and stretched. His arms looked a lot less scrawny than when he'd first come to Sabbath Hollow. He held himself differently, too—at the same time straighter and more relaxed. With all his heart Manning prayed his going wouldn't change that.

He shook his head. "Can't say."

"Does that mean...you're leaving? For good?"

"I wish I didn't have to, Tem. Maybe when you're older you'll understand why."

"No, I won't. I'll never understand it and I'll never like it! Neither will Rina. She doesn't know what a carpetbagger is, but I do. It's a Yankee who comes here to make a pile of money, then skedaddles back up North."

Perhaps the boy was trying to shame him into staying.

"You'd better get home to breakfast, Son."

"How come you call me that? I'm not your son."

"No. But I'm as proud of you, and I think as much of you as if you were."

"Then don't go 'way. If you do, I'll..." The boy seemed to be conjuring up the direst threat he could imagine. "I'll run off and go live with Uncle Lon—so there!"

"No, Tem. You stay away from your uncle Lon, you hear me? I don't think he's really a bad man, but he wants

something so much he doesn't care anymore what he has
to do to get it—lie, cheat, steal.'' Were he and Lon all that
different at heart?

"I want you to promise me you'll never let that happen
to you, Tem. If you want something you can't get by honest
means, let it be, no matter how much you hanker for it.''

"I'll promise if you'll stay.''

"I can't. I'm sorry that makes you feel bad, but this is
how it has to be.''

"Because of my ma? I thought she liked you now. I've
seen her kiss you and she says your name the special way
she says Rina's and mine—like it tastes good. If she's being
mean to you again, I'll—''

"No, Tem. Your ma's not making me go.'' So much for
his resolution to tell the brutal truth. "It's something else
I need you to look after your ma and Varina once I'm gone
You'll be the man of the family.''

"I ain't a man!'' The child threw his arms around Manning's legs and began to wail. "I'm just a little boy, and
you hadn't ought to leave, you danged carpetbagger!''

Apart from watching Tem's father die, and tearing his
mother to pieces by telling her about it, Manning had never
done anything harder in his life than detach himself from
the sobbing child and walk away—leaving a great chunk
of his heart raw and bleeding in the dust behind him.

Just like when he'd burned his hands, the pain made
Manning blind and deaf to everything around him. He
stumbled up the lane and onto the main road, heading for
Mercer's Corner.

He almost walked right into Lon Marsh's sleek bay.

"I don't like the looks of this, Carpetbagger,'' Lon
growled. "Where're Caddie and the young'uns? Have you
got my deed?''

All Manning's hurt ignited into rage. "It isn't *your* deed
and it never will be!''

He knew this was all his own fault. Lon Marsh had done nothing more than exploit the situation for his own ends. Still, it felt good for once to blame somebody else.

"I told Caddie the truth and now I'm leaving. But I'm not going far, so don't entertain any fool ideas about getting your hands on Sabbath Hollow. I almost gunned you down once to run you off Caddie's property and I wouldn't hesitate a second to do it if you harm a hair on my family's heads."

From his lofty perch, Lon glared down. "Damn you straight to hell, Yankee! Did my brother send you here just to bedevil me?"

"I guess neither of us is getting what we want out of this, Lon. Let's think of it as a lesson in character building." Manning skirted the horse and continued on his way to town.

Behind him a revolver cocked. "Not so fast, Yankee. If I'm not going to get compensation for my brother's death, I reckon I'll have to settle for revenge."

Why hadn't the man just pulled out a gun and shot her the way he'd shot Del? Caddie wondered. It probably wouldn't have hurt as much as what he'd put her through.

Or had she put herself through it?

Once her initial shock and outrage had begun to subside, she'd tried to separate what Manning had said from her own assumptions. It was useless. Once she'd realized he was responsible for Del's death, and that he'd only come to Sabbath Hollow to salve his conscience, she'd stopped listening to the words that came out of his mouth in favor of the ones that swirled inside her own head.

She remembered his last words though. They'd been branded onto her heart with red-hot irons. *I had no right to love you, but I couldn't help myself.*

Could she believe him? After everything that had happened with Del and now with Manning, could she trust him? Even if it was possible, against all pride, was it too late for them to start over?

Varina padded into the kitchen, rubbing her eyes. "Where's Tem?"

"Isn't he upstairs?" A clammy hand squeezed Caddie's innards hard.

"Uh-uh." Varina shook her head vigorously. "He was gone when I woked up. Did Manning take him fishing early and leave me behind? If they did…"

"No, dear. Tem's not fishing. I'll go fetch him in for breakfast. Can you dress yourself, like a big girl?"

"Can I pick which clothes?"

Caddie was already halfway out the door. "Fine, just as long as it's not your Sunday best. I'll be back in a few minutes—now scoot!"

Outside, she called Templeton's name several times with no response. At least none from the boy. After her second try Sergeant came loping around from the front of the house. The dog let out a loud bark every time she called after that.

"Will you hush so Tem can hear me?" she scolded.

The dog whined and his ears dropped a little, but his tail whipped back and forth in an ingratiating manner.

"Can you find Tem, boy?"

Sergeant barked. Off like a shot, the dog circled around the house and up the lane. Caddie panted along behind him, praying Tem wasn't in any danger. After the boy's drastic reactions to her past quarrels with Manning, she dreaded to think how this irreparable breach might crush Tem's sensitive spirit.

How could she have been so selfish as to send Manning away without even considering her children's feelings? They adored Manning and he adored them. What might have begun as an obligation to their dead father had rapidly grown into something deep and genuine.

Could the same be true of his feelings for her, or was she just trying to fool herself again?

Up ahead on the road she could make out a small figure running toward her. Thank heaven he was all right!

Caddie ran to meet him, arms outstretched to offer a mother's comfort. As Tem came closer, she could tell he'd been crying, hard.

"Come on, precious. It's going to be all right."

Tem resisted her effort to gather him close. Sniffling and swiping away tears with the back of his hand, he cried, "Manning's going away, Mama!"

Caddie's heart lurched in her chest as if it had just begun to beat again. Tem had said *going,* not *gone.*

"You have to stop him." The boy grabbed her sleeve and pulled her up the road. "He'll listen to you. I know he will."

"But, Tem, honey, we'll never catch up with him."

"Sure we will. He's talking to Uncle Lon right now. Just 'round the next bend."

Lon. If her world was crashing down around her yet again, chances were good Lon and Lydene had a hand in it.

"Very well, then. I'll go talk to him. But I need you and Sergeant to go back to the house and watch Varina. Who knows what mischief she'll get into on her own? I'll bring Manning back to the house if he'll come, and we can all talk to him."

And listen. With her ears this time, and her heart, instead of her oversensitive pride.

"Go on, now."

"Don't be long, Mama."

"I won't." To prove it she picked up her skirts and hurried down the road.

As soon as she rounded the bend she saw them—Lon seated with lordly grace on his fine bay mare and Manning standing his ground, the rucksack slung over his shoulder. For an instant she wondered where he had spent the night. Then she knew.

"What's going on here?" she called out in a breathless voice as she approached them.

Manning answered first. "Go home, Caddie!"

He hadn't spoken to her in so peremptory a manner since that morning after the first night they'd spent together. Had she just imagined his reluctance about leaving last night? Or after the hysteria with which she'd greeted his confession, had he decided he was well rid of her?

Then Caddie saw the gun in Lon's hand and she knew Manning had been trying to protect her. From the very first minute they'd met, he'd been trying to protect her from someone or something. Most recently he'd been trying to protect her from the truth he knew would hurt her so badly, even though the lies were gnawing him to pieces.

"Don't run off, Caddie," barked Lon. "This Yankee claims he told you how he killed Del, but I reckon he just slunk away without saying anything."

What was Caddie doing here? Though Manning burned to know, and his whole being ached with joy at seeing her one last time, he wished she'd turn around and scurry back home like he'd ordered her. If any harm came to her on his account, he'd never be able to live with that corrosive knowledge.

Caddie flung her reply at Lon. "He told me."

Astonishment got the better of Lon's rage for about five seconds. "In that case, maybe I ought to give you the satisfaction of shooting the varmint."

"Hand me the gun."

Both men stared at Caddie for an instant, slack-jawed. Manning tried to get his mouth to work so he could warn her that Lon's offer was a trap. With him dead and her in jail, nothing would stand between Lon and Sabbath Hollow. Or between Lon and the children.

That thought knocked the air out of Manning as handily as a hard jab in the belly.

Caddie held out her hand for the pistol, but Lon shook his head. "Tut-tut, now. Do you take me for a fool, woman? How do I know you wouldn't blow a hole in me, instead?"

"I'd be sorely tempted, Lon, you can be sure of that."

"After all that's happened, you're not still mooning for this Yankee, are you?" Lon sneered. "Why, he doesn't care a fig for you and those young'uns. If he did, he would have jumped at the chance I offered him to take the three of you away from here and nobody the wiser—Sabbath Hollow back in Marsh hands where it belongs."

"The chance *you* gave him?" Caddie looked as if she'd been struck by a bolt of lightning out of a blue sky.

"I found that damn letter he took off Del." Somewhat awkwardly with his left hand, Lon fished the paper out of his coat pocket and threw it to the ground at Caddie's feet. "I gave him twenty-four hours to talk you into leaving Sabbath Hollow or I'd show it to you. The carpetbagger here had to go get noble and stupid. If he gave half a damn about y'all, you'd be on a train out of the state by now."

Manning couldn't keep silent a moment longer. "That's not true, Caddie."

Let Lon put a bullet in him. He couldn't stand having Caddie think he'd chosen this course because he didn't love her enough to cheat her children out of their birthright.

She chewed on her bottom lip, and Manning thought he spied a faint glitter of moisture in her eyes.

He shut his mouth. After the way he'd deceived Caddie since coming to Sabbath Hollow, what could he say at this late date that he had any right to hope she might believe?

"Put your gun away, Lon, and I'll give you what you want." With an air of regal defiance, Caddie hurled the words at her brother-in-law.

"Huh?" Lon scratched his chin, clearly not grasping her intent.

Manning did, and it staggered him. After all that had happened, Caddie was willing to forfeit her dearest dream...for him. If Lon Marsh gunned him down right now, he would die a perfectly happy man.

What he couldn't do was live with the burden of that sacrifice. "No, Caddie, I won't let you do this."

"I don't see how you can stop me." She probably meant to sound tart. The look on her face told Manning this decision might have been quick, but it hadn't been easy.

"Think of Templeton...Varina..."

She shook her. "They need a pa who loves them the way you do a whole lot worse than they need any piece of land." Caddie sounded more resolute with every word. "And I need a live husband I can raise my children and grow old with more than I need to hang on to memories of a past that's dead and gone."

"Hush up," snapped Lon, "before you make me puke. Let's go back to Sabbath Hollow so you can sign that deed over to me."

Something about Lon's voice and posture told Manning that this bargain had sucked most of the sweetness from his triumph.

Despite what Caddie had said, Manning realized there was something he could do to stop her. He could rush Lon and disarm him, or take a bullet, canceling this unholy transaction.

Before he could act, the woods beside the road roared to life. Sergeant burst out, baying like all the hounds of hell. Hot on the dog's heels, howling like bloodthirsty barbarians, raced Tem and Varina.

What happened next took seconds. But to Manning it felt as though the hourglass of time had squeezed tight in the middle, passing only one single grain of sand after another.

Templeton carried Manning's rifle in a way that showed he hadn't a clue how to fire it. Manning knew the weapon couldn't be loaded. The hatchet in Varina's hand scared him far worse.

Not as bad as the whole attack scared Lon's horse, though. The big bay reared, its powerful front hooves flailing. In an instant, they would plunge back to earth, striking down the slender boy who froze in the horse's path.

Manning sprang forward. Tem's cry echoed in his ears as he tackled the child to the ground, shielding him from the bay's lethal hooves. Before the thunder of pain and darkness came a single lightning bolt of exultation.

Having taken the life of one Marsh, Manning now gave his up for another. His soul belonged to him again.

"Am I going to lose him?" Caddie searched Doc Mercer's eyes, not caring how pitifully scared she sounded.

The doctor glanced toward the half-open door of her bedroom. "I wish I could give you a reliable answer one way or the other, child, but I can't. I've set his arm. It was a clean break, which is a mercy. His body's bruised some, but that could just be the way he hit the ground. I can't tell if he's bleeding inside. If he is…well…"

"What about his head?"

Avoiding her eyes, Doc Mercer began to unroll his shirtsleeves. "What doctor knows any fool thing about head wounds? I've seen patients with skulls pounded to a jelly come around the next day right as rain. Others just take a little knock in the wrong spot and they waste away without ever waking up."

"Is there nothing you can do?"

"Nothing anybody can do, child." The doctor reconsidered. "Except maybe *Him*." He nodded heavenward.

"And him." He inclined his head toward the bedroom door. "Often it all comes down to the patient's will to recover."

Caddie tried to digest that information and decide whether it was good news or bad. Manning had been willing to surrender his own happiness, even his life for what he believed best for her and the children. But could he wrestle free of the guilt that had dogged him?

Could he ever bring himself to believe that the very best thing for her and Tem and Varina was *him?*

Doc Mercer was saying something. Caddie tried to shake herself free from the dank fog of fear that had settled over her.

"Is it true what I heard—that Forbes killed Del?"

"The war killed Del, Dr. Mercer. Manning just happened to be holding the wrong gun."

"Well, well, well." The doctor shook his head. "And he came down here to look after you and the young'uns? Who'd have thought a Yankee would have it in him to do something like that? I don't reckon I'd have done the same in his place."

They both stood there for a moment, lost in thought. Then Doc Mercer asked, "You planning to set the law on Lon? I don't defend him by any means, but for what it's worth, I think he's learned his lesson. When he saw Tem in front of that horse, I think it jolted him back to his senses. He's going to be laid up for a spell from his horse throwing him. Once he's back on his feet, though, I doubt he'll give you any more trouble."

"I haven't decided." Caddie pressed her fingers to her throbbing forehead. "It depends on what happens with Manning. He'll probably want to give Lon another chance if…"

If he wakes up. The unspoken words gagged her.

The doctor patted her shoulder. "Might as well hope for the best, child. Send for me if there's any change."

"Thank you, Doc." Caddie dredged up a tired smile. "I'll do that. If you wouldn't mind seeing yourself out, I'll go back and sit with him some more. Might it bring my husband around sooner if I talk to him?"

"It can't hurt."

It might not help, either. As she watched Doc Mercer descend the stairs with a heavy tread, Caddie sensed those words had been on the tip of his tongue.

She turned her back on that thought and returned to her seat beside the bed. Even if it made no difference to Manning, talking would help her.

"I reckon I'm being selfish, wanting you to wake up." She stroked his sound arm. "At least this way you're not in any pain."

His face looked so serene, purged of the tension and remorse that had oppressed him from the first day they'd met.

"If you could just open your eyes for a minute or two, give some sign that you know me, I'd let you go back to sleep and not pester you anymore. So, if you can hear me, even a little, will you try to wake up? Or if that's too much, just hang on. Whatever you do, don't slip away."

A sob retched out of her. She battled for her composure and won. What could she say that might lure Manning to open his eyes, that might strengthen his will to keep on breathing?

Perhaps if she could cut the ties on that awful load of guilt, before it dragged him down to oblivion…

"You might have fired the shot that killed Del, but I'm the one who shoved him in the path of your bullet…"

Once she started, the words heaved out of her and she couldn't have stopped them any more than she could have

poured blood back *into* a gaping wound. She talked about
Del and their marriage. About finding him with Lydene.
About the bitterness that had festered between them after-
ward.

"He joined the cavalry to get as far away from me as
he could. Looking back, I hardly blame him. Even that last
letter I wrote. *Your faithful wife, Caddie.* I couldn't resist
rubbing it in. Yet you said he talked about me when he lay
dying. He sent you to take care of me and the children."

Her words choked off and it took awhile for her to begin
speaking again. "I had plenty of chances to forgive Del, to
tell him I was sorry for what went wrong between us. Now
it's too late and I'm going to have to live with that. I know
you can find a way to live with what happened, too. You
just have to try. Please."

One of Manning's eyelids flickered. Had he intended
that, or had it been some reflex? Caddie held her breath,
waiting to see if it would happen again. It didn't.

She lifted his limp hand and pressed it to her cheek,
wondering if she would ever feel his caress again.

He couldn't feel anything. He couldn't move or speak.
It was as if his mind had taken up residence outside his
body.

The sound of Caddie's voice reached him, though, and
he held on to it like a filament of golden thread that might
lead him out of a baffling maze. He concentrated on her
words and tried to move his consciousness toward them.

When she spoke of her first marriage, Manning was certain the pain in her voice would wring an answering sigh
from his senseless hulk of a body. Discovering that she'd
carried her own burden of guilt for Del Marsh's death
somehow eased his.

He heard a rising tide of desperation in her voice.

"I know it would probably be a whole lot easier to slip

away, but the children and I need you. Tem especially. I've told him it wasn't wise for him and Varina to do what they did this morning, but that it was very brave. I told him if anything happens to you, it'll be Lon's fault, not his. But you know what he's like—" Her voice broke.

"He's like you. He'll carry this around with him for the rest of his life, and I know you don't want that."

He was almost there. Manning could feel it. The pain in his head and his arm. And his heart.

Sense warned him to avoid pain. Love told him it was part of the price for being alive.

"Don't you dare leave me, Manning Forbes. You may be a Yankee, but you are no carpetbagger! Damn I hate that word."

"So do I." His mouth was so dry and his tongue so awkward, Manning wasn't sure Caddie would understand his words.

She must have, though, for she laughed and sobbed and gasped for breath. She squeezed his hand so tight that for a moment it made him forget his other pains.

"Can you open your eyes?"

About as easily as he could turn the mill wheel with his bare hands—but he managed. The sight of Caddie's face was worth the effort.

"You're beau-tiful," he croaked.

She laughed through her tears. "Liar!"

"I've got...to sleep awhile, but I'll be...back."

"I'll be here when you wake up again." The brilliant light of her smile almost blinded him. "From now on. For-ever."

"I like...the sound of that."

She caressed his cheek. "So do I."

"Care to...seal that...promise with a...kiss?"

"Uh-huh." Her lips alighted on his—tender, warm and indescribably sweet.

Deep in his chest, Manning's heart beat strong and sure. And whole once more.

Epilogue

Northern Virginia, Autumn 1866

"Home," whispered Caddie Forbes as the old buckboard rattled over the rise looking down on Sabbath Hollow. As the shadows of evening gathered, she listed slightly, resting her head on her husband's shoulder. Templeton leaned against her on the other side, fighting to keep his eyes open. Varina snuggled in Caddie's arms, sound asleep.

When she and the children had come here in the spring, Caddie had been buoyed by a sense of relief and false optimism. She hadn't felt the soft, enfolding happiness of true homecoming that she experienced now.

Down in the hollow, Sergeant commenced to bark as he tore up the lane toward them.

Manning chuckled. "The way that dog's carrying on, you'd think we'd gone to California rather than a wedding in Mercer's Corner."

"A double wedding," Caddie reminded her husband, trying not to sound too smug in her satisfaction.

Once Dora Gordon had overcome her deeply ingrained modesty and laid siege to Jeff Pratt's pride, the young man had been wise enough to offer his unconditional surrender.

Instead of just witnessing the marriage of Ann and Bobbie Stevens, Jeff and Dora had also taken their vows today.

"Who do you think looked better pleased?" asked Manning as he reined in the horses. "The brides and grooms, or Mrs. Pratt and Mrs. Gordon?"

He climbed down from the buckboard with stiff, awkward movements that betrayed the lingering effects of his injuries.

"I wonder if they'll be as pleased when they hear Jeff and Bobbie mean to move the whole clan into Gordon Manor," Caddie quipped, gently rousing Varina and helping her down from the wagon.

Caddie had worried how Jeff's and Dora's mothers would tolerate the Forbes family attending the wedding, once the whole story of Manning's past became common knowledge throughout the community. To her surprise, Mrs. Pratt had been quite civil, Mrs. Gordon downright gracious.

Some of the other guests had stared at first or whispered to each other when they thought Caddie wasn't looking. Still, things must have gone better than Manning had expected, for he'd relaxed visibly as the afternoon wore on. So had Caddie after she overheard that Lon meant to sell up and resettle in Texas.

"Come along to bed, children." She ushered Templeton and Varina into the house with Sergeant trotting along at Tem's side. "It's been a lovely day, but a long one. Leave the horses, Manning. I'll see to them once I get the young'uns settled for the night."

She returned a short while later to find the team unharnessed, fed and watered. Manning sat on the steps to the verandah, perhaps because he was too tuckered out to go any farther.

"Did you not hear me, Manning Forbes, or did you just not listen?" An anxious tightness inside her made Caddie's voice sharper than she'd intended. She settled onto the step beside him. "I said I'd see to the horses. Just because you're on your feet now doesn't mean you ought to overdo it."

"Don't fuss, woman." The warmth of his tone told her he liked being fussed over. He leaned against Caddie, resting his head on her shoulder. "Doc Mercer says I'm healing just fine."

Caddie's tight nub of worry slowly unfurled into fragile-winged desire. With all that had happened, they hadn't made love since she'd learned the truth about Manning. Would the knowledge change the precious passion they'd found? Poison it?

She raised her hand to stroke his hair. "Bodies mend faster than hearts and souls."

Manning leaned into her touch. "We've all got a lot of healing to do, Caddie. Me, you, the children. Most everybody in this country, one way or another."

A breeze sighed through the leaves of the dogwood bushes and the big old oak, as night enfolded the Virginia countryside. Overhead stars shimmered like teardrops on the face of heaven.

Slipping his sound arm around Caddie's waist, Manning pulled her even closer to him. "We're lucky we have the perfect tonic to restore us, here at Sabbath Hollow."

"And what might that be?" Caddie knew, but she still wanted to hear him say it.

He tilted his face to meet hers. Just as their lips came together for a deep lingering kiss, Manning whispered the word, almost as if he was afraid to speak it any louder.

"Love."

Her head was spinning by the time they drew apart again. "Would you care to retire to bed and take a little dose of that tonic, Mr. Forbes?"

The night had grown too dark for her to see his smile, but she could feel it.

"That sounds like just what the doctor ordered, Caddie-girl."

* * * * *

Be sure to look for
Deborah's next historical,
CUPID GOES TO GRETNA,
a novella in THE LOVE MATCH
Regency anthology
with Deborah Simmons and Nicola Cornick,
on sale in March 2002.

This Mother's Day
Give Your Mom
 # A Royal Treat

Win a fabulous one-week vacation in Puerto Rico for you and your mother at the luxurious Inter-Continental San Juan Resort & Casino. The prize includes round trip airfare for two, breakfast daily and a mother and daughter day of beauty at the beachfront hotel's spa.

INTER·CONTINENTAL
San Juan
RESORT & CASINO

Here's all you have to do:

Tell us in 100 words or less how your mother helped with the romance in your life. It may be a story about your engagement, wedding or those boyfriends when you were a teenager or any other romantic advice from your mother. The entry will be judged based on its originality, emotionally compelling nature and sincerity. See official rules on following page.

Send your entry to:
Mother's Day Contest

In Canada
P.O. Box 637
Fort Erie, Ontario
L2A 5X3

In U.S.A.
P.O. Box 9076
3010 Walden Ave.
Buffalo, NY
14269-9076

Or enter online at www.eHarlequin.com

PRROY

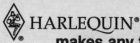

Lookin' for some spicy Westerns seasoned
with just the right amount of sizzling
romance and rollicking adventure? Then help
yourselves to these Harlequin Historicals novels

ON SALE MARCH 2002

A MARRIAGE BY CHANCE
by **Carolyn Davidson**
(Wyoming, 1894)

SHADES OF GRAY
by **Wendy Douglas**
(Texas, 1868)

ON SALE APRIL 2002

THE BRIDE FAIR
by **Cheryl Reavis**
(North Carolina, 1868)

THE DRIFTER
by **Lisa Plumley**
(Arizona, 1887)

 Harlequin Historicals®